LOOTERS & LEECHES

A Sage Adair Historical Mystery

Also by S.L. Stoner
In the
Sage Adair Historical Mystery Series
Of The Pacific Northwest

Timber Beasts
Land Sharks
Dry Rot
Black Drop
Dead Line
The Mangle
Slow Burn
Bitter Cry
Unseen
Preservation

And

In the Maggie Kubiac Mystery Series

Repercussion

LOOTERS & LEECHES

**A Sage Adair Historical Mystery
of the Pacific Northwest**

S. L. Stoner

Yamhill Press
www.yamhillpress.com

S. L. Stoner
Yamhill Press
www.yamhillpress.com

Looters & Leeches
A Sage Adair Historical Mystery of the Pacific Northwest

A Yamhill Press Book

The original Sage Adair Historical Mystery series cover design was created by Alec "Icky" Dunn. The *Looters & Leeches* cover art is by Vladimir Stefanovic, at VladixArt, vladimir.stefanovic@hotmail.com

Interior and Cover Design by Slaven Kovačević at: *slaven980@gmail.com*

Edition ISBNs

Softcover 979-8-9986887-0-6
Ebook   978-1-7320066-9-0
Library of Congress Control Number: 2025907909

Publishers Cataloguing in Publication

Looters & Leeches /S.L. Stoner

244 pages cm – (A Sage Adair historical mystery of the Pacific Northwest) 1. Northwest, Pacific—History—early 20th century—Fiction, 2. Detective and Mystery Fiction, 3. Action and Adventure—Fiction, 4. Progressive History—Fiction, 5. Municipal Corruption- History—Fiction, 6. Dr. Harry Lane, 7. International Workers of the World (IWW)—Fiction, 8. 1905 Lewis & Clark Exposition—Fiction

This Book is Dedicated to

Bernie Sanders

Born 86 years after Harry Lane
And a Continent Apart
Yet Still
Cut From the Same Bolt of Cloth

And

To George Slanina,

Always and Forever
Life's Greatest Gift

ONE

March 23, 1905

THEY STEPPED ONTO THE CROWDED North End sidewalk, leaving the midnight miasma of smoke, drunken caterwauling, and tinny notes behind them. Outside was lively with the drunken timber workers and staggering sailors who filled the night with raucous sounds as they drunkenly sought their "houses and lots,"—meaning whorehouses and lots of beer as a logger once told Sage.

A light spring rain made the boardwalk slickly treacherous beneath lowering, leaden clouds signaling harder rain was coming. A chill breeze from the east gorge wafted tendrils of wood and coal smoke through the air. This fitful early spring night in Portland, Oregon made John Sagacity "Sage" Adair alias, John Miner, yearn for summer's dry warmth.

Turning to his two companions, he clasped their hands with both of his, feeling affection and admiration. Their response was equally warm. Finally, they turned away, heading for their beds after a long and arduous day.

Sage watched them leave, wishing he was going with Meachum and Vincent but grateful he was not. The road those two traveled was strenuous, dangerous, and lonely. His road could be hard and risky, but it was also full of pleasurable moments and rarely lonely.

A furtive movement caught his eye just as he turned in the opposite direction. A figure had stepped onto the boardwalk from between the buildings just as his two friends passed. Gaslight glinted on something in his hand.

He shouted "Watch out" and began running as that hand raised.

Meachum must have heard Sage's shout because he whirled. Too late. The gun barked once, then again, and again. Vincent collapsed while those around him dove to the ground, jumped into doorways, or leapt away behind the horses and wagons crowding the street.

Meachum's momentum slammed him into the gunman and both crashed to the boardwalk in a writhing tangle. The assassin's gun rose above Meachum and slammed down. Meachum fell away. The gunman scrambled to his feet and fled across Burnside, weaving around traffic stalled by the excitement. Sage's wanted to give chase but his friends were hurt, maybe dead.

As he reached them, Meachum tried to rise, looking up at Sage with unfocused eyes half-blinded by the blood streaming from a head wound.

"You all right?" Sage asked.

"Vincent, go to him. He's shot." Meachum mumbled as he crawled toward where an unmoving St. Alban lay in a widening pool of blood.

After a frantic feel of Vincent's neck, Sage found a pulse. "Get one of those wagons!" he shouted at the gawking bystanders. Surprisingly, a man charged into the street and stopped a cab.

Meachum staggered to his feet and other men ran forward to help. Sage turned Vincent onto his back and pressed his palms against two arm wounds. He was dimly aware of the cab turning around until it faced west toward the nearest hospital. Seconds later, multiple hands reached for Vincent, lifting him up and away.

Sage jumped up and scrambled into the cab, Meachum entering behind him. Seconds later, Vincent was gently lifted and laid across their laps. Sage cradled Vincent's head, saying, "Hang in there Vincent, we'll soon be at the hospital."

The cabbie unhesitatingly hawed his horse into a fast trot.

Sage and Meachum exchanged panicked glances. "He's strong, he's young," Sage said though aware of Vincent's gasping lungs. Once his eyes adjusted to the dim interior, Sage's fingers fumbled across Vincent's torso and felt momentary relief. No bullet had hit his friend's center mass. But blood streamed down Vincent's left arm. Sage took the handkerchief from his pocket and pressed it against the shoulder wound.

Vincent must have also turned at my shout, Sage thought. Still, the blood flow was alarming. Vincent was unconscious. Shock and blood loss could kill. Sage snatched a second handkerchief from his pocket and handed it to Meachum who pressed it against Vincent's wrist wound.

The twenty-four blocks to the St. Vincent hospital seemed unending. Overhead, the cabbie shouted warnings as he drove the horse pell-mell, recklessly weaving between walkers and wagons. The cab jostled and clattered over cobbles as scattering people cried out. Sage was only dimly aware of the journey, his eyes, and thoughts fixed on the man who lay across their laps with a face turning ever paler.

The cab slowed as it climbed the hospital's steep drive until finally stopping at a gap in the wall. Beyond stood the hospital's front doors. Meachum jumped from the cab, staggered to the doors, and disappeared inside.

The cabbie dropped from his perch and began easing Vincent's limp body off Sage. Meachum and four men ran down the steps to gently lift Vincent out of the cab and onto a stretcher.

Seconds later the hospital orderlies carrying Vincent disappeared inside. Momentarily befuddled, Sage, Meachum, and the cabbie stood beside the exhausted horse whose sides were heaving and its eyes rolling. The cabbie snatched a towel from a wooden box and began wiping the horse down while murmuring praise into its twitching ear.

Sage touched the man's shoulder. "You are an excellent driver. I can't thank you enough." He pulled money from his pocket and handed it to the cabbie. As Sage turned toward the hospital entrance, Meachum's legs collapsed. The cabbie grabbed him and shouldered his weight before he hit the ground.

Sage slung his arm around Meachum's back and the three staggered toward the hospital doors. Once inside, the nun at the reception desk ran for help and soon Meachum was rolled away between two swinging doors.

Sage and the cabbie exchanged relieved looks. "Your friend's taken a wallop to his head, he has. A'bleeding like a stuck pig he is. Might be concussed," remarked the cabbie.

The British accent caused Sage to really look at the cabbie for the first time. The man was wiry, slight, and middle-aged with a weather-worn, beaky face. Dark blue eyes, similar to his own, returned the survey.

Seeing a smile on the cabbie's thin lips, Sage said, "If my friends live, it will be because of you."

"Well now, any of us cabbies would have done the same," the man said before shyly glancing away.

Shoving a hand into his pocket, Sage pulled out every remaining coin his fingers encountered and held them out to the man who looked down and shook his head. "Ah, no. You already paid for the ride when we were outside. Much as my missus might celebrate this treasure, it is far too much."

Sage laughed. "Well, that may be, but I am also hiring you to do another task. It will be longer and more onerous—especially since those clouds look like they're about to drop their load."

"I got me a good rain slicker. I'm your man wherever you might send me!" the cabbie exclaimed, grinning as he pocketed the money.

"Do you know Dr. Harry Lane?" Sage asked.

"Doc Lane? Why sure! All of us cabbies know him. He's who we all go to when we need doctoring. Our families too."

"Can you fetch him? I fear it's a long trip because he lives on the eastside, on Holgate at the corner of 28th."

The man laughed. "You needn't tell me that. I've fetched him many a time from his house when other folks needed doctoring. He's always willing to come if he's ta' home. If he's out tending someone, that nice wife of his will tell me where to find him, don't you fear."

The cabbie departed, leaving Sage with nothing to do but wait on the lobby's hard wooden chair. He didn't know which man was worse off. Meachum's skull took such a wallop that he could be badly injured and getting worse. Vincent had lost so much blood that he might never regain consciousness.

After a long worry about the two men he finally gave up—their fate was out of his hands. He looked at the large pendulum wall clock, surprised to note it was only a quarter to one. His world had changed dramatically in less than an hour. Outside, strong wind gusts drove a heavy downpour against the window panes. That poor cabbie, Sage thought. He's earning every cent I paid him and then some.

One o'clock came and went and still he waited. He'd learned nothing about either man's chances and was too afraid to ask. He'd wait for Harry. He trusted Harry Lane.

He rested his head against the wall, lowered his hat over his brow, and closed his eyes. But he didn't sleep. With a sigh, he decided to ponder the night's events. Why had someone shot at Vincent and Meachum? He knew there was some explanation—they even talked about a potential assassination. The question was: which man—Meachum or Vincent—was the target? Or had the assassin intended to murder both of them?

He opened his eyes, rose, and crossed to the nun at the reception desk. The early morning hours were quiet. He was the only other person in the waiting room. Looking down, he noticed her coifed head bent over a bible. When he cleared his throat, she used a finger to mark her place and looked up inquiringly. He noted she was young, pretty, and green-eyed with a face of tawny brown. "Excuse me, Sister," he said. "Might the hospital possess one of those new telephonic machines?"

"Oh, my yes. We depend on it to summon those doctors who have one installed."

Sage was glad he wouldn't have to send the poor cabbie back out into the rain on yet another errand. At some point, the man needed to get home where it was warm and dry. That relief was followed by shame— why hadn't he thought of the telephone sooner? "Does Dr. Harry Lane have one of those telephone instruments?"

She shook her head. "We surely wish he did. He's our most popular doctor but none of the telephone companies have run wires as far as his house."

"Well, Sister, I was wondering. The police station is equipped with a telephone. Would it be possible for you to call the police station and ask them to summon Sergeant Hanke here? Tell them to inform Hanke that there were two attempted murders and John Miner is here at the hospital with the victims."

"Why certainly," she said. "The instrument is in a nearby office. Please watch the lobby while I make the call. Unless a doctor comes in, keep everybody here in the lobby. You're John Miner you say?" Sage nodded and felt a familiar twinge of guilt at the necessary lie. Hanke knew both his real name and his alias.

She carefully closed her book and disappeared behind the swinging doors. Sage stared at the doors, wondering what was happening beyond them and feeling frustrated. "Damn it Harry, where the bloody hell are you?" he asked aloud.

After he'd circled the lobby a few times, the nun returned. "They said they would summon the sergeant immediately," she told him.

Sage thanked her and sat again. He wasn't a patient man at the best of times and this wasn't one of them. The wait was excruciating.

He sighed and ordered himself to breathe deeply and evenly to experience the calm in his solar plexus his teacher, Fong, always talked about. When that calm proved elusive, his thoughts returned to the night's events, trying to recall them, one minute at a time. Maybe he could discover the why and who of the attack.

TWO

March 22 and March 23

THE NIGHT'S EVENTS BEGAN WITH the door whapping open and a drunk staggering out. Sage sidestepped and caught the door before it closed. The stink of stale beer, smoke, cheap pomade, and sweaty bodies rolled out to smack him in the face. Not his favorite mix of odors, but tonight it was a necessary and welcome one. He'd been glad when a messenger arrived to summon him. Although in code, the note was easy to decipher. His friend, Meachum, was in town and wanted to meet at Fritz's Theater.

Once inside, Sage faced a bouncer whose look pierced before sliding over him to the next customer. Fritz's interior resembled the city's other skid road saloons, filled with drunken men and loose women. Like nearby Erickson's, it offered burlesque shows that catered to out-of-towners—mostly men who worked the woods, fields, and sea. But Fritz's was smaller and more tawdry than its block-sized competitor.

Sage cast an eye over the scene. Narrow aisles snaked between tightly packed tables and chairs. At the rectangular room's far end, a stage's painted backdrop offered a bucolic countryside scene, complete with leafy trees, blue sky, and distant cottage. He thought it an ironic homage to the abandoned dreams of customers intent on drinking and gambling their futures away.

On the stage and behind wire mesh, a shaggy, blackface performer yowled along to a ragtime tune pounded out on an upright piano. While the performers' efforts added to the din's whoops and screeches, the tune was barely indiscernible.

A U-shaped gallery hung above the main floor, wreathed in the tobacco smoke piling against the tin ceiling. Sage gazed around, seeking alternative exits from the overcrowded, claustrophobic shoebox. Some time ago, Fire Chief Campbell warned Sage that the Fritz, with its faulty wiring, was a conflagration waiting to happen. Campbell had tried and failed to close it down. He said the owner had too many friends in high places.

Unease rippled through him. The fire threat aside, he always wanted a second way out. He saw no exits but maybe there was one backstage. At least, the gallery had an outside fire escape. It hung off the building's front and was reachable from the gallery where he was to meet Meachum.

He crossed the sticky floor to the stairs. The uneven treads were tricky, being both gouged and crowded. More than once he pressed against the wall, giving way to descending drunks and the women they clutched to their side. Few offered a boozy-breath apology after stomping on his toes.

Gaining the gallery, he scanned the rows of curtained booths that extended along either side and across the far end. Most booths sported "Private-Do Not Enter" signs hanging from hooks screwed into the wooden partitions. The plentitude of signs meant the saloon was having a lucrative night. He focused on a curtained booth tucked into the furthest corner. It was Meachum's favorite booth. That's where he headed.

At his knock on the partition, Meachum's voice told him to enter. Pulling the curtain aside, Sage stepped forward and paused. Meachum was not alone. His hesitation gave way when he recognized the second man. It was Vincent St. Alban!

Sage yanked the curtain closed and reached both hands toward Vincent who rose from his chair to meet him. "My Lord! Vincent! You're a sight for sore eyes. What are you doing here in Portland? When did you get here?" Sage didn't wait for an answer before grabbing the man in a fierce hug that told him St. Alban's shoulders were too bony and his frame too slight. Vincent pulled away, turning his face aside to cough.

As Vincent continued to hack, Sage looked toward Meachum who mouthed the words "It's okay." Meachum's tired craggy face lit in an easy grin. Affection for the labor organizer filled Sage as they shook hands. This Colorado man spent months away from home, family, and his beloved woodworking shop, taking up the uncertain life of riding the rails, to spread the dream of one big union.

His companion, Vincent St. Alban, was making an equal sacrifice. While Vincent was always known as "the Saint" his nickname had taken on a stronger meaning in recent years following his heroic acts in Colorado's mining country. During the Smuggler Mine fire, Vincent repeatedly ran into the smoke-filled mine to rescue the trapped men. He'd saved very few because most immediately died from asphyxiation. Still, his brave effort made him a legend among the West's hard rock miners.

Twenty-four men died that day. They died because, when it took control, the Boston corporation eliminated the fire guard position. That guard would have known to slam shut the sealing doors the instant a fire broke out in the trolley house at the mine's entrance and no one would have died.

Vincent's valiant effort cost him dearly. Sixty straight hours of searching that smoke-filled death trap ruined Vincent's lungs. Tonight, the pale face, scrawny body, and hacking cough meant his health was worsening.

Once Vincent's coughing ceased, the three took seats around the small table. St. Alban was a small, wiry man, with a boyish face, large gray eyes, and a gentle manner. At first glance, he seemed neither remarkable nor charismatic. And yet, he was both. He exuded intelligence, capability, honesty, steadfastness, fearlessness, and kindness in equal measure. Sage was taller and older, yet he would have followed this slight man anywhere.

"Still got that cough, I see," Sage said.

Vincent shrugged. "It isn't all bad, this cough. It reminds me why we must keep fighting. Otherwise, more men will die, leaving their families to do without. I lost my mentor and best friend in the Smuggler." Grief momentarily darkened his eyes.

Sage met St. Alban after the disaster, during a protracted labor strike at the Smuggler mine. The Boston corporation had made numerous changes, all profit-driven. Those changes killed not only the twenty-four but had also killed or maimed a score of others. Those not physically harmed found their earnings reduced to starvation levels.

Sage knew mining. As a nine-year-old, he'd worked the drifts in an Appalachian coal mine. His job had been to crawl into wall cuts, drill holes, and fill them with dynamite. A methane explosion happened when he was deep inside one of those slits. Crawling out, he discovered everyone dead except the mine owner's five-year-old grandson. Lashing the boy to his chest, Sage carried him up an air shaft to safety.

In gratitude, the mine owner rewarded Sage by fostering him and paying for his education. Though he graduated from college, Sage had endured many years of separation from his mother. Before they'd reunited, Sage went to Alaska during the early gold rush days and made a fortune after which he looked for his mother and found her.

Their reunion was all he could have hoped for. They discovered they were of one mind, both eager to join the labor movement's fight for economic justice. So, when they learned of the Colorado miners' struggles, he headed west to Telluride. He found the miners in an uproar the day he arrived. A few days prior the mine owners' thugs had shot an unarmed miner dead. As Vincent and Sage talked, word came that a crowd was converging on the Smuggler mine, intent on burning down the crusher mill at the mine's entrance. The messenger warned that the owners' thugs were heavily armed with rifles while the strikers carried only pickaxes and shovels.

Vincent ran for the door. Sage followed. When they reached the mine, Vincent instantly calmed the irate miners, using words that sent them peacefully home. Impressed, Sage vowed he and Mae would do whatever Vincent wanted done. Their task turned out to be working as undercover labor operatives in Portland, Oregon where Sage's false persona was that of the Mozart's Table owner. He had bought and opened the elite restaurant with his Klondike gold. Mae Clemens was the restaurant's manager. Though, for the last three years, they'd only communicated with Vincent by letter and telegram.

St. Alban had given Meachum a different task. While he too worked as an undercover labor operative, his mission was far more onerous. Meachum rode the rails as an itinerant worker, supporting working-men's fights and selling the idea of one big union—Vincent's big dream.

Tonight, in Fritz's Theater, they'd spent an enjoyable hour drinking weak beer and telling stories until Meachum got down to business, "Vincent just came from California where he's been recruiting folks to attend the convention that's happening in a few months.

"I was doing the same in Washington. I just came down from Seattle to meet him. We're taking the train to Chicago to organize our first convention. It will be a union that every worker can join. We'll maybe call it the Industrial Workers of the World—IWW for short. I've been recruiting itinerant workers and loggers here in the Pacific Northwest. Vincent has been talking to the loggers and miners in California and the Southwest. Big Bill Haywood is ginning up support in the Rocky Mountain mine fields. Others are doing the same thing all across the country.

Meachum leaned across the table his brown eyes alight. "We plan to keep the membership cost very small. We'll issue IWW cards to every member. The cards guarantee that we will help one another, much like the Masons do."

"I remember hearing talk about that idea," Sage said. "I'm glad it will finally happen. Will the members have to drop membership in their other unions?"

"Never! Most of the other unions promise that they will affiliate with the IWW. The only one refusing to affiliate is the AFL. That's because that ole cigar maker, Gompers, is afraid he'll lose power. 'Course, that's no surprise. Gompers accommodates the bosses way too often."

Meachum moved on to the topic that involved Sage. "I decided to travel to Chicago with Vincent. Someone needs to watch his back because the Mine Owners Association just put a price on his head."

Sage raised an eyebrow and looked at St. Alban who waved a dismissive hand, "I can't be worrying about that. But I have to admit, Meachum is good company. I'm glad to have him with me."

Meachum shook his head at St. Alban's casual dismissal of the threat before saying, "Anyway, there's another reason I wanted to see you beyond the three of us having a good chinwag. When I got here yesterday, I made the rounds. I wanted to see if there were any mumblings about Vincent. In one saloon, I overheard something you need to know."

Sage straightened, frowning at Meachum's ominous tone. "What do you mean?"

"This afternoon, I landed in the Portland Club and was nursing a beer. Three men were meeting in the booth next to mine. I couldn't see them because of the high seat back but I heard them."

Meachum swallowed beer and continued, "It was pretty clear they're planning to kill someone."

"Why do you say that?"

"One fellow, fairly well-spoken, said it would be best to make it look like an accident. Another one agreed and said it should happen when nobody was around.

"Then a rough, gravelly-type voice said he'd do his 'best' but they had to decide whether they wanted the fellow dead before the election and if so, to decide which was more important: That it look like an accident or that fellow 'be dead.'"

"Whoa, that's pretty plain, alright."

"Yup, that's what I thought. They finally agreed that dead was more important than making it look accidental."

"I don't suppose they named any names?"

"Nope, nary a one. Didn't even speak their own names when they were talking."

Sage sat back in his chair, silently puzzling over who might be the target. "Did you see any of them?"

"Well, that's the weird part. The two well-spoken ones left first. I think they paid the fellow some money in advance because I heard them promise to give him the rest once the job was finished. They should have passed by me on their way out but they didn't. They must have snuck out the back door. I stayed put because the rougher fellow ordered another beer. I figured I'd try strolling past the booth to eyeball him. But before I could do that he got up and left. Luckily, he strode right past me. I followed him out."

"Where'd he go?"

"He hopped a streetcar and rode out to the Lewis and Clark Centennial Exposition fairgrounds being built north of town. He flashed a card at the gate and got let inside. I didn't have a card so I turned around and headed back into town."

"Can you describe him?"

"Well, he's shortish and stocky—got wide shoulders, dark hair, and deep-set muddy brown eyes. His nose is fat and red like he drinks a bit too much."

Sage laughed. "That description fits half the men down there on Fritz's main floor. Nothing distinguishable?"

Meachum grinned, "Yup, there was something. I saw a white blaze in the hair above his left temple, just like yours. Unlike you, though, he'd don't dye it dark."

Sage fingered his dyed streak. He started dying it after deciding it was bothersome to temporarily blacken it whenever he needed to be John Miner. Fortunately, the would-be assassin hadn't done the same.

Sage's recollecting came to an abrupt halt when Sergeant Hanke burst through the hospital doors. Sage quickly told him what happened. The sergeant immediately left for Fritz's where he hoped to discover witnesses to the shooting and obtain a description of the shooter since all Sage remembered was that the man looked to be tall and lanky.

His departure left Sage still sitting on the hard chair, awaiting news of the two patients. Sage returned to his musing. This time, he pondered which of his friends had been the assassin's target. Vincent St. Alban, who had a price on his head? Or, was it Meachum? Was it the man Meachum had trailed to the Exposition fairgrounds? But, the man Sage saw was not the stocky man Meachum described.

Sage's thoughts were interrupted when the hospital's doors swept open and Dr. Harry Lane barged into the lobby. "I should have known you'd be the one to roust me out of my warm, comfy bed," Harry declared with a grin as he pumped Sage's hand in greeting.

"The cabbie was supposed to tell you it was me summoning you here."

"He probably did. He shot a passel of words at me before I was fully awake. All I heard was 'urgent.' I can don trousers, shirt, coat, and grab my bag while still asleep. Years of practice."

He waved the bag in his hand, and added, "Of course the bag's unnecessary, given that he brought me here to the hospital."

Harry plopped onto the chair beside Sage. "Obviously, you aren't the one who needs doctoring. What's happened?"

Once Sage quickly filled him in, Harry jumped up. "I best go get some information. Wait here. Watch the bag." With that, Harry disappeared behind the swinging doors.

Ten minutes later, Harry reappeared. Sage stood and searched his face. Harry began with the reassurance, "Your friend with the head injury will be fine. They'll keep an eye on him for a while to make sure there's no bleeding into the brain."

Harry paused and his face turned grim. "Damn good thing you got me here. The doctor on duty is no surgeon. He was fixing to amputate your other friend's arm. One bullet smashed St. Alban's wrist while another made a mess of his shoulder. Given that I got surgery training at a major New York hospital, the doctor agreed I should try saving that arm."

Harry squeezed Sage's shoulder. "You look dead on your feet, my friend. Head home and come back tomorrow afternoon. The operation will take hours and Mr. St. Alban will be unconscious until past noon. I best be getting on with it," he said. Grabbing his case, he disappeared behind the swinging doors.

Sage exited the hospital at three o'clock in the morning, He was dead tired. It would be a long walk home since the streetcar wasn't running and all the cabs would be parked outside the North End saloons.

To his relief, a solitary cab stood before the hospital, its horse's head hung low. He recognized the white patch on the animal's forehead. That was the cab that had brought them here to the hospital.

Like the horse, the cabbie was asleep. He lay under a blanket on the passenger's cushion. When Sage tapped lightly on the cab, the man woke and jumped down quickly.

"I thought you might need a ride," he said as he climbed onto his perch and gathered the reins. "Where are we going next?"

"You were right. I surely do need a ride. Thank you for waiting," Sage said. As he climbed wearily aboard, he gave Mozart's address. Just before the cab began rolling he called, "By the way, Sir, what might be your name?"

"Folks call me 'Sprig' because my last name is Flowers and I'm a bit on the small side," replied the cabbie from his overhead perch.

THREE

March 23, 1905

SAGE WAITED ON THE SIDEWALK until the cab rolled off. Skyward, dawn was pearling the sky gray. He was bone weary. Glancing up, he noted that Mozart's was dark except for a flickering behind the lace curtains of his third-floor room.

After letting himself in through the front door, he headed to the restaurant's kitchen. Taking bread from the safe and meat from the icebox, he stood in the dark kitchen munching, still wondering which man had been the target. Sandwich gone, he gave up and headed for the stairs.

As expected, his mother was dozing in the armchair beside the flickering candle, sewing in her lap. When he entered, she roused, her fingers fumbling for needle and thread.

"I was worried, Sage," she said.

"Yeah Ma, I'm sorry about that. Everything was going fine until just after midnight. Then it all went to hell. I thought of sending you a message but didn't know how to get it to you. If you were asleep, you wouldn't hear the messenger pounding on the door three flights below. While I still don't like the idea of wiring this building for electricity, I think we should subscribe to one of those telephone exchanges. It would have been handy tonight. I could have let you know I was alright."

"What do you mean everything went to hell?" As always she picked up on the key point, though he knew she'd file the telephone idea away for future reference.

He told her about the shots fired at Meachum and St. Vincent and the conundrum of not knowing who'd been the target. He also told her about Meachum overhearing a second assassination plot.

Now wide awake, she said decisively, "Sounds like we best get the crew together. I can't think many men are running around with white streaks in their hair. You're the only one I've seen. As for that fellow who shot St. Alban—do you think he's the same fellow Meachum overheard?"

"Lord knows, we have to figure that out. Our problem is that Meachum watched the Portland Club man disappear into the Exposition grounds. Hundreds of men have come here to build those fairgrounds. They're constructing the exposition buildings and landscaping everything. So many new arrivals flood the train station every day that everyone with an extra room is renting it. There are an unlimited number of hotels, rooming houses, or private homes where he could stay."

She frowned and changed the subject. "I don't suppose you got a good look at the fellow who fired the gun?"

"Nah. His back was to me, and when he fired, he wasn't standing under a light pole. There was nothing remarkable about him except, when he ran across the street, he looked to be tall and skinny. Not like the Portland Club fellow Meachum described."

"Did you tell Sergeant Hanke about the shooting?"

"Yup, sure did. He came soon as he got my message. The hospital has a telephone and so does the police station. His apartment's close by. After they rousted him out of bed, he turned up. He's going to station a guard outside Meachum and Vincent's rooms."

Mae rose from the chair, sewing in hand, and said, "Right now, your head better hit that pillow over yonder. Sleep in late. I'll wake you up before the restaurant opens and have Fong and Herman here. We'll figure out what to do then."

"Maybe see if Lucinda can also come? She always gets involved anyway."

Mae Clemens smiled and patted his cheek, saying, "Of course, we can't forget to include our favorite lady, can we?"

In the brief moment before sleep overtook him, Sage thought about "their" lady, her dark gold hair, dancing blue eyes, and stylish elegance—while inside that attractive package lived a kind heart, sharp mind, and playful sense of humor. He was grateful that his woman ranked high in his mother's affections. That was Mae Clemens, unshakably steadfast and loyal. She loved, without discrimination. As she was fond of saying:

"Everyone puts their trousers or pantaloons on the same way, one leg at a time…makes no difference if they're donning flour sack cotton or silk. It's their insides that count."

He awoke with a start, just five hours after falling asleep. The clock ticking on the dresser said it was ten thirty. Perfect. He hurriedly dressed, hoping to spare his mother the stair climb, and was soon entering Mozart's dining room. There he found the typically serene Fong setting out dishes and cutlery for the noon-hour service. Upon seeing Sage, his narrow, aesthetic face lit with a smile that made his black eyes twinkle.

Herman Eich sat at a corner table and Sage felt affectionate warmth at the sight of the Jewish ragpicker poet. He was one of the most unusual and ethical characters Sage had ever met. College-educated but living in a lean-to, surviving by collecting, repairing ,and selling other people's castoffs—all while writing rather good poetry.

Today Eich's bearded face was intent as he scribbled in his new leather-bound notebook—a gift from Mae, his sweetheart. Sage smiled at the idea of his fifty-something mother having a beau. He was happy for her, she deserved it. Her life had been one of constant toil—raised in Appalachian coal fields, working in coal sorting sheds, losing a father and brother to her own husband's betrayal, her remaining brother dying of black lung, and then all of that sadness culminating in having to surrender her son to the mine owner's fostering. Instead of defeating her, she'd grown stronger until she was tough as fire-forged steel.

Sage fetched a cup of black coffee from the walnut buffet and joined Herman. Just as he sat, the kitchen doors swung open and Mae entered with a bowl of scrambled eggs in one hand, plated toast in the other. Fong trailed behind, carrying a tray holding dishes, jam, and cutlery.

While they all dug in Mae said, "Lucinda got my message and said she'll get here as soon as possible. I imagine she had a late night as well."

Mae was correct. Lucinda Collins was the city's most noteworthy madam. She operated the city's most exclusive parlor house, offering women, drink, and gentlemanly card games to the city's wealthiest men.

Mae turned to Sage. "I told Mr. Fong and Herman about what happened last night. I also sent an inquiry to the hospital. The reply just came that both Meachum and Vincent are recovering fine. I knew you'd be worried."

"I'll visit them both after the dinner hour. Doc Lane said that's the soonest they'd be able to have visitors."

"Best you bring Meachum fella here," advised Fong. "He can stay in my room upstairs. Nobody think of him here."

Sage nodded. "That's a good idea, Mr. Fong. That way, we can protect him until we figure out exactly what is going on."

Herman cleared his throat. "Do we need to have someone standing guard at the hospital? Just in case St. Alban was the target?"

"No, Sergeant Hanke promised to assign someone to guard him."

A soft knock on the front door announced Lucinda's arrival. After she strode in, there was a flurry of getting her settled. She and Sage exchanged brief smiles before she greeted everyone else.

Sage gazed affectionately at these people his mother called, "our crew." The only missing member was Solomon. His absence was unavoidable since his maitre'd duties at the Portland Hotel were already underway. Besides, they didn't know whether he'd be needed.

Sage quickly ran through the night's events for Lucinda's sake, ending with, "Last night, Meachum said the mine owners put a price on Vincent's head. He thinks that the bastard running the Dickensen agency is planning to collect that reward."

"I haven't thought of that detective agency since our little Central Oregon adventure," Lucinda mused. "Do you suppose we could send a telegram to Charlie Siringo? He might know the name and description if it's an agency assassin."

"Can we trust him?" asked Mae. "He still works for that despicable agency."

"Charlie's his own man. If something they want doesn't sit right with him, he doesn't do it," Sage said.

Sage and Lucinda exchanged a long look laden with memories of their perilous Central Oregon time. It had included Sage's embarrassingly wrong jealousy of Charlie. The tweak of a smile on Lucinda's lips told him she was also remembering that particular foible as well.

"I'd trust him with my life," Sage added. Lucinda nodded in agreement.

Fong stirred to say, "Number one, we find assassin before Vincent leave town. Otherwise, assassin leave town with him. But what Mr. Meachum heard, that sound like they plan to kill a local politician. What he say exact?"

Sage thought about Meachum's words and said, "He overheard three men. They wanted someone killed but also wanted it to look like an accident if possible. They also said it had to happen before the election."

"Well, that sounds like they're planning to murder a politician," Lucinda said thoughtfully.

"Yes, but which one?" Herman wondered aloud.

"Well, it's got to be the June 6th city election. That's a little over two months away." Mae noted, adding, "There's a passel of folks running for office in that election. How do we know which one?"

They exchanged looks of consternation. She was right. All the precinct, judge, and city offices would be on the ballot. "There must be scores of men running for something," Sage grumbled.

Mae's tone was matter-of-fact as she said, "Well, that means we have no choice. We have to find the guy with the streak in his hair."

Sage thought and said, "He must have some connection to the fairground construction since Meachum saw him flash a card and stroll right in."

"I best take my cart and set it up near the main entrance. I've some refurbished household goods that the workers might want. Not everyone is a newcomer. Some are union men moving into those new houses on the east side. They need furnishings of every sort," Eich said.

"Okay, we might get lucky and you'll spot him. As for me, after the noon dinner hour, I'll head to the hospital to see if Meachum can recall anything else."

He turned to Lucinda, "Are you still in touch with your friend, Xenobia Brown, Charlie's new wife over there in Prineville?" When she nodded, he said, "Could you send her a letter, asking her if Charlie knows which Dickenson thug might be hunting Vincent?"

Lucinda patted his hand reassuringly. "I will do that today." She rose, saying. "I best get back to the house. A guest got a little too frisky last night. Lots of shouting and screaming. I need to reassure the girl that she'll never see him again. He's banned."

She and Herman exited, leaving Sage, Mae, and Fong to set up for Mozart's noontime dinner hour.

The last of the patrons would soon be gone and the closed sign was on the door when Sage sat drinking coffee at the small kitchen table. He hoped it'd chase away his brain cobwebs before he headed to the hospital.

May came into the kitchen, laden with dirty dishes. She sent him an exasperated look. "I thought you were leaving for the hospital! If you're going to sit around reading the newspaper you might as well help Fong, Homer, and I clear the tables. Not to mention there's the washing up to do."

Sage raised a halting hand. "I promise that I am going to the hospital. I'm reading this newspaper in preparation. I need to know more about the upcoming election before I see Meachum. I might find something that'll jog his memory."

She sighed and flopped down onto the chair. "Sorry for snapping. I didn't get much sleep last night so I'm cranky. What is it that you're learning?"

"Well, since our assassin's deadline is the election, I've been reading the *Journal* trying to figure out the dates. Today is March 23rd. Candidates have to declare by March 29th—in just 6 days. That's followed by the primary election on May 5th. The general election is just a month later on June 6th. So the first question is, whether the assassin is supposed to strike before the primary or before the general election?"

Mae sighed. "I forgot there'd be two elections because male voters get to pick the candidates in a primary election for the first time instead of the party conventions picking them."

"Yup, a big win for democracy and a big loss for the party machines. But, it makes it harder for us since we have two election deadlines to worry about instead of one. If the plan is to kill someone before the primary, we have a problem."

Sage turned the page and tapped a list. "Right now, there are open positions for mayor, treasurer, city attorney, municipal judge, councilmen and precinct captains. Johnson's *Journal* is predicting a total of over 100 candidates. There's no way we can figure out which one of them might be the target. There are too many candidates and too little time.

"On the other hand, our odds are much better if they plan to wait until after the primary. That might give us enough time to find the assassin. If the primary is the deadline, we have too little time."

"I'm wondering whose oxen might be gored if the wrong candidate were to win. Surely nobody's going to murder someone over a precinct position. Seems like we can narrow the possibilities down to just those positions that have some kind of power," Mae suggested.

"That is brilliant! I think you're right. Looking only at positions that exert power over others would narrow the field considerably. Hmm." Sage returned his attention to the newspaper while Mae headed toward the sink with an armload of dirty dishes, a satisfied smile on her face.

❀   ❀   ❀

Meachum sported a bandaged head, a black eye, and a frown when Sage slipped into his hospital room.

"How are you doing, my friend?" Sage asked as his friend's frown changed to a smile.

"Well, my head feels like a crate of eggs been dropped off a wagon. But getting better every hour."

"He clubbed you good with his gun butt."

"You chased him off?"

"I guess. Sorry I didn't reach the two of you soon enough."

Meachum waved his apology aside. "How's Vincent?"

"Well, I thought I'd go see him next. The nurse said Doc Lane spent three hours putting his arm back together. His shoulder will likely mend okay. Unfortunately, the wrist was shattered. She said Lane did his best but the hand will likely be gimpy for the rest of his life."

"Poor Vincent. First his lungs, now his arm. Sure don't know why such a good man must suffer so."

Silence followed that lamentation. What could be said to an unspoken question that had no answer, Sage wondered but still tried, saying, "He sure sets a helluva worthy example for the rest of us." That observation earned him a rueful nod.

Sage broke the silence by noting, "Well, at least Vincent will live. If it hadn't been for you diving into the shooter, that might not be the case. You saved his life."

Meachum's lips twisted in self disgust. "Too little, too late, is how I see it."

"Don't," Sage admonished.

Meachum sighed. "Well it is as it is, I guess. Spilt milk and all that."

Sage decided they'd whined long enough. "Our crew is up and running. We've made some decisions. You're coming with me to stay at Mozart's. Doc Lane said he'd release you tomorrow provided you promise to stay in bed for a few days once I get you home.

"The crew also intends to find your attacker before Vincent leaves the hospital. The biggest unknown is whether we are looking for two assassins or just one. There's the fellow you overheard in the Portland Club and the one you took to the ground last night. Do you have any idea if they were the same man or not?"

Meachum gazed out the window into an uneasy sky as he searched his memory.

When his gaze returned to Sage there was worry in his face. "Two different men," he said. "The one in the Portland Club was stocky and short. The one I knocked down felt ropey and tall."

"Damn. I feared you'd say that."

Meachum gave a tired sigh. "Yup. There's two assassins on the loose, not just one."

FOUR

March 26, 1905

Two days before, Sage had collected Meachum from the hospital and delivered him to Mae at Mozart's so he was only here to visit Vincent. Alarm bells began ringing in his head when he saw the vacant chair outside St. Alban's room. Where was the police officer who was supposed to be keeping watch? Hanke would hear about this he vowed breaking into a run.

When he burst into Vincent's room, Sage had worked himself into what his mother would call a "proper snit" only to halt abruptly. Vincent had surprising company. There was no mistaking that shock of unruly hair silhouetted against the window's light.

"Harry!" Sage exclaimed.

Chuckling, Harry Lane said, "Your scowl would send a cougar scampering. I told the officer to fetch some breakfast. He was on night duty. I promised to stay until he returned."

Sage grinned at Vincent and laughed. "You caught me, Harry. I worked up a full head of steam when I saw that empty chair. I'm doubly glad to see you."

Sage nodded at Vincent's bandaged arm. It hung in the air, elevated by a cord and pulley system. "How's your patient?"

Lane patted the blanket atop St. Alban's foot, "He's coming along nicely."

A grin brightened St. Alban's pale face as he said, "John, Dr. Lane and I have been having a most enjoyable visit."

Lane nodded enthusiastically. "Vincent has been telling me about the one big union he plans to start this June."

"I bet he has. It's his favorite tune. You're in favor of it?" Sage asked.

"Hell yes, just as much as you are, I suspect. I visit people's homes to treat them, so, I see how they live. Union folks are always much better off. Not rich, you understand, but noticeably better off. At least they have food on their tables and decent roofs over their head."

"Exactly! Sounds like we can count on you to help sell the idea, Dr. Lane!" Vincent's delight was genuine but then he sobered. "How's Meach doing?"

Sage shrugged. "Fine. Itching at the confinement but realizes the most important thing is to keep you both safe until you're away on the train. He was still sleeping when I left the restaurant. Mae is making sure he follows the doctor's orders. She wakes him up every few hours. I suspect neither of them has gotten much sleep. Fortunately, this was the last night she had to keep waking him. We'll both see you this afternoon. It'll be his first day out of Mozart's."

The three of them chatted until the officer returned.

After saying their goodbyes, Sage walked Lane out. Once they were out of earshot he asked, "How's Vincent really doing?"

"Well, I checked under the bandages and there's no infection so that's good news. The bad news is that, while he'll be able to move that arm, his hand will stay fairly useless."

Lane stopped walking to say, "Adair, I think your friend is an admirable man. Losing the use of his hand must be devastating but he doesn't complain or feel sorry for himself. And, those damaged lungs," Lane shook his head, his face sorrowful.

He sighed and added, "The pain he endures is hard to imagine. But all he wants to talk about are his dreams of making life easier for folks. Wish there was more like him."

"There's more than you think. Lots of men and women are doing their best in quiet ways. I've met them. In fact, you're one of them," Sage declared before changing the subject. "At least you were able to save his arm."

"Yup. And, he's thanked me more than once."

"How long will he stay in the hospital?"

"Another week to ten days. The biggest concerns are infection and gangrene. Wouldn't want to see my beautiful handiwork go to waste," Harry said, with self-mockery twisting his lips.

They exited the hospital doors and halted beneath the entrance portico, Sage asked, "You going to run for mayor's job?"

Harry wrinkled his patrician nose and waggled a finger at Sage, saying, "I wish I got paid a nickel every time someone asks me that question."

Sage shrugged. "Folks say you are the only Democrat who can beat Williams and his Republican machine."

"Yup, I've heard that too."

"Well, the candidate declaration cutoff date is just two days away."

"Yup, that's the other thing I hear. Over and over, I might add."

"You're not going to tell me, are you?"

Lane's face turned pensive as he gazed across the city from the hospital's portico. He broke his gaze and turned to Sage with a wry smile. "Well, since I haven't even told my lady wife what I plan to do, she'd skin me alive if I told anyone else first." He glanced down at the street as a cab drew up.

They shook hands as Lane said, "I've got to go. I'm late for a room full of scheduled patients. Glad to know you're watching over St. Alban. Like I said, he's a fine fellow. Besides, if someone shoots him dead, there goes all my amazing handiwork." With that, Lane turned and trotted down the steps, raising his arm to hail the cabbie.

Sage watched the vehicle carry off a conflicted man. "Poor devil still hasn't made up his mind," he murmured. "He'd make a good mayor because he can't stand to see people suffer, whatever the cause." Lane was well-known for treating and not charging the poor for medical treatment and medicines. Many referred to him as Portland's "Poor People's Doctor."

And, Lane gave his impoverished patients superior care. Unlike most Portland doctors, his training extended far beyond just two years at Willamette University in Salem. He'd undergone specialty training in San Francisco, New York, and Europe, giving him far more skills than those of most Portland doctors. He could have catered to the wealthy. They would have embraced him, and drawn him into their inner circle because of those skills and his elite lineage as the grandson of Oregon's first governor. But, that life was not for Harry Lane. He eschewed wealth's trappings. Instead, his was a humble life of service.

Loud shouts, issuing out the hospital doors interrupted Sage's reverie. He wheeled and charged inside. There he saw people running to and fro across the lobby, darting through the swinging doors.

"What's happening," he demanded of the alarmed nun in the lobby.

"I don't know. Someone yelled 'fire' and a woman screamed. I can't leave the desk to learn what's happening."

Doors slammed in the distance followed by more shouting. Sage whirled as the policeman assigned to St. Alban's room burst from the near stairwell. Hand on his weapon, he shouted, "What's the problem? I'm a police officer."

Sage's heart stalled. "You left Vincent unguarded? You idiot!" he yelled and raced for the stairs.

He charged up the stairs, two steps at a time. He slammed out the corridor door in time to see a figure slip across Vincent's threshold. Seconds later he crashed into the room just as a man pulled a pistol from beneath his coat. Sage launched himself through the air. The violent collision sent the weapon flying. It hit the floor and slid beneath the bed as their bodies careened into the wall.

Sage hit hard. The attacker shoved him aside and broke for the door just as the police officer charged in. The assassin grabbed the startled officer's arm and slung him toward Sage. By the time the two of them untangled and Sage ran into the hallway, the man had vanished.

"Damn it all to hell!" Sage swore. He re-entered the room to hear the officer apologizing, "I'm so sorry, Sir. I should have realized it was a phony distraction. If it hadn't been for your friend, you would. . ." His voice trailed off as if suddenly struck by the implications of that outcome. He stared at the attacker's gun he held in his hand.

When he turned to Sage, his face showed horror, fear, and panic. For the first time, Sage realized that the officer was quite young which meant inexperienced. The earnest, freckled face touched Sage. Partly because he too made some near-fatal mistakes when he was just starting out. During his initial Klondike experiences, he'd survived only because of the kindness of older, more experienced men.

Sage raised a hand to stop any more apologies. "It's alright and understandable. Lesson learned. What's your name?"

The young man gulped. "Dan Carter," he said.

Sage stuck out his hand, thinking the incident was a good thing. It guaranteed the young man's diligence going forward. He found the young man's hand damp to the touch. "My name's 'John Miner.' I'm pleased to meet you," he said.

He sent St. Alban a questioning look and received a nod in return. "Patrolman Carter, I need to tell the sergeant what happened. That way he'll know the danger is real and he'll keep you here. But I won't make a fuss. I'll explain the confusing situation and tell him to take it easy on you. I know him well. He'll understand. I best go see him now. I'll take that gun to him as well."

The young officer looked relieved, and handed Sage the gun, murmuring a heartfelt thanks before stumbling in his eagerness to exit the room. Once they were alone, Sage turned to Vincent. "Are you alright?"

His question elicited a laugh. "Fit as a fiddle and twice as entertained. I never imagined you could fly. You must have flown ten feet."

"Well, 'panic either freeze or peps up,' according to my teacher, Mr. Fong. You haven't met him yet. He makes me practice the "pep up" part all the time."

Vincent's eyebrow quirked inquiringly and he repeated, "Mr. Fong?"

Sage smiled ruefully. "He's my teacher and my employee and my best friend."

"What's he teach?"

"A fighting style he calls the snake and crane. An Asian way of fighting. He stands only a few inches over five feet and I could pick him up with one hand. Yet, I've seen him take down men twice my size without breaking a sweat. The first time I realized he could fight, he saved me from three goons kicking the stuffing out of me."

"Sounds like an interesting fellow. I'd like to meet him."

"Since he's helping search for your assassin, you probably will."

As Sage climbed the steep stairs to police station's front doors a sudden certainty arrested him. He hadn't seen the assassin's face but he'd felt his body—thin and ropey very unlike like Portland Club fellow Meachum described. Also, the hospital room assassin was tall.

So, the hospital room incident told him two things: At least one of the two targets the other night had been St. Alban—otherwise, there'd have been no second attempt. And, the other thing he realized was that Meachum was correct: Two assassins were loose in the city.

Once they were seated in the sergeant's office, he told Hanke about the attack and his certainty that two assassins were running around Portland aiming at least two different targets.

"So, St. Alban would be dead if you hadn't turned up when you did," Hanke said with a frown.

"Yes. But go easy on the kid. He instantly grasped the situation. He won't ever make that mistake again. He's well and truly chastened. I believe he's the best man for the job from now on. There's no doubt but that he's taken the lesson to heart."

"You're probably right. Carter's a brand new hire—fresh off an eastern Oregon ranch. Hasn't even formally reported to the station for training. I thought guard duty at the hospital was a good way to ease him in before the others steer him wrong. I should have realized the assassin would create a distraction to lure him away. I neglected to warn him about a trick like that, so it's my fault."

Sage raised a hand to wave Hanke's guilt aside. "It's over now and all is good. More worrisome is that there's also a plot afoot to kill an unknown local politician before the election. You don't have enough officers to guard every candidate.

"That's true. But, Mae's idea of focusing only on those offices that exercise power is a good one. It narrows the field considerably. Still, that leaves multiple candidates to worry about. As you say, we're looking at four citywide positions and one judge position because each exercises power."

Hanke lowered his face and scrubbed it with both hands. Dropping his hands, he said, "After the candidate declarations on the 29th, there's just four short weeks before the primary election. How the devil can we discover who he's targeting before then? Saying the guy is stocky and has a streak in his hair isn't very descriptive. For one thing, a hat will hide that streak as you well know."

Hanke fell silent as he absently picked up a pencil to turn it about in his fingers. He dropped the pencil and said, "Good lord, think how many men have come into town to work on the exposition. Hundreds, maybe thousands. I don't have enough officers to check on all of them. The best I can do is circulate your sparse description and tell them to be on the lookout."

Sage agreed it was unlikely that ordering the patrolmen to keep their eyes peeled would yield results. "I understand. It's a nearly impossible task. You are right. The town is overrun with strangers. Our crew will also be looking. But, surely they can't be intending to kill someone before the primary, before they know who'll be the final candidates. Why pay for an unnecessary murder?

"The general election must be the deadline, not the time before the May 5th primary. That means, right now, we must focus on St. Alban's assassin. Searching for the second one can wait until after St. Alban leaves. Until then, we'll keep eye out for the one with the streak in his hair, knowing that the greatest danger from him will come after the May primary.

❋ ❋ ❋

Lucinda Collins was in the back parlor, idly sipping coffee and thinking of John Sagacity Adair. She wondered if she'd see him today. Probably not. He'd be too busy with their new mission.

Her thoughts drifted to her mother, wondering what she would have thought of her daughter's man. Though she was many years' dead, Lucinda was sure she would have approved of Sage. She'd always spoke of "tall, dark, and handsome men" as if that were the ideal standard for a mate. Dark-haired Sage Adair was all of that, with his six-foot height, perfect nose, penetrating dark blue eyes, and easy smile.

But her mother always conditioned her ideal by quickly adding, "But remember my girl, 'Beauty is, as Beauty does." Sage excels on that point, as well, she mused.

What a ridiculous position the two of them were in. Circumstances kept her from accepting Sage's marriage proposals. God knows she wanted to. Even dreamed of it.

Lucinda let a familiar fantasy slip into her thoughts—one where they lived together, in a home with their children. She had only a few more years before children would be out of the question.

Her mother always said her only child was her greatest gift and then she'd hug long and hard. Lucinda still could feel the power of those encircling arms on that last day and their gentle release at the end, when her mother's eyes locked on a distant somewhere, a tiny smile on her lips, as a gentle sigh carried her away.

"Oh boy, am I maudlin. Many more of those thoughts, and I'll be wetting my hanky," Lucinda declared to the empty room. She stood, grabbed her cup, and marched toward the kitchen. Once there, she got busy blackening the stove, her favorite household task.

The task only partly sidetracked her thoughts. Her mother often strived to make their old iron stove look new. That's how she'd restore her spirits after Lucinda's father's fists let loose—she'd scrub and polish until she found peace. Today Lucinda launched a vigorous attack, seeking that same calm while feeling her mother's loving spirit surrounding her.

A noise made her turn. At the kitchen door, if summoned by her thoughts, stood a grinning Sage with a smug Elmira at his side. For some reason, her housekeeper adored the man.

Once her apron was doffed and her dress smoothed, Lucinda led Sage into the front parlor. After they were settled on the couch, Lucinda said, "I received a telegram from Xenobia. She and Charlie Siringo will be in town soon."

"Wonderful! Did she say anything more? Like why they are coming?"

"Just that 'Charlie will help.'"

Sage relaxed. If Charlie Siringo helped, they'd have a better chance of capturing St. Alban's would-be assassin. The cowboy knew the methods and the people of the Dickensen agency. If that agency was involved, as they suspected, ole Charlie would prove invaluable.

FIVE

March 28th, 1905

HE ENTERED THE KITCHEN WITH his thoughts on coffee and the two newspapers in his hand. He'd already scanned the front pages. The big question in both was whether Harry Lane would run for the mayor's office. Tomorrow the candidates had to declare. The *Oregonian* called the good doctor "coy" and clearly hoped he wouldn't. The *Journal* was urging him to run. One thing for sure, 'ole Harry was stirring things up.

"Herman!" Sage exclaimed at seeing the ragpicker poet sitting at Mozart's kitchen table.

"Good morning, Sage. I trust you slept well," Herman responded.

Sage poured himself coffee and took the seat across from the ragpicker. "I've slept better." He noted another *Journal* lying beneath the ragpicker's hand. "Anything important happen? I've only seen the front page."

"No, not in the paper. But there is a reason I am here and not at the fairground. Something occurred there but too late to hit the newspapers." The flash of teeth midst the beard said Herman was amused.

"And," Sage urged, feeling anticipation spark.

"You'll like this. The union carpenters walked off the fairground jobs last night."

"All of the carpenters?"

"No, just the union fellows."

"Hmm. See anyone with white-streaked hair among them?"

Eich shook his head. "Nope, nary a one, and believe me, I looked. They'll be picketing today, trying to persuade the other unions to join their cause."

"And, why did they strike?"

"Something about wages and non-union workers. I thought perhaps, you could ask Leo." Eich waited, though his raised eyebrows signaled he thought Sage should talk to the carpenters' union president. Certainly, their entire crew was in Leo's good books. There'd been a strike during which the boss was murdered. Leo's arrest quickly followed. They'd all worked hard to discover the murderer and exonerate Leo. He was now a close friend of theirs.

"I'll talk to him but I'm not sure how that will help us find the assassins," Sage said.

"Well, I thought he might ask his picketers to keep an eye out for our guy. They will be manning every gate whenever the grounds are open."

"What a great idea. I should have thought of that."

"Well, I've had all night to think on it," Eich said, rubbing his weary face.

An hour later, Sage headed to the carpenters' union hall. As expected, it buzzed with activity. Pausing at the third-floor meeting room's threshold, he saw men nailing picket signs together while their wives painted slogans on the white cardboard. Sage smiled at the sight. These folks were doing an efficient job.

"John Adair!" exclaimed Leo, charging forward, his round face alight with a genuine smile. "You come to volunteer for the picket line?"

Sage laughed. "I wish, Leo. But, no. I've got my own fish to fry. Do you have a minute? Is there somewhere we can talk?"

Leo nodded and ushered him into a tiny office containing only two hardback chairs and a small table shoved into a corner. Leo gestured around, "Sorry. There's but two offices and our dispatcher needs the bigger one. I'm out with the men most days so I don't need a big office. Besides, I'm not much for paperwork," he added.

Sage grinned. "Yup. I know what you mean. It's my least favorite thing to do." He briefly explained about the fellow with the white streak in his hair and the danger to some unknown politician.

"Well, if the threat's against one of them already holding an office, my heart and my head would tussle over whether to send flowers or not. They're a bunch of union-hating, corrupt scoundrels."

"Which would win?" Sage was curious.

Leo's smile was rueful. "I'm afraid that is one of those decisions that can only get resolved in the moment of its making. I hope the heart. Besides, if I step away from my anger, even my head knows it's best to honor the law—despite its imperfect evolution. Assassination can't shape democracy—even if it's motivated by the desire to create greater good. Sadly, we voters have to make mistakes if we're to learn how to separate the warped from the straight."

Sage mulled that over until Leo stirred to say decisively, "Certainly we'll help. I'll talk to the men. If they see the fellow we'll send word. They'll be manning every gate so there's a good chance they'll spot him coming or going."

Sage stood and shook Leo's hand. "There's a reward if they follow and discover where he's staying. But he's very dangerous. Make sure they know that."

As they said their final goodbyes Sage felt suddenly embarrassed and said, "Say, I forgot to ask, why are you striking?"

Leo stopped to shake a new arrival's hand before replying, "Three basic things. We want the standard $3.50-a-day wage everyone else gets on the West Coast. We also don't want to work with non-union carpenters. Most of them don't know which end of a hammer to use. Their work is shoddy and we're getting blamed for it.

"And, after winning an 8-hour day a few years back, we sure don't want to be forced to work nine-hour days without overtime like they're demanding."

Leo's lips pursed and his nose wrinkled as he added, "As expected, the rich men promoting the fair squeeze every dollar, except for the ones they put into their pockets."

"Well, your wants sound reasonable. What are your chances?"

"We think good. Not like back in 1903 when the strike lasted over two months. The extravaganza's opening day is less than six weeks away. There's still a wagonload of work to be done. It's going to run until mid-October. Good reviews at the opening mean more visitors to the end. More visitors mean more customers for those rich men's hotels, restaurants, shops, and the real estate sales they plan to make to the workers and fairgoers. Not to mention all the gambling, drinking, and whoring under-the-table dollars the newcomers will drop into their troughs. I can't imagine how much this city will grow because of the fair."

Leo's smile held glee. "In the meantime, they'll have an even worse day tomorrow. The other building trade unions have agreed not to cross our picket lines." Leo rubbed his hands in anticipation. "I predict we'll be back at work come the end of next week."

Sage left Leo and strode back to Mozart's, hoping that Leo's optimism was justified. From the crowing talk he'd heard at Mozart's, he too believed the fair organizers cared only about financial gain regardless of how it was achieved. They'd turned down the most logical site for the fairgrounds—a huge eastside city-owned park directly across from downtown. That park was acres big, a long rectangle bounded by the 11th and 12th avenues, Belmont and Hawthorne streets. He'd overheard them agreeing that their grow-the-city-quick-exposition couldn't take place there, one excuse being that it was in the area many called Union Town because so many homeowners were better-paid union men.

But that excuse rang hollow. Undoubtedly, their real reason was profit-driven because they'd picked a shallow, unused swamp at the city's far northern edge. Not surprisingly, some of the fair promoters had financial connections to the swamp's owners or to those owning the hillside overlooking it. Owners of the land under the water would be paid rent and would regain their improved property once the fair ended—a very good deal for them. Those owning the hillside lots would see their land values increase.

He considered whether the politician targeted for assassination was someone who'd interfere with the promoters' money-making schemes. He decided that was unlikely. The extravaganza was too far advanced. At this point, no one could stop the fair from happening.

Reaching Mozart's, he glanced in the front window and saw Lucinda. She sat sidewise to him and was laughing with two people. One was a woman and the other a lanky fellow slapping a familiar, well-worn, cowboy hat against his knee. Charlie Siringo and Xenobia Brown had arrived. Sage hurried inside. He strode quickly across the room to hug Xenobia and shake Charlie's hand with both of his.

Mae and Fong joined the group, bringing coffee and sweets with them. Once greetings were over, Mae and Fong rose to prepare the dining room for the noon trade. At their departure, Sage and Charlie exchanged a look, followed by Sage saying, "Charlie, let's you and I go upstairs and talk." To Lucinda and Xenobia, Sage said, "Please excuse us, ladies. Lucinda, please tell Xenobia what's going on."

Once they were seated at the bay window table in Sage's third-floor room, Charlie said. "Miss Lucinda wrote about what's going on with Mr. St. Alban. Even though I've officially quit the agency, I'm still in touch with a few of the fellas. Before we left home, I confirmed that the Mine Owners Association put a price on the Saint's head.

Charlie leaned forward, his eyes narrowed. "One thing is darn sure— as long as Jasper McKinney's running the agency he'll keep stirring things up between the unions and bosses. As they say, 'Money makes the mare go' and McKinney's cracking the whip."

Charlie flicked his hand as if swatting that thought away. "So, that's a given. I expect knowing that won't help us find the scoundrel who tried to kill Meachum and St. Alban. Anyone see the fellow who fired the gun? What'd he look like?" he asked.

Sage described the long-legged figure he'd glimpsed running across the street.

"And that Meachum fellow, the one who tangled with him, never got a look at his face?"

"I'll ask him again. What he said was that it happened too fast and his eyes stayed fixed on the gun. He'd be here with us right now but he's out combing the saloons and gambling houses for our two assassins."

That last comment straightened Siringo from his relaxed slouch. "Two? Lucinda only told us of one."

"We think the man who tried to kill St. Alban is employed by the mine owners. The description of the second assassin is markedly different." Sage described the shorter, stocky man with the white blaze in his hair. "You can keep your eye peeled for him too if you want. We sure can use your help."

Sage explained what they knew, concluding, "That's why we doubt the second assassin has a connection to the Dickensen agency. We think he's somebody completely different who's been hired by some local men to kill a local politician. In the meantime, like I said, we could surely use your help identifying the assassin who tried to kill the Saint."

Siringo stretched out his legs, leaned back in his chair, puffed cigar smoke, and contemplated the ceiling while Sage waited.

After a long beat, Charlie lowered his jaw and directed a level gaze at Sage. "Yah know, Dickensen corrupts its agents from the git-go. My very first check, I was ordered to pad my expenses 'cause the client was wealthy." His lips twisted. "We all had to do it. After awhile, that extra money in my pay check tasted real sweet. But, deep down, it turned my stomach. Now, even though I refuse to pad my time, they still call on me sometimes even though I'm not an employee anymore. That's because I'm the only one they know who can play the cowpoke. Most of their other detectives are too citified to pass."

Charlie's narrow lips tightened. "A cowpoke ain't what's needed in this here situation so McKinney has plenty of galoots in his stable to choose from. Still, knowing it's a tall, skinny fellow helps. Only a few Dickensen agents fit that description—one fellow in particular. Let me check to see where him and the likely others bunk these days."

Meachum turned up in the late afternoon. "Any luck?" Sage asked him.

"Nah, I started out at the breakfast places and then moved to the watering holes. There sure are a lot of saloons in this town. No way that I can search every one of them and the gambling dens and the whorehouses.

Sage chuckled. "Yup, I have to stifle my chuckles when I hear the chamber of commerce fellows boasting that, unlike Seattle, Portland is very civilized and respectable. Hah! Seattle's just more honest about it. Our policeman friend, Hanke, who you met in the hospital, claims there's over 400 saloons and 500 whorehouses. Not to mention the gambling dens. Plus, almost every North End alley sports a shooting gallery where would-be sharpshooters try to win prizes."

"I don't understand. Why does this city have so many of those places?" Meachum wondered aloud.

Sage laughed. "It's quite simple my dear man. When the purveyors of vice are caught violating curfew or other ordinances, they only pay a fine. That money goes into the city's coffers. Half the city budget comes from their licenses and those fines—all money swindled from those having the least to spare. And, there's also the fact that some of the city's wealthiest men own those places. If there's a raid, they pull strings and their place is back in business, lickety-split."

"Good lord. Here I've always thought Denver was the wild and wooly place!"

"What were folks talking about today?"

"Well, the saloon owners are sounding off about the Democrats. They're afraid if one of them gets the mayor's job he'll close the town down—no more saloons, whoring, or gambling. They claim the vice men have joined up with some of the building owners and the cigar makers union to fight any Democrat or 'closed shop' candidate."

Sage's ears perked up. Was that the target—some politician who wanted a closed town, meaning no more twenty-four-hour saloons offering gambling and prostitution as well as liquor? "Hear any other complaints?" he asked.

"Yup, seems they got problems with the city's women. They griped about that Traveler's Aid woman, Lillian Baldwin, meeting the trains and steering women away from saloon work. And, they're unhappy about the Women's Club ladies who are raising a fuss about curtained booths in the saloons. The ladies want them outlawed, as well as inside stairways running from the saloons to the cribs on the second floor. Portland's frisky women have got them upset."

"Did they mention the name of any politician in particular they're worried about?"

"Matter of fact, they did. Your friend, Doctor Harry Lane is at the top of their list. He's the Democrat who scares them the most. They think he's the only one who can beat the old guard in the mayor's election."

Sage sat back in his chair. He could see why some elements in the city wouldn't want the feisty doctor sitting in the mayor's chair. Of course, that worry wouldn't exist if Harry didn't declare by tomorrow's deadline. Sage wasn't sure what he thought about that.

SIX

March 29, 1905

"HEY LAZY BONES, BEST GET yourself up and at 'em," Mae said as she set a tray on the table before whipping aside the curtains and sending daylight stabbing into his eyes.

Sage groaned. He and Meachum spent the night trolling dives 'til near dawn, searching for the two assassins. He'd drunk too much bad beer followed by too little sleep.

"What time is it?" he mumbled.

"It don't matter. You best get up, drink the coffee I just brought you and read the newspaper."

"Newspaper? Did Harry declare himself a candidate?" After everything he'd overheard last night, Sage had very conflicted thoughts about Harry changing jobs. There was a lot of nasty opposition to the idea, especially from the saloon and gambling den operators. Still, Harry Lane would be a godsend to the city.

Mae eyed him and smirked. "Guess you'll best get your fanny sitting on that chair and find out."

"You're a hard woman."

Her face softened momentarily before she brusquely declared, "One who's borne a lazy man if today's any measure!"

Once she was gone, Sage tossed back the covers, slipped into a robe, and headed for the table. Flipping to the *Journal's* front page he got an immediate answer to his question. The headline blared, "Lane Declares Candidacy!" He could imagine the glee with which

Ben Johnston had written that headline. The brief article beneath that headline began:

> The candidate stated taxation of the rich will be an issue. Dr. Lane also said that he was for enforcement of all laws and the honest handling of city contracts.

Typical Harry, covering all the ground in a few blunt sentences. Sage looked up as his mother entered the room once again. "What's he talking about when he says 'honest handling of city contracts'?" he asked.

"Well, I suspect he's talking about the fuss over the Tanner Creek sewer repair."

"You mean the sewer that caused all that flooding last year? The one that covered the Multnomah Athletic field with 5 feet of water?"

"Yup. The city engineer says the sewer's fixed but the rich folks who've got to pay for it are raising heck. They say it wasn't done right. That it won't last."

"Interesting. Maybe I should learn more about it."

"Good idea," she said. "Anyways, I got no time to talk about sewers right now. I hauled myself upstairs to tell you that a messenger came. Harry Lane's wife, Lola, will be here in half an hour. She wants to talk to you. So, you best get moving. You can't meet her wearing a bathrobe and your hair looking electrified."

"Okay, I'll get dressed but she's used to unruly hair. Harry's hair pokes up every which way half the time."

"Yeah, well, you're no Harry."

He'd just downed a slice of toast when Lola Lane tapped on Mozart's front door. She was a middle-aged, put-together woman wearing a modest walking suit, her dark hair tucked neatly beneath a simple hat. She'd pass largely unnoticed on the street. He suspected that was her intent.

He led her to the table where coffee sat waiting. Once both were settled, he said, "Mrs. Lane, is there something I can help you with?"

She looked at him direct, her gaze steady. "First of all, please call me Lola. We know too many of each others' secrets to stand on formality. And secondly John, you are correct. I am here to ask a favor."

Sage grinned, "Alright, Lola it is. I've always liked the sound of Lola Lane…kind of musical."

She laughed. "Harry agrees with you. He calls me that all the time." She paused, gathering her thoughts. Sage studied her. Not a beautiful woman but sweet-faced as his mother would say. Her erect posture reminded him that Harry once said she'd been a school marm.

She looked him, a wistful smile on her face. "Before I ask the favor, let me tell you a few things about my Harry." There was tenderness in how she said his name. It matched the tenderness he always heard in Lane's voice whenever he spoke of her.

"Harry and I played together as children. We had our disagreements, like all children, but I knew back then that he was special—bright, fun, fearless, but tender-hearted too. I think his first ten years living in Corvallis, before the family moved here to the city, are what made him the man he is today."

She paused, seeing his questioning look. "Ah, you don't know about that. Well, as a child, Harry spent time with the Indians. He likes to say they taught him about caring and sharing." She smiled and confided, "So, you see, my Harry is not like other white men."

Sage thought about that. She was right. Harry Lane was unique. He nodded, encouraging her to continue.

"An inner light guides Harry. His convictions give him immeasurable courage. He says there are only two questions: 'Is it right? And is it good for people?'."

Her lips twisted, "Sometimes, the answers to those questions cause him to take foolish risks."

"You think running for mayor is one of those foolish risks?"

She gave her head a vehement shake. "Oh, no. I think it is a risk but it's not foolish. The people need him. As a doctor, he roots out infection and heals. As mayor, he'll root out corruption and heal the city. He needs to do it. Otherwise, he'd regret it for the rest of his life. And, I'd be living with a sad and frustrated Harry. That's something I won't do."

Her expression turned pensive, almost dreamy as she continued, "As a Unitarian, Harry believes the prophet Jesus laid out a clear path to follow, a path of social justice. He'd never say it, but I suspect that, deep down, Harry believes if he sticks to that path, he'll be protected, always safe. That's why he's never hesitated to expose himself to diseases of every sort."

Sage straightened, sensing that Lola had reached the point of asking for the "favor."

She reached inside the black pocketbook she'd placed on the table to pull out two folded pieces of paper that had once been crumpled. Wordlessly, she pushed them across the table to Sage. He unfolded them, placing them side by side. They both said the same thing. "If you run for mayor, you will die."

He looked up, "Has Harry seen these?"

She nodded. "He let me see the first one before he tossed it in the fire. These last two he kept from me. I fished them out of his waste basket." She looked down, momentarily silent. When she raised her eyes they were steady and shone with fearful entreaty.

"Please, don't let them kill my Harry."

Typical chaos roiled within the *Journal's* offices. Men sitting at desks clacked away at type writing machines before surging to their feet, snatching the paper from the machine, and charging toward the stairway down into the building's basement where the presses hummed.

As expected, he found Ben Johnston in his tiny corner office, sleeves rolled up as his ink-stained fingers sent a fountain pen scrawling across paper.

Sage liked to believe the pleasure on the newspaperman's face was genuine and not just because Sage was one of the paper's primary investors.

"My goodness! John Adair! It's been a raccoon's age since I last saw you!" Johnston declared, standing up shake hands.

"Good afternoon, Ben. It's been a busy few months. I notice you've had a lot to stay on top of given the upcoming election."

Johnston cackled gleefully. "It's been fun, especially today. I bet the Republican machine men groaned when they saw our front page. Not that many of them read the *Journal* since their mouthpiece is the *Gazette*."

"You think they are worried about Harry Lane running for mayor?"

"If they're not, they should be. Harry has friends in both parties and the best reputation of any man in town except maybe Pastor Lamb and Rabbi Wise. Plus, Lane's not a prohibitionist. He admits he takes a drink now and again."

"You think a closed town is an election issue?"

"Yup. Harry will lose votes to the Democrat teetotaler candidate on the ballot who promises to close it down. But, Lane won't lose many votes since he also plans strict enforcement of the vice laws. He says there'll be no more increasing the city's coffers with license fees and fines. He wants to tax the rich."

"I saw the numbers you printed in the paper. There's a heck of a lot more registered Republicans in this town than Democrats."

"True, but there's a huge schism in the Republican Party. Mayor Williams has three men running against him in the primary election. Harry only has one, George Thomas. And even Thomas promises to help elect Harry should he lose to him—as he most assuredly will.

"Mayor Williams is in a different situation. There's every indication that his primary opponents will swing their supporters over to Lane's side."

"Why do you suppose there's such a schism among the Republicans?"

"More and more Republicans are fed up with the corruption and self-dealing of Williams and his cronies. People are dog tired of the gambling, prostitution, and saloons flaunting the law. They don't take kindly to encountering that everywhere they go."

The two men fell silent before Johnston stirred. "Okay John, we've done the niceties. I say this, without any rancor, what exactly are you doing here? You never come to see me unless it is to ask a favor. What is it that you need from me? Spit it out. I'm a busy man."

Sage laughed. "You nailed me. What I need is to tell you something in confidence and get your opinion." He raised a halting hand, "And, yes, there will be a story in it if I'm right and can do something about it. But, in the meantime, mum's the word."

"Sounds mysterious." Johnston sounded skeptical but his intense gaze said he was interested.

"We believe there's a plot afoot to assassinate Harry Lane."

Johnston's expression blanked as his face paled. "Good god. That can't be right."

Sage quickly told Johnston about the conversation Meachum overheard. Then he followed up by showing the threatening notes to him.

Johnston resisted believing. "Well, your guy said he didn't hear who they were targeting. And, the mentally unbalanced are always sending anonymous notes. They never amount to anything."

"I hope you're right Ben, I really do. But can we take that chance?"

"Hell, no." Johnston leaned forward. "How can I help?"

"Let's forget crazy people right now. It's likely that somebody is funding the conspiracy. So I thought you might have a handle on who stands to lose if Harry wins. And, also, who has the money to fund the attempt?"

Johnston swiped a hand down his face as if to wipe away thought. "There are so many, I don't know where to start."

"Maybe I should write them down," Sage suggested jokingly.

Johnston didn't think it funny. He reached into his desk drawer, pulled out pencil and paper, and handed them to Sage. "Yup, you better get ready to write," he advised.

Charlie Siringo turned up during Mozart's tea hour. "I just got a telegram from my friend at Dickensen. He knows where all the likeliest are, except for one." Siringo looked glum.

Sage, feeling overwhelmed from his visit with Ben Johnston, didn't want to dance around. "Please give me the bad news straight. It can't be worse than what I've already heard today."

"Why? Did someone shoot that St. Alban fellow again? I thought there's a police guard at the hospital."

Sage told him there were many more reasons to think that the second assassin planned to go after Harry Lane.

"Criminy, you sure got a way of complicating your life," Siringo said. "I'll tell you straight. My news is that I suspect the man we need to look for goes by the name of 'Tom Horn' ."

"What do you know about him?"

"Have you time for me to tell you a little story about Mr. Horn?"

Sage nodded.

Siringo took a big swig of his coffee, swallowed, and began talking. "For a while I was Dickensen's only cowboy detective. When I refused to do dirty work, they hired Tom Horn, out of Arizona. Some big Wyoming ranchers wanted the small ranches around their spreads. So, they contacted Dickensen. Tom Horn and some other scoundrels were sent up there. They murdered at least ten ranchers that I know about. Every darn one was an innocent man just trying to make a decent life for his family. It was Tom Horn who led that scurvy bunch of killers."

"Damn," Sage said. "Will Horn be a hard man to find and catch?"

"I know he will. My agency contact tells me he's taken to wearing disguises. It's gonna be dadgum hard to run him down—especially since you've got all these strangers in town because of that fair."

Siringo waited a beat before saying, "And, so that's why I'll stay in town a bit longer. I'll recognize that villain, even if he wears a bucket for a hat."

"Charlie, I can't ask you to do that, though I am happy to pay for your time if you do stay."

"Wahl, I can't take money direct from you since I consider you a friend. But, how about if you spring for me and Xenobia's lodgings? We might enjoy spending time in the big city. And, while we're a' touring round, we can be looking for Horn. That way, you and I will be even-steven for all the help you gave me in Prineville. Tell you true," he added, "there's no damn way I'd leave you and your friends to deal with Tom Horn without me. Like I said, you're my friend. Besides, it sounds like fun. Nothing will give me greater pleasure than putting Tom Horn down into the dirt." Charlie Siringo stood, slapped his cowboy hat on his head, gave Sage a silent nod, and headed out the door.

SEVEN

April 1, 1905

TWO DAYS AFTER LANE DECLARED his candidacy, Sage entered the kitchen to find his mother chuckling and shaking her head over the newspaper.

"What's so funny?" he asked, sitting across from her.

"Oh, this Tanner Creek sewer mess up. I'm chuckling because that sewer is what empties the rich folk's houses in the Regal neighborhood. You know, the one up near City Park. They've got to pay for the repairs and now their hired lawyer is making a big fuss."

"About what?"

"He claims the work is so shoddy that the whole thing will collapse and flood in the first big rain. Says the contractor shouldn't be paid a dime."

"I thought the city engineer, that Elliott fellow, approved the work."

"Yup, exactly." She sent him a pointed look.

Sage didn't want to think about sewer problems, especially since Mozart's was far from Tanner Creek. "I put the closed-for-the-noontime meal sign on the door. Is everyone able to come?"

Mae nodded. "Yes. Unlike you, Meach was up and at 'em early this morning. He and Charlie met for coffee. They're out looking for that Tom Horn fellow. I think Meachum feels it's kinda urgent since the hospital is releasing Vincent next week. He wants to find Horn before they leave on the train to Chicago. He says Portland's the best place to corner Horn because here, there's Charlie and the rest of us to help."

"When will they leave for Chicago?"

"He thinks this coming Friday—six days from now."

By twelve-thirty, all ten of them were assembled in the dining room. Gathered around a big table was the regular crew—Sage, Mae, Fong, Lucinda, Eich, Hanke, and Solomon and the three additions of Meachum, Siringo, and Xenobia Brown.

Deep affection swelled his heart as Sage gazed at their faces. Each one had proven he, or she, was willing to 'do right' as Harry Lane would say. For some of them, it was a sacrifice. Today, Angus Solomon was present at the risk of losing his job as maitre'd of the Portland Hotel's dining room. And, Charlie and Xenobia had traveled across half the state to be here.

Once everyone's plate was full, Sage described the situation in detail, finishing with, "I think Meach, Charlie, and Xenobia are best suited to look for the St. Alban assassin. Meach, because he tangled with the fellow, and maybe has already seen Horn trailing him and Vincent. Charlie, here, knows Horn and will see through any disguise." Looking at Charlie's new wife, he added, "Xenobia is good cover for Charlie and, for sure, two pairs of eyes are always better than one."

Xenobia grinned at his effort to include her and declared, "Not to mention, I'm a damn good shot!"

Charlie laughed aloud. "A better one than me, I'm ashamed to say!" Xenobia's face brightened at his admission and she gave him a consoling pat.

Their acceptance of that plan achieved, Sage moved on to the more troublesome chore. "With those three handling the St. Alban situation, it's up to the rest of us to figure out who wants to kill Harry Lane."

Solomon cleared his throat. At Sage's nod, he said, "How certain can we be that Harry Lane is the target? And, if he is, how likely is it that they'll try to kill him before the primary election? That's not until May 5th, thirty-five days from now and the general election is more than sixty-five days away. Protecting Lane for such a long time . . . well, that will be hard to do. He runs all over town treating patients at all hours."

Everyone silently mulled over those questions until Eich spoke up. "Solomon's right. How certain are we of the target and when they'll make the attempt?"

Sage said, "Mae, Fong, and I believe it's Harry they're after. Meach overheard the election being mentioned and Lola has given us two threatening notes someone sent to Harry. Besides, if it's someone else, then who?

"And, let's be honest, it's Harry's safety that matters most to us. Certainly, if we learn it's someone else they're targeting we'll try to protect that person. Until then, everything we know points to Harry as the politician in danger."

No one argued with Sage's conclusion.

Mae spoke up. "Okay now that us chickens are in agreement that we'll be keeping Harry safe, there's Angus's second question to answer: When's the attack going to come?"

Solomon's deep voice sounded once again. "If you don't mind, I'd like to offer my opinion on that issue." Hearing no objection, he continued, "John stopped by the dining room yesterday to alert me to the situation, so I have had time to mull it over. I believe nothing will happen until after the primary. There's a chance the Democrats will choose Harry's only real competition, that George Thomas fellow.

Solomon delivered his conclusion quietly, "No one will chance killing one of the two likely democratic contenders before knowing which one of them is the actual contender for the mayoral position."

That observation sat with the group for a while until Eich spoke up. "What are the odds that George Thomas fellow might win against Harry?"

Sage had discussed that probability with Ben Johnston. He repeated Johnston's opinion, "Thomas has a slim chance because he's a prohibitionist and wants a completely closed town, one with no saloons, gambling dens, or prostitution. There's a minority of folks in both parties who think the same—most don't. Still, for a Democrat to win, he has to pull a huge number of Republican votes away from Mayor Williams.

"Johnston says most people think only Harry has the widespread popularity to do that. Thomas would pose no threat to Williams or his Republican machine because there's no way he could win the general election."

Hanke, his normally placid face earnest, spoke for the first time, "You can bet Williams will win his primary. He has the *Gazette* pushing it, his entrenched political machine working it, and most of the town's wealthiest men who sit on his executive committee funding it. Money is no object for them."

"What is executive committee?" asked Fong, speaking for the first time.

"It advises the mayor. It includes some of the city's richest lawyers, bankers, manufacturers, and real estate men. Most folks think they tell Mayor Williams what to do. When they tell my police chief to jump, he just asks 'how high?' Far as I'm concerned, they run the city with Williams in the role of kind, grandfatherly, front man."

Sage wanted to move things along because the most difficult questions still lay ahead. "So what's the conclusion? Is Harry in danger before the primary?"

Fong again participated. "I think Angus right. Killer wait until sure Lane a problem."

Once again there was a nodding consensus. Sage breathed out slowly. So, they'd concluded that Harry was the target and the time to worry was if he won the primary.

Before he could speak, Fong said, "Better we not wait until after primary. We keep eye out now for killer but not need to search."

"Mr. Fong is right, we need to stay aware, but the real search begins if and when Harry wins the primary," Sage said as he pulled a folded paper from his pocket. "Still, we need to start thinking about who might be funding the plot. So, I asked Johnston who'd hate it if Harry Lane was elected mayor. I warn you, it's a long list. Hard to believe such a lovable fellow has so many enemies. "Anyway, I think we need to narrow it down to the most likely. If everyone agrees, I'll read the list and then we can go back and discuss them individually."

"How many are on that list?" Lucinda asked.

Surprised exclamations greeted his answer, "Seventeen."

At their astonished exclamations, he laughed and said, "Yup, shocked me too. Mae, Fong, and I think three of those are highly unlikely. You just let me know if you disagree.

"So, I think our most unlikely suspects are his Democratic opponent George Thomas, the cigar and beer unions, and the Chinese garden people. Thomas because he's a congenial man who has already said he'll support Harry if he wins. The unions are unlikely because their issue is that they don't want a closed town but then Harry isn't for that either. I think the least likely are the Chinese garden people. While they are probably miffed that Harry shot up their fertilizer jars . . ."

He stopped and looked at Fong who explained, "Oh they plenty mad about night soil jars but they know he not do it because he mean. Besides, they get sick, Harry Lane is doctor they want for Western medicine. He never be their target."

"Okay, that takes us down to the next ten who are slightly more likely. They're possible but not strong candidates for planning and funding an assassination. We have the rich, Harry's thinks they need to be taxed more. He also is against all the street vacations awarded to the rail and streetcar companies. He says they're robbing the city.

Sage paused to swallow water and nodded toward Hanke, "Present company excepted, Sergeant Hanke, but Harry vows he'll put a stop to police officers accepting bribes. He also says he'll raise their wages."

Hanke shook his head, saying ruefully, "Best of luck with that."

Sage understood Hanke's frustration. The city had too few policemen working for way too little pay—the worst combination possible.

He consulted his list and kept going, "Harry pushed for stricter pure food laws and for hiring more market inspectors to catch those adulterating foods. Some shopkeepers fought him on that. But that issue is already over. The laws have been passed and Harry's not involved anymore.

"Then there's the public ownership concept. He wants the public to own the river docks and the electric company. You can imagine how happy that idea makes the current owners.

"Harry feels the same about garbage collection—he wants it publically owned, not a private franchise. For sure he's vehemently opposed to the shanghai crimp, Larry Sullivan, getting the garbage franchise. Harry constantly harps about Sullivan and his shanghaiing operation. So, Sullivan's got two reasons to dislike Harry. And, Sullivan certainly knows unsavory men capable of murder.

"Last on the list of possible but, unlikely, conspirators are the men putting on the Exposition. Harry's accused them of crooked self-dealing in their selection of the location and in their hiring of the construction companies."

Eich's brow furrowed as he questioned, "Yet, you are saying that none of those you just listed are likely to be behind the assassination attempt? It sounds to me like all have both the money and motive to launch an assassination."

Sage nodded slowly. "You are right, Herman—they do. But, we think, and Ben Johnston agrees, that any attempt by Harry to affect their interests will be checkmated by what is certain to be a majority Republican city council. Except for overseeing the police, they have the majority control needed to overturn his vetoes of their decisions. More importantly, the mayor has no unilateral power to create ordinances controlling franchises, street vacations, the dock, electric or garbage ownership, or anything affecting the fair.

The city council has to approve almost every action he tries to implement. That'll never happen. In this town, what the rich men want, the rich men get—their handpicked city council will guarantee that.

"The only exception on the list is the police department. He does get to pick his chief of police who could fire officers. But, the patrolmen on the street knows Harry wants to raise wages. So, we think even the sworn officer bribe-takers will adopt the wait-and-see approach."

Lucinda leaned forward to ask, "If what you say is true, then who is left?"

Sage glanced at his list. "Crooked bureaucrats, crooked contractors, vice profiteers, and the so-called special police assigned to the North End vice district."

"Why those four? And what are the "special" police?" asked Xenobia.

Sage raised four fingers, turning them down as he made each point. "Both the bureaucrat and contractor crooks not only face social and financial ruin, they also could end up in jail. As for the vice profiteers, they are making enormous sums of money. One saloon operator brags that he clears over twenty thousand a month from liquor, prostitution, and gambling. And, the rich man who owns the building gets a chunk of that. That is exactly why, whenever there is a police raid, everyone knows about it beforehand. And, anyone arrested for show, is back on the street within a few hours. The strings running from the vice dens to the town's wealthy are many and durable."

Sage lowered the last upright finger and said, "And that brings us to the last potentials: the special police. These are untrained men who are not sworn officers but are still getting paid by the city. Theirs' are patronage jobs. If some fellow to whom Williams is beholden wants a job for his nephew, lickety-split that nephew becomes a special police officer assigned to the North End. Every one of them licks the gravy off every type of vice game down there. However, what the old mayor giveth, the new mayor can taketh away. And, the specials and their vice pals know it."

Sage tapped the newspaper lying on the table before him and said, "Harry's already launched a salvo against all four of them in his candidate petition. Let me read it aloud to you. He writes:

> I will, during my term of office, conduct the same in a business-like manner, keeping before me at all times the interests of the whole body of citizens. I guarantee that there shall be no Tanner-Creek sewer or other like scandals during my administration, but a strict and careful investigation will be made of every contract before it is let, and every job of work, before it is accepted or paid for, and I will faithfully and to the best of my ability enforce all vice laws and ordinances of the city.

Sage laid the paper aside. "So, in the first sentence, Harry declares there will be no favoritism or patronage. In the second, he warns the bribe-taking bureaucrats and crooked contractors that their time is over. And, in the final sentence, he serves notice on those benefitting from vice—the owners, operators, and those special police officers on the take—that no bribes or fines will be allowed instead of enforcement."

Sage gazed around the table. Each facial expression mirrored his conflicted response to Harry's bold message—pride and delight in his unequivocal stances and fear over the turmoil he was stirring up. Thinking it best to move on, Sage asked, "So, how about we start divvying up the tasks?"

EIGHT

April 3, 1905

BEFORE DAWN, MONDAY MORNING, SAGE headed toward the carpenters' hall beneath an umbrella as a cold rain beat down relentlessly. He was out early because Leo would be on the strike line once dawn broke.

He was feeling "chipper as a chipmunk with a full stash of nuts" as his mother would say. They knew what needed to be done and had ideas on how to do it.

Everyone had contributed good suggestions making Sage once again appreciate their habit of collaboration. By the end of their Saturday meeting, all agreed that only three teams were needed. Sage and Eich would investigate the issue of crooked bureaucrats and contractors. Hanke, Lucinda, and Fong would focus on the city's vice lords and Special police. Charlie, Xenobia, and Meachum, besides looking for the St. Alban assassin, would keep their eyes and ears open for any mention of harm planned for Harry. Meanwhile, Mae would run the restaurant. The scowl on her face said she wasn't happy with that task but she reluctantly agreed that someone needed to keep things going.

At meetings' end, Sage left to hunt down Sprig Flowers, the cab driver who'd so ably driven the gunshot St. Alban to the hospital. He found Flowers and his cab in the North End. After quickly explaining the threat to Lane and Sage saying he'd pay, Flowers agreed to park his vehicle wherever Harry was and drive Harry wherever he wanted to go, whenever he wanted to go. He said his adult son, Branch, could fill in for the late-night runs. It was not a cheap solution but it was one Sage could easily afford and would give Sage and the others peace of mind.

Of course, the next step was getting Harry to agree to their plan. And, to meet that challenge, Sage had a secret weapon, Lola Lane.

Today though, his task was to find a way to get next to the sewer repair contractor. He needed to learn who at city hall took bribes and who paid those bribes. Leo, as president of the carpenters union, might know. And maybe Leo could suggest a way into the contractor's world.

When he stepped into the carpenters' hall, Sage saw picket signs already stacked high at the top of the stairs, the room full of carpenters and their wives, and Leo standing atop a table finishing up a rousing speech.

Leo concluded, "Okay people. We all need to show great vigor walking the line. But, do not start physical altercations, no matter what the verbal provocation. However, if someone pushes you, push back just enough to stop their behavior."

A shout sounded from the back, "What if someone hits us or pushes the women?"

Leo laughed, "Well if that happens, all bets are off. Defend yourselves and help your brother or sister but never more than needed to protect and end the attack. News reporters will be there and you know the *Gazette* loves to portray us as ignorant, violent thugs, no matter who starts it."

After Leo was done giving instructions to the strike captains, he turned to Sage. "Boy, howdy, you're getting to be a regular here! You come to walk with us?"

"Ah, Leo, you know I would if I could but I still have to keep my personal beliefs hidden if I want certain folks to spill the beans around me."

Leo laughed. "I was just teasing. Right now, we don't need any help." He glanced around to make sure no one stood close and leaned in to say quietly. "I got a message from the exposition backers that they want to meet and dicker. I haven't told my folks. Too much hope early on can create unrealistic expectations if the resolution drags out."

"Well, you said the fair committee can't afford any delays at this juncture so let's hope they're sincere in wanting to resolve the problem."

Sage saw that the crowd was thinning out rapidly as people snatched up picket signs and headed down the stairs. "Look Leo, I need to get a job with that contractor who did the Tanner Creek sewer job. Harry thinks something about that job stinks and it's a big issue in his campaign. Also, I need to know how corruption happens on city construction contracts. I know you're too busy right now, but maybe we can get together later?"

"It might be few days before I can meet," Leo said. "But, as for you working for Riner Construction, I might have an idea. But it will cost you some bucks."

"Tell me."

"I recently sent a young fellow out to a Riner job. They needed a carpenter's helper. I assume you don't know how to do much carpentry."

Sage shook his head. "I know all about producing the logs that get cut into lumber but not much about how to nail things together."

"That's okay. Helpers just tote, saw, hold, and run errands. Most anyone can do that, though I have to warn you, it's hard physical labor. You'll be mighty tired at the end of the day."

"Logging's pretty physical work. I'm not afraid of it though I'm not used to physical labor these days. But, since you already sent somebody to the job site, how can you also send me?"

"Ah, that's the part that will cost you. The fellow I sent will be paid $2.50 a day, six days a week. He's a good kid but his wife's just had a baby and she's having trouble taking care of it. It was a hard birthing. He asked me if I knew anyone who might be willing to volunteer to help her since they have so little money. How about you do the work and turn your earnings over to him so he can stay home to help his wife?"

Sage grinned. "Perfect solution, Leo! When can I start?"

"Tomorrow bright and early. Be here by six. I'll get word to him and you can meet and agree on the plan. I suspect he'll be relieved and grateful. And, if you're lucky, it won't be raining."

Sage wasn't looking forward to his next meeting. He was skipping his hosting duties during Mozart's supper hour to visit the Lanes instead. That was at Lola's suggestion. He'd gone to see her in the late afternoon. She'd quickly agreed with the plan to use Sprig Flowers and his cab. She suggested he return for dinner, saying Harry always tried to be home by six-thirty p.m. Once Harry ate, he'd be in the best mood to consider Sage's plan. "Don't let him pooh-poo the idea," she instructed, adding, "I'll make sure Harry agrees or else."

Sage didn't ask what her "or else" threat might be. Every couple created their own ways of resolving conflicts and those ways were none of his business.

Harry answered Sage's knock, greeting him with a big grin around a cigar clenched in his teeth. "Well, hey there John. You're a sight for sore eyes. So happy to see you! Lola said you'd be coming to dinner. Come in, come in. Shake off the wet. I bet this rain has the creek banks overflowing. I can't imagine what's happening inside that Tanner Creek sewer."

They had a pleasant meal and a few guffaws over Republican reactions to Harry's candidacy. Once dessert was served Sage broached the subject of the Tanner Creek construction project.

Harry shook his head but admitted, "You know, I don't know a heck of a lot about that situation—just what I read in the newspapers. It sounds like a corrupt deal. You say you're going to look into it? While I'd surely like to know more, I am a bit puzzled as to the reason for your interest. The Mozart's building is far from it so you won't be stuck paying for it like those rich fellows on the hill."

Sage looked at Lola and she nodded. Taking a deep breath, he launched into his primary purpose for being in Harry's house. "Look Harry, I know about the death threats you've received."

Harry flushed and he shot an accusing look at Lola. She answered his silent accusation with a steadfast gaze and lifted chin.

Sage jumped in, hoping to forestall any domestic recriminations. "Yes, Lola told me about the written threats but I already knew something was being planned." He went on to recite what Meachum had overheard in the Portland Club.

Although Harry dismissed that worry with a hand wave, his wrinkled brow said he found the information troubling. Still, he protested, "Look, John, even if the threats are genuine, there's no way you can protect me. I am out and about constantly. If someone wants to take a shot at me, there are boatloads of opportunities. I suppose these lazy critters might decide to protect us here in the house," he said, gesturing at the two big dogs lying stretched out within begging distance of the dinner table, "But away from home, it would be well-nigh impossible."

Sage nodded in agreement but said, "Well, we met as a group. You know most of the people. We intend to find the would-be assassin and discover who is funding the plan. One thing we agree on is that you are fairly safe for now. That will change when you win the primary on May 5th.

"Still, until then, we need you to take precautions while we try to track down the who and why. That's why, to keep you safe, we've hired a cabbie and his son. Between them, they'll be at your beck and call, day and night until after the general election. The cab will park outside your house and office, ready to ferry and wait for you wherever you need to go whether on a house call or to attend a meeting. The idea is that, by having a cabbie on hand, you'll be safer. You won't be standing on curbs waiting for one and you'll know the driver. It's not a lot, but it's something."

Harry burst out, "Good lord man! That's crazy! I can't let you do that. It will cost a fortune!"

"Harry, believe me, I can well afford it. I don't operate Mozart's because I need the money."

Harry cocked a questioning eyebrow at Sage's statement before raising another objection. "But sometimes, I get called out in the middle of the night."

"Yes, we know. The cabbie, Sprig Flowers, has a son eager to do the night shift."

"I can't have those poor souls sitting out in front of my house all day and all night!"

For the first time, Lola spoke, her voice a gentle wheedle. "Harry dear, there's that small room off the front hall. I'll fix it up with a cot and some bedding. It's only temporary, just until after the general election. Once elected, you'll have police protection. "

Harry shot her a rueful look. "You've been conspiring against me, wife!"

Lola's eyes filled with tears as she stretched out a hand to touch her husband's. "Harry you are everything to me and the girls. I don't know how we could go on without you."

"Oh criminy, Lola, you know I can't stand to see you cry." Shaking his head, he turned to Sage, a corner of his mouth quirked. "Okay, we'll try it out. But, I reserve the right to cancel the arrangement if it cramps my activities too much."

While Harry escorted the dogs out the kitchen door, Lola said quietly, "I notice you didn't tell him about Mr. Fong."

Sage responded, "Well, that won't start in earnest until after the primary. I figure we get him used to Step 1 before we introduce Step 2."

"Good idea." She stood and began clearing the table just as Harry returned.

"What's a good idea," he asked suspiciously.

"Oh, that we give the night shift fellow breakfast," she responded airily before disappearing into the kitchen.

Harry looked suspicious but Sage kept his face blank even as he wondered whether all wives learned to be such fast prevaricators.

Hanke knocked on Mozart's kitchen door just as they were closing down. After carefully hanging up his dripping mackintosh he took a seat at the kitchen table He pulled a handwritten list of names from an inside pocket as he said, "This lists the police detectives and the special police officers who are on the take in the North End."

Sage looked first at the long list, Puzzled, he asked, "So soon? You certainly gathered these names faster than I expected."

"Nah, I've been making that list for some time. Just about every North End detective is dirty. There hasn't been a single raid where the operator wasn't forewarned.

"As for the special police, that list was a bit harder to get. The chief doesn't tell us their names and they operate separate from the rest of us." Hanke hesitated before saying, with a slightly red face, "The records gal seems a bit sweet on me. We made a trade. I took her to dinner and she took the names off their wage sheets."

Sage eyed the twenty-five names in silence before saying, "I'll copy this list and hand it out to everybody."

"Tell them to keep it close. It's best if the men on that list don't know what we're up to. It'd be like jabbing a nest of cobras with a stick," Hanke warned unnecessarily.

NINE

April 4, 1905

FORTUNE IS SMILING TODAY, HERMAN Eich mused. He paused to bathe in the light streaming through a gap between the thinning clouds. Birds started to twitter and flower buds opened. Nature was heralding the end of yet another spring drizzle. He'd been prevented from venturing out yesterday because of a heavy downpour. It would have been useless. His conversations with house servants usually took place outside, at the mansions' back doors. Even the friendliest servants wouldn't stand chatting in the rain. Despite that reasonable excuse, he'd felt guilty knowing the others were out searching while he stayed snug in his lean-to, repairing his porcelain bits.

Trudging along, hands gripping the shafts of his cart, he let his thoughts drift back to the Sunday meeting. His mind's eye traveled slowly across the faces of those who'd gathered. Such beauty in their strength and dedication, he mused. An Emerson poem came to mind, and stepping to its cadence, he began softly reciting aloud, only adding "women" because New England's transcendental poet forgot them. Not something he could do.

> What makes a nation's pillars high
> And its foundation strong?
> Not gold—only men and women can make
> A people great and strong;
> Men and women who for truth and honor's sake

Stand fast and suffer long.
Brave people who work while others sleep
Who dare while others fly
They build a nation's pillars deep
And lift them to the sky

In a nutshell, that's what he and the others gathered around that Sunday table were trying to do: build the country strong and true. If pride can swell a heart then the thought of my friends is what swells mine, he told himself.

Eich reached the slope's steepest part. Above him loomed mansions from where the wealthy could gaze upon the city that had made them rich. Eich found such displays of wealth shameful when so many others lived in hovels or slept on the streets.

Reaching the hillside bench of mansions, he headed for the first kitchen door. There the cook threw open the door, her face a smiling welcome. "Why, Mr. Eich! You are a happy sight. We were just saying it's been some time since we've seen you!"

Opening the door wider, she gestured him inside, exclaiming, "Come in, come in. I have fresh coffee on the stove. Mister and Missus are gone for the day. He's to work, she's to some tea party or such and they aren't expecting guests for dinner. So, we can have ourselves a proper visit."

Thereafter he enjoyed a pleasant conversation with the cheerful cook and young housemaid. Unfortunately, they knew nothing about the Tanner Creek sewer situation. As he stood to leave, a few fresh-baked cookies were slipped into his pocket.

It wasn't until his fifth stop at a mansion's back door that he gleaned significant information. He and the household's cook sat on the side porch in wicker chairs while resting their eyes on a garden of blooming flowers and sprouting leaf buds. The sky had cleared leaving them bathed in warming sunlight. He shifted in his chair and began fishing, "I suppose your employer is a trifle annoyed about the whole Tanner Creek scandal."

She chortled and exclaimed, "Lord, have mercy! That man's beyond annoyed, I can tell you that. Why, he made this house the meeting place for all thems that be upset. I've heard aplenty, let me tell you."

Glancing sideways, he saw her cheery face turn prideful as she said, "The mister always asks me to serve if there be guests in the house. He says our maid Sylvia has two left feet and fumble-fingers. He's right but she's a sweet gal and hard working. The missus refuses to fire her."

"I wonder how he found out the sewer job had problems."

She chuckled and said, "That were a funny thing. Mayhap I know how it came about. One night this fellow knocked on the door. When I answered it, he said he needed to see the mister, that it was important. It not being my place to decide such things, I went and told the mister. He came out, listened to the man, and then took him into the library."

"You couldn't hear what the stranger had to say?"

"Well, afore they went into the library I heard him say that new sewer down below is going to collapse. Anyways, after that, there's been meetings aplenty. Mostly neighbor men come but, an attorney was at the last one."

"And, you serve coffee and such to them when they meet?"

"That's right. And, I'm a 'listening because I got no choice since when they're upset, they talk loud. They say won't pay for something that's going to collapse."

"Have you heard anything else interesting?"

"Wahl, they're worried the contractor will sneak back to cover up the problems. And, one of them's so worried he's down there every night. They're trying to make the mayor let them send down their own inspectors. One said the city engineer's 'crooked as a dog's hind leg'. "

Additional probing yielded nothing further but Eich was satisfied. He led her to his cart and lifted the tarpaulin covering his goods. After carefully fingering the restored porcelain bits, she plucked up an especially lovely bowl. It was nearly flawless, his repair scarcely noticeable. She fumbled in her apron pocket for money, telling him it was to be a wedding present for a favorite niece.

He refused her coin. Some time ago he'd learned she supported an apartment and three grandchildren on a measly $3.50 a week wages. Their mother had died and their father had "gone the way of the drink, like so many men do these days," she'd told him.

After a token protest, she accepted Eich's gift, telling him, "Next time you come back, I'll make sure to provide treats to go with your coffee," she promised.

As his cart rolled down the sidewalk, a sense of well-being filled him. Their talk had been fruitful. He'd learned something important to share with the team, thanks to a serving maid with two left feet and fumble fingers.

Hours later Eich waited in Mozart's kitchen for Sage to appear. Mae waited with him, her nimble fingers peeling the last of the cellar potatoes. He thought about how he'd loved her face from the moment he first saw her. She was one of those people—the longer you knew them, the more beautiful they seemed.

Sage had once commented that her face carried the nobility of a ship's figurehead. In the dim light of the building's only electric bulb, he had to agree with Sage. Her face showed such character, with its fine brow, penetrating eyes, and generous mouth above a determined chin. He thought her a great beauty.

He felt the familiar roiling in his thoughts: Keep his simple lean-to and ragpicker life, or create a more ordinary one with Mae Clemens. He felt that push-pull almost every day, especially when he was with her, like now. As for her, he didn't know whether she'd even accept a proposal. She never raised the subject so he didn't either—taking the coward's way out.

"If you don't try Ida's canned peach pie, her heart will break," murmured the noble figurehead when she looked up with a wry smile and glanced toward the cook busily preparing Mozart's supper menu.

He laughed. "I will definitely eat her pie," he said, sliding it closer. "Any idea when Sage will bless us with his presence?"

"That's a bit tricky. He's just started working for the contractor who did the Tanner Creek repairs. He hoped to return before the supper hour but figured they'd work him until sundown."

Eich shrugged and forked in a bit of peach and pastry. He didn't have to fake his "mmm" of pleasure. "This pie is top drawer, Miz Ida!" he called to the cook who smiled at the compliment.

Sage's feet dragged as he walked from the streetcar stop to Mozart's. Who'd think toting boards, moving ladders, and picking up scrap could be so exhausting? Thank god, the union carpenters won their eight-hour-day fight a few years back. He smiled, remembering that they'd helped with that win.

He was satisfied. The day had gone well. He'd left Mozart's as the sun rose. As promised, Leo and a young man awaited him inside the carpenters' hall. Once he heard the proposition, the bright-eyed fellow readily agreed, expressing his gratitude and vigorously shaking Sage's hand before departing.

Leo clapped Sage's shoulder and said, "You've done that little family a very good turn. He says because of the baby's colic, neither he nor the wife get enough sleep. Now they can trade off."

After leaving the union hall, Sage caught the streetcar to the Irvington neighborhood where the Tanner Creek contractor had a construction job. He soon found the work site where a small apartment house was being built. He asked for the foreman and was directed to a middle-aged, bulky man with an aggrieved expression.

"You look a bit old for this type of work," commented the foreman, Oscar Muckleroy. "Truth be told, if Leo hadn't sent a message personally requesting that I take you on, I wouldn't. I see that you also failed to bring tools."

Sage apologized for his lack of tools, saying they'd just been stolen. That earned him a shake of the head and the order, "Go help Emil, he's over there building that work shed. You can't mess that up too much. Do exactly what Emil tells you to do. He'll decide whether we keep you or not."

Emil proved to be much friendlier. When Sage later asked if Muckleroy was always so grumpy, Emil said something interesting, "Actually, it's kinda strange. He's a good and fair boss but he's turned sour this last month."

"Trouble at home?" Sage pried.

Emil shook his head and said another interesting thing. "Nah, he and Betty live just a few doors down from me and Esther. Betty told my wife that she can't figure what's got him so unhappy. He's sour at home as well." That was the end of what Emil was willing to say.

Despite the hard work, Sage enjoyed the day. Emil was cheerful, kindly, and a pleasure to watch. Every measurement was perfect, every nail was driven straight. At day's end, they stood admiring the sturdy shed they'd built. "The building owner plans to use it for storage so we built it right sturdy. It'll last," he told Sage.

Sage tried probing a bit more. "Did Muckleroy work on the Tanner Creek sewer project?"

"We all did. It took 120 men working three shifts, 24 hours a day. I sure wouldn't want to do that again. It was a nasty, nasty job."

"Maybe Muckleroy's worried about that scandal involving him."

Emil sent Sage a penetrating look before shrugging. "Don't know. Could be," was all he said before stooping to toss his tools into a bag. "Best not to think on it," he said, before commenting, "You work pretty good for an old fellow. You coming back tomorrow?"

When Sage said that he was, Emil clapped him on the shoulder and strode off, tool bag swinging from his hand.

Sage mulled over the little he'd learned. So, Muckleroy's grumpiness was something new. Maybe the change in Muckleroy is connected to the Tanner Creek scandal. But, how he could find out?

It was full dark when he stepped through the back door into Mozart's kitchen. He was in a hurry. There was little time to get upstairs and change clothes before the customers began streaming in for dinner. Spotting Mae and Herman waiting in Mozart's elegant dining room, he asked that they accompany him upstairs. They waited in his room while he went down the hall to bathe and dress in his suit and bow tie.

Once he joined them at the window table, Herman quickly shared what he'd learned from the cook, adding, "If a person was of a mind, he might go into the sewer and see, firsthand, what kind of job was done. I've got to admit, I'm curious."

"How does one get into it?" Sage asked.

"Climbing down through one of the manholes."

Mae spoke up. "I've been reading in the *Journal* about those manholes. Evidently the plans called for only four of them but, according to the paper, there are six. Riner has dinged the city extra for them. That city engineer, Elliott, is backing Riner up."

Sage shot her a grateful look, glad she was staying on top of the reports like she'd promised. That's not all. She said she'd eavesdropped on Mozart's female clientele, saying, "Some of the ladies were talking about the sewer over tea this afternoon. Their husbands are insisting that the city not pay the contractor because of his shoddy work. They hired Erskine Wood's law firm."

That was a curious development. Wood was a former law partner of Williams. "Did you hear anything else?" Sage asked.

"Well, I know that the city engineer had an inspector on site every day. The ladies think the city engineer, his inspector, and that Riner contractor are all corrupt."

Sage pondered that. "Hmm. Add that to what Eich just learned and it sounds like an independent inspector might be involved fairly soon. Given they're some of the city's richest men, I bet we'll learn what's happened soon enough."

Mae exchanged a look with Eich before saying, "Might be a good idea to take a look for yourself."

Sage's mouth fell open. "Me go down into the sewer? I can't think of a worse place."

Mae sent him her raised eyebrow look and he caught her meaning. A coal mine and its sorting shed were worse places. They both knew that.

TEN

April 4, 1905

THE CARRIAGES AND CABS DRAWING up to drop off well-dressed women raised eyebrows amongst the city's wealthy matrons strolling beneath the trees in the adjoining park blocks. Certainly, the three-story stone house with its mansard roof was sufficiently elegant to justify the opulent dress of its female visitors. But, everyone knew it was a parlor house, a brothel, a bordello, or whatever catchy name one used to designate a place where women sold their bodies. The city's so-called decent women always made a show of passing it with averted eyes and hissed comments.

The decor inside was so sumptuous that the arriving guests momentarily paused to take it in until Lucinda Collin's warm greetings drew their attention. Soon, she was ushering them into a dining room already set with china and silver.

Her warmth was genuine. She liked and admired these women. Like her, they paid well, took care of the girls in their charge, and didn't tolerate abuse. They also hated pedophilia, having helped run four such despicable places out of business.

Usually, their group gathered once a month at a nice restaurant but today was special. It was not their regular time to meet and for the first time, they'd been invited to Lucinda's parlor house where most had never been.

Minutes later, Lucinda sat at the table's head, smiling fondly at the dozen women sitting around her large dining table, eating excellent food, and chatting comfortably. It was a jolly group. The times were good. More cash was flowing into their purses from the influx of Exposition workers. They gleefully agreed that, once the fair opened, its visitors would mean even more money.

Hester, a particular favorite of Lucinda's, was the first to ask about the day's business. "Lucy, this has been delightful but I think there must be a reason that you invited us to your lovely house and fed us like royalty. How about you tell us what you need us to do?"

Lucinda laughed. "Yes. You've called it right, Hester. Simply put, we think someone plans to kill Harry Lane. There's a good chance it's one of the city's vice men and his financial backers."

Exclamations greeted her announcement.

The first woman's words earned a nod from every woman around the table when she said, "Well, I'm of two minds where Harry Lane is concerned. On one hand, he promises to shut down vice, which means our businesses. But, on the other hand, he's helped more than once when one of my girls has taken sick. He treats them kindly and with respect, which is rare among the city doctors. Besides, he's a damn fine doctor."

Lucinda welcomed that response. "Well, I agree that there is a risk that Harry might try to close us down. But he seems fair-minded. He's talking about arresting the customers as well. I do know he also intends to fire the bribe-grasping cops and detectives. That will help everyone's bottom line. I guess the question is whether you'd prefer to have Williams to continue as mayor or Harry Lane."

The women around the table exchanged looks and seemed to reach consensus. Hester voiced their opinion, "Okay, we all agree that Harry's the better man. We have to hope he doesn't ruin our businesses and that he focuses on those really awful cribs and the back alley women and their pimps. Besides, who knows? Maybe he'll also do something about the landlord leeches. I'm sick to death of them. They charge us five to seven times more than what they could get from a legit business. As for the crooked cops, they're slime and too many of them get rough with my girls."

A second woman said eagerly, "I heard that Harry likes the idea of a tin plate on every building, naming its owner. That happens, and those landlords will sell. Then we can try to buy our own places like you've done here."

This triggered another woman to say, "That's the best thing to do. Thanks to Lucinda's loan, I bought my own house. It's small, but at least it's mine. Now I only have to deal with the corrupt cops. And, of course, the problem with that is that if they raid me now, I don't have a wealthy landlord to make them drop the charges."

Hester spoke again, "So, Lucy, how can we help save Harry?"

"We need to find the assassin before he strikes. A man was overheard talking with others in the Portland Club about his plan to kill Harry. The killer's stocky, short, with a light streak in his hair at his left temple. Once we find him, people will trail him to his backer. We have to identify them, otherwise the backers will just hire someone else."

The women tossed around some ideas until one noted that the assassination meetings would likely continue to happen at the Portland Club. The others agreed. The main problem was that they all ran brothels, not the girls working the saloons.

They mulled over that conundrum until one said, "I got it! One of my girls has a friend who works in the Portland Club. Apparently, the place caters to a slightly higher class customer so her earnings are pretty good—fifty cents per customer instead of the usual twenty-five."

Lucinda brightened. "Do you think she'd help us?"

"That's where we're in luck. My gal says her friend is tired of servicing up to 40 men a day. Plus she's gotten gonorrhea twice because she can't take time to use an antiseptic between customers. So, she's begged my gal to see if I'd take her on. I would have earlier, but my rooms have been full until yesterday, when one of my gals left to marry a farmer. So, I have room to take on a new gal."

Everyone around the table leaned forward to hear her next words which didn't disappoint. "I'll have my gal bring her around. If she is presentable, I'll tell her she can come live with me provided she stays working the Portland Club through the election and tell us about any meetings between the white streak guy and anyone else. I'll also find out if she's seen the fellow and maybe who he's meeting."

Lucinda had a sudden idea and said, "Would you mind if I met her and brought a friend? We'd like to ask her some questions. Maybe she won't have to keep working there through the election."

The woman thought there'd be no problem with that. After quickly agreeing all would keep an eye out for the suspected assassin, the party broke up. Soon all were aboard and leaving in their waiting carriages.

Lucinda helped Elmira clear the table. Once they were done, she asked Elmira to sit. At Lucinda's request, the housekeeper had listened to the discussion. "Well, what do you think?" she asked.

Elmira grinned, "I think you ladies made a good plan. I didn't want to say anything but, you know, lots of black and Chinese folk work in those saloons washing dishes and toting barrels. It may be they'll see that fella you be looking for. Since we black folk number less than 1,500 in the city, men, women, and children, it'll be easy for me to get the word out. Mr. Fong can do the same with his people."

"Great idea! I'd never have thought of that. You'll ask your folks to be on the lookout?"

"Sure enough, I will," Elmira said before heading for the kitchen adding, "I best help with the washing up if we want to open on time this afternoon."

Lucinda went to the side buffet for a pen and paper. She'd send a message to Sage. Maybe he'd turn up in response. She wouldn't mind seeing John Sagacity Adair every day of her life. "And, that's the problem, isn't it Lucy Collins?" she said aloud.

An outraged Sergeant Hanke stormed into the chief's office. "That raid last night was a waste of time. The saloon keeper had the stairs to the second floor blocked off, the shooting gallery in the alley was mysteriously gone, and there was no money on the card tables. Heck, they were pretending to play for match sticks! They were warned about the raid!"

Chief Hunt raised an eyebrow. "How do you suppose that happened?"

Hanke bristled and fumed, deliberately emphasizing his exasperation. "It's those damn special police. We found two of them sitting in there, swilling free beer. They claimed to be policing the joint and swore nothing untoward was going on. Well, that's true. Nothing was going on because they'd warned the saloonkeeper."

Hunt sighed and said, "I can't think of the last time we had a successful raid. Even if we arrest the saloonkeeper and a few prostitutes, they're out once they pay the fines and never see the inside of the courtroom."

"Yeah, and who's responsible for that? Their bigwig landlord or the brewery owner. I'm beginning to think we should just give up and let the whole North End go to vice."

Hunt shrugged. "Well, that can't happen. Those fines and fees make up half the city's budget."

Hanke knew Hunt was right. The rich successfully fought tax increases so the city's money had to come from somewhere. Still, he found the idea repulsive because those fines and fees were passed on to the customers—many of them poor and alcoholic.

He moved on to the real purpose of his visit. "And what about those special so-called policemen? According to my sources, every single one of them, and most of the detectives assigned to the North End, are raking in bribes and getting free booze and women."

"Look, I understand your frustration. But, you know I can't do a thing about the special police. The mayor sends me a name and I have to hire the man. Every one of them is somehow connected to one of the mayor's friends. When I try to transfer a bad apple out of the North End, I get told I can't do that. The mayor's executive committee, his rich buddies, raise a fuss. In one form or another, they benefit from that vice money. They even made a rule that the specials could only be deployed in a red-light district. That means I can never transfer them out."

"Chief, how am I supposed to keep our trained patrolmen honest? They are trying to raise families on a measly $80 per month. They know those untrained special cops are raking in hundreds. Hell, a good share of my men likely already sweeten their pockets with a bit here and there. It would be far worse if I couldn't keep from working inside the North End."

Hunt raised a hand, saying, "I know, I know. But that's the way it is. That's how this city works."

"Do you think things will get better if Harry Lane is elected mayor?"

Hunt sighed deeply. "Well, I know I won't keep my job. He's criticized me more than once. I've heard he wants to enforce the vice laws instead of taking fines and looking the other way. And he's been damn critical of the special police arrangement. I can't believe he'd continue it, not unless he wants to use it to pay off some of his supporters."

Hanke tried not to show that Hunt had finally given him the opening he needed. "You're right. Lane tries to do exactly what he says."

Hunt nodded thoughtfully. "Exactly. He's promised no favoritism or nepotism. That'd pretty much do away with the special police."

"Have you heard any of them mentioning Lane? None of them will talk to me because I've been outspoken about what worthless curs they are."

"Yup, they seem to hate his guts to a man. They know which side of their bread is buttered. They'll do their best to get Williams re-elected."

❀ ❀ ❀

"Any luck finding the tall, skinny fellow, Horn?" Sage asked as he, Meachum, and Charlie sat around St. Alban's bed. The patient looked much better with his face pink and his gray eyes once again lively.

Charlie cleared his throat to say, "Wahl, I did get a bit of helpful news from my buddy who works for Dickensen. He wrote that since I last saw that lowdown Tom Horn, he got into a fight with some fellow who bit off the bottom of Horn's left ear. My buddy says it's real obvious."

"That must have hurt," Meachum commented with a smile.

"Not near as much as the fellow who did the biting. Horn drilled him in the forehead. He's dead as a doornail."

The men exchanged frowns but it was Vincent who spoke up. "Any hints of where this Horn fellow might be?"

Charlie was the one who answered, "Wahl, I think you could say we've narrowed things down a bit. We've made the rounds, dropped a few of Adair's coins here and there. Somebody's gonna see him sooner or later."

Vincent looked skeptical. "I agree with the idea of finding him. It will be far more dangerous if he gets on the train with us to Chicago. But boys, I have to tell you, I'm getting on that train come this Friday. I can't afford to dilly-dally over leaving here. If we're going to have a successful convention and create our one big union, we've got to get to Chicago so I can help pull it together."

Charlie stood, slapped his hat on his head, and gestured to Meachum. "Come on partner, we got us a lily-livered snake to trap. Can't have him shooting holes in this feller a second time."

Once they were gone Vincent looked at Sage and said, "That Charley Siringo is something else."

"Yeah. And, he's not someone you'd want to mess with. I've seen him in action."

Leaving the hospital room, Sage saw that the young policeman, Dan Carter, was still assigned to guard Vincent. He snapped upright and alert upon seeing Sage. That was reassuring too.

Once outside, Sage headed toward Mozart's, mulling over how best to carry out the unpleasant task he and Eich planned for the next night. Deep in thought, he didn't notice the lanky figure lurking beside a nearby porch column, his fingers thoughtfully massaging a mutilated ear.

ELEVEN

April 5, 1905

BEST LAID PLANS AND ALL that. Their foray into the sewer was delayed by heavy rain such that, when they lifted the manhole cover late that night, it was to see swift water filling the pipe below. Sage felt both frustration and relief. Neither he nor Eich had been looking forward to the task. They lowered the cover and separated, each heading for a warm bed.

Rain the next day made for a miserable worksite. With a grin, Emil informed him carpenters never stop work for the rain. It being Oregon, they'd starve if they did. So, the crew kept hard at erecting the small apartment house atop its newly set foundation. Oddly, Oscar Muckleroy, the foreman was absent and when asked where he was, Emil looked momentarily perplexed before shrugging.

After examining the foundation, Emil pronounced it acceptable. He told Sage that the building's owner was an experienced developer who knew construction, adding, "Good thing too! Looks like they poured decent concrete."

Seeing Sage's puzzled look he said, "Ain't always the case, unfortunately," making Sage realize, once again, that he still had a lot to learn about the construction business.

Early the next morning, on the way to the job site, he stopped by the union hall. Upon seeing Leo, he said, "I saw in this morning's *Journal* that congratulations are in order. You called it right. You must be delighted the strike ended so quickly."

Leo grinned, "Not as happy as the men and their wives. We got everything we asked for, thanks to the other trades refusing to cross our picket lines. We brought the exposition work to a standstill. So, the promoters agreed to assign all the nonunion contractors and their workers to separate sites so our men don't have to work with them. And, we got the hours and wages we wanted. Some of those nonunion workers now say they want to join up. So, it was a big win all around."

"Leo, that is great to hear. I wish I could hang around to celebrate but I have to get to the job site. I'm finding I'm pretty ignorant when it comes to carpentry and construction. Emil, the fellow I'm working with, said something about concrete I didn't understand. I was hoping you could educate me. I figure they must have used concrete on the Tanner Creek sewer job."

"For sure they did. What do you need to know?"

"For one, what's the difference between cement and concrete? When I called the foundation cement he just shook his head at me."

An understanding smile flashed across Leo's face. "Cement is a binding agent. It's a combination of clay and limestone. When cement is added to rocks, sand, and water in the correct proportions, it becomes concrete. That's the building material in foundations, sidewalks, street curbs, and such."

"So, why would Emil say the owner knowing construction meant the foundation was good?"

"That's easy. Cement costs more than rocks or sand. So, a crooked building contractor can save on material costs by using too much sand and rocks in the concrete and not enough cement. It looks okay, but crumbles and deteriorates over time, sometimes quickly, depending on how much sand he's used. A developer's specifications won't permit that, but if someone isn't watching, the switch can occur. Sounds like the developer on your job site pays close attention."

"Aren't city inspectors supposed to be keeping an eye out for that kind of cheating?"

Leo's lips twisted. "They are supposed to, but you need an honest inspector. Sometimes one is hard to find."

As Sage rode the streetcar and trudged to work, questions filled his head. He wondered how many ways a contractor might cheat on a construction project. Maybe that's what happened with the Tanner Creek sewer. He couldn't stay to talk further with Leo but the union boss agreed to meet later that day to further enlighten Sage.

The rain never let up. By the time he and Leo entered a cafe, Sage was soaked and his feet felt like blocks of ice. Fortunately, because Muckleroy was again mysteriously absent, Emil was in charge and let everyone quit early. Portland's April weather was always an unpredictable mix of delight and deluge.

Over hot coffee Leo filled him in on how a sewer project could go wrong, cautioning, "I'm not a bricklayer and carpenters usually don't get involved in sewer work except to install temporary supports for the project. That said, when I was out at the exposition site today I spoke with the Bricklayers Union president. He said the Tanner job was predominately nonunion because most of the union folks were busy working the exposition. But, he said he'd heard rumors about it."

"What kind of rumors?"

"Mostly that its construction doesn't meet the project specifications."

"How can that be? The paper said an inspector was on site every day. And the city engineer gave it his blessing. He's told the city council to pay the contractor. As you know, that contractor is the very fellow I'm working for, Riner."

"Exactly. And it could be that their approval tells you more about the inspector and engineer's honesty than it does about the quality of the job."

Sage leaned forward eagerly to ask, "In what ways could a contractor like Riner cheat?"

"Well, if those rich folks get their way and an independent inspector goes down into the pipe, we will know for certain but there's many ways. The first thing you need to know is that although they call it a "pipe," that sewer is not a pipe. Instead, it's an enclosed canal. Bricks form the ceiling and walls and stone pavers the floor. Mortar and concrete hold it all together. So there's lots of different materials involved.

"A crooked contractor will short the materials, use inferior materials, erect defective walls, and floors, fail to properly tamp it in from the outside—those are just a few of the ways Riner might have padded his profits."

Leo paused and thought. "And then, one must wonder how he could have landed the project in the first place. We got a real problem when it comes to city projects."

"What do you mean?"

"If the city engineer is crooked and expects a piece of the action, he'll inflate the projected cost of the project. Rumor is the engineer, William

Elliott, does that. In Tanner sewer case, the engineer convinced the city council to accept Riner's bid even though it was above the project estimate."

"Also, I've heard the contractors collude on the bids. Before the contract is let, the biggest contractors get together and agree on who will win the bid and at what price. They'll settle on the lowest bid price to be submitted. It is always above the city engineer's estimate. Next, they decide which of them will submit that winning bid."

"How can the contractors collude in advance of the bidding? I thought the city's calculations are supposed to be secret."

"Exactly. But experience tells us that they aren't. All it takes is a quiet word from a crooked city engineer.

"I don't understand. Why do the contractors give up the chance to win the bid? And why would the city engineer do that?"

"Well, they rotate who gets to make the lowest bid. And, every contractor who colludes gets a portion of the profits. My bricklayer friend said he heard that Riner plans to pay them $500 apiece out of the profits from the Tanner sewer job. They'll get paid for doing no work."

"And, the city engineer? What does he get?"

"He benefits when he overvalues the job because it increases the profit. That means he gets a kickback from those profits. The higher they are, the more he gets. So, it is in his interest for the contractor to excess bid on materials, job quality, and such."

"You think our city engineer would do that?"

Rather than answering the question, Leo used his thumb and forefinger to pinch his nostrils shut like he'd caught a whiff of something rotten. Removing his fingers he said, "That's Elliott's reputation."

Sage wrinkled his brow, pondering Leo's explanation. "I don't understand why Mayor Williams and his executive committee would tolerate blatant corruption. It seems like it would come back to bite them."

"Adair, surely you don't think all that kickback money goes just into the engineer's pockets, do you?"

Later that night, Sage left Mozart's. With rain making for a sparsely attended supper hour. He left early, heading to the hospital to check on St. Alban. He discovered Sprig, the cabbie he'd assigned to watch over Harry, parked outside. Sprig said he'd left his son to watch Lane. As Sage climbed aboard, he gestured for Sprig to join him on the covered seat.

Once they were settled Sage asked, "How's it going? Is Lane behaving himself?"

Sprig chuckled. "That Harry Lane is one comical fellow. He likes his jokes, he does. He always makes me laugh. And, he insists on tipping me and the son for every trip even though I told him you were already paying us above the going rate. Says he was raised to carry his own water. That's kinda peculiar since lots of times he don't charge sick folk nothing. I seen that because sometimes he asks me come inside to help."

"Have you seen any suspicious characters lurking around his house or office?" Sage had told Sprig about the threat but nothing more.

The cabbie rubbed a bewhiskered chin. "I can't say that I have and I've been keeping an eye out like you asked and my son too."

"You don't mind having to stick with him?"

"Heck no! It's an honor. When he's home he makes us wait inside. Says he doesn't want to tend to any more patients. It's warm and comfortable. Even the horse gets to stay in a shed out of the rain. And that Mrs. Lane, she's a right fine woman. Brings me cookies and insists on feeding me dinner, no matter how late we get back."

"Is your son okay with working all night?"

"He's happier than a pig in mud. Thanks' to your generosity he bought the rig he's been saving up for. Doc Lane ain't called out all that much in the middle of the night. And, my boy's getting fat from Mrs. Lane's breakfasts."

"I don't suppose you might have one more trip in you before heading home?"

"Why, Mr. Adair, it'd be my pleasure. I was waiting here because I figured you'd want to head up to the hospital."

"You figured right. I need to check on my friend. I am most grateful to find you here."

Upon entering Vincent's room, Sage found Meachum, Siringo, and the patient deep in the throes of planning.

Meachum turned to Sage, satisfaction in his voice. "We've found Horn. Mr. Fong's out now keeping an eye on his movements."

"Where'd you catch up with him?"

"Like me and Charlie figured, Horn's been circling around this place—looking for a way and time to sneak in. We took turns watching the hospital's front and back doors and finally spotted him lurking around like a cow pie fly."

"Cow pie? Meach. I think you've been hanging around our cowboy here a bit too much."

Charlie followed their laughter by saying, "You think there ain't cows in Colorado where Meach is from?"

More laughter but then Sage sobered. "You three seem to be in the thick of discussing what to do."

"Yup. We got some ideas on how to catch the galoot. Sergeant Hanke says we have to catch him in the act if we want him jailed," Siringo said.

"We figure he'll come in with the visitors when it's busy. Then hang around until things quiet down. Once the visitors are gone, that's when the nurses go into the rooms, to ready everyone for sleep. That's when we figure he'll make his move."

"I'm not too keen on the single policeman being enough to stop Horn."

"Wahl, we feel the same. So we got a plan for that, but we'll need some help from Hanke."

"Hanke will help. But, it'll have to be a believable show. We can't risk Vincent's life," Sage cautioned.

TWELVE

April 6, 1905

SAGE FOUND SERGEANT HANKE IN his customary spot at the small kitchen table, a plate of Ida's leftovers before him. "Why, good afternoon Sergeant," Sage said as he took a chair.

"I hope you don't mind me stopping by." Hanke paused to smile at Ida as she poured more coffee into his cup and said, "Though Miz Ida's excellent cooking lures me here like a rosy-lipped siren."

Ida's round face flushed with pleasure as she said, "Pshaw" and patted him on the shoulder before heading back to her stove.

Hanke leaned forward to say softly, "I have some business to conduct as well. I came up with an idea and thought to get your opinion."

Sage nodded at him to continue.

"You remember that new officer at the hospital? The one you said shows promise, name of Dan Carter?"

Sage again nodded and waited.

"Once St. Alban leaves, I want to send Carter into the special police ranks to work undercover. Maybe he can discover whether any of them are involved in the assassination plot."

Sage felt compelled to caution, "That could be very dangerous for him. He's awfully young to be put in that situation."

"I know that's a worry. I warned him and he still wants to do it. He's a tough kid, and smart. Besides, he's promised to only listen, not instigate or investigate. I don't know what else to do. I sure the heck can't stick my nose into the special police ranks. They know me. Plus, that unit is run out of the chief's office. Hunt's so trussed up by political patronage that I can't trust him to tell me the truth."

"Well, won't the chief know you've planted a cuckoo in the nest?"

"He would. That's why I'm here. We have to get Carter assigned to the unit the normal way: Rich man asks Mayor Williams. The Mayor orders Chief Hunt."

Sage frowned. "I don't have any influence with Mayor Williams. Sure he's an infrequent customer, but I doubt he'd pull any patronage strings on my behalf."

As Sage was speaking, Hanke was nodding. "I didn't figure you could do it. But, Harry has the connections that could make it happen."

"There is no way Williams is going to do Harry Lane a favor. Not when they are likely to end up competing for the same job!" Sage wondered what had happened to Hanke's common sense.

Hanke's subsequent explanation proved he hadn't lost it. "Please, Adair, give me some credit. Harry Lane's best friend is R.W. Montague. He's a partner in Erskine Wood's law firm. And as you know, that firm represents some of Portland's wealthiest and most powerful: Corbett, Ladd, Ainsworth, Reed, Benson, and others. Some of those men are on Williams' executive committee. Montague can ask one of them to put Carter's name forward to Williams. If that happens, Williams will order Hunt to put Carter into the special police unit."

Sage mulled that idea over and decided Hanke just might have a workable plan. "Well, Harry would have to agree to ask his friend, Montague, to help. You know Lane pooh-poohs the idea that he's in danger. Then Montague would have to get one of his clients to ask the Mayor to make Hunt appoint Carter. Lots of favors in that chain of events."

"Well, you're the silver-tongued devil. I'm sure you can make it happen," Hanke said with a grin. Then he sobered. "I think we best get Carter inserted into the special police ranks soon, before the primary. That way, they'll be less suspicious of him since it's unlikely they'll talk about assassinating Harry until after he wins the primary."

Before Hanke departed, Sage detailed their plan to trap Tom Horn, St. Alban's would-be assassin. The sergeant quickly agreed to play his designated part in the effort.

As it turned out, Harry was willing to impose on his friend, Dick Montague, though he cautioned, "As you know, I don't believe in this whole assassination hoo-hah you and the wife got going. But, I do think there are mostly bad actors in the special police ranks so inside information will be very helpful. Especially if I become mayor. So, I'll ask Montague if he'll tap into his client list and get your man into that unit. We can tell him the truth of why we want to do it. He already knows about the assassination threat since my dear wife spilled the beans to him."

Harry was a fast actor. Just a few hours later, during the gap between the noon dinner hour and the tea time service, someone knocked on Mozart's kitchen door and Mae came to get him upstairs. He entered the dining room to find Harry, his friend, Dick Montague, and amazingly, Charles Erskine Wood.

Sage's footsteps stuttered briefly before he strode forward, hand outstretched. "Colonel Wood, what a delightful surprise to see you here."

Harry laughed and explained, "When I told Dick what you were up to, he said that Erskine was just the fellow to handle things. Don't worry. They've both promised to keep your involvement strictly secret."

Sage turned to Wood and waited.

"I suspect you are wondering why I, having been in a law firm partnership with George Williams, am willing to stick my neck out to help George's opponent."

Sage could only nod thoughtfully.

After they were seated, Wood began, "Let me tell you straight out. I would give George Williams the shirt off my back and the shoes off my feet if he asked me for them. He's a genial fellow and has been a good friend of mine for years. That said, I am all too familiar with his weaknesses as well. He is easily manipulated by the wealthy. Particularly since his wife spends like money grows on trees. That's proven to be a very bad combination."

For a moment Wood fell silent and Sage watched him, thinking that his tall stature, heavy-lidded eyes, strong brow, and full beard made for a man who looked both handsome and formidable.

Wood finally stirred himself to speak again. "We need a man like Harry Lane to govern this city. It's become as corrupt as the Eastern cities. We need William's political machine to die because, more and more, all it does is serve the greedy, self-interested, and incompetent. This Tanner Creek sewer scandal is a perfect example of why Portland's government needs to change.

"George is upset that our law firm represents the homeowners who object to paying for the sewer repairs. But, I believe exposing the shoddy work is how we will put an end to such blatant corruption—that and putting Harry into the mayor's office."

"You know about the conspiracy to make sure that never happens?"

"Yes, Harry and Dick filled me in about the assassination plot. Like Harry, I find it hard to believe and I hope you are wrong. But, the reason I am here is because I also agree with Harry that the special police force is a major impediment to ending our city's worst vice operations. So, I'll do what I can to help. I have many influential acquaintances through my long-term Arlington Club membership. Some of them are beholden to me for one thing or another. I'm certain we'll get the young police officer inserted into the special police unit. Expect to hear from me tomorrow."

Wood stood and turned toward the door.

Sage stood to follow as he raised a halting hand. "Mr. Wood, one more moment, please." He quickly explained about their investigation into whether Tanner Creek crooks might be involved in the plot against Lane and asked, "Do you think Mayor Williams will agree to the outside inspectors taking a look?"

Wood's lips twisted. "I told George that he's a fool to keep fighting it. Those angry homeowners are some of the town's wealthiest, Ladd, Ainsworth, and others. He's resisting very strongly. That makes me wonder what the heck George has got himself into. In the end, he'll have no choice because the public outcry is getting louder every day."

"Can we help you by doing a preliminary survey while you await permission to conduct a more formal one? Take a look ourselves and tell you what we find?"

"You're willing to go down into the sewer?" Wood chuckled. "I don't envy you that experience. But sure, such information would be very helpful. It'd also give our inspectors a leg up on the task."

"Okay then, expect to hear from me. Once the rain stops, we intend to take a look-see. Hopefully, all the rainwater will flush out the stink."

Wood shook his head, Sage's hand, clapped on his hat, and took his leave, saying, "You're an interesting man, John Adair. I admit that I'm curious as to why the owner of the town's most exclusive restaurant is involved."

Later that evening, Sage climbed the hospital steps once again. Tomorrow morning Vincent was to be discharged. He planned to catch the afternoon train to Chicago. Horn knew of the discharge plan because Hanke reported that one of the nurses saw a stranger reading patient charts. She chased him off but Vincent's was the chart he'd been reading. It notes he'll be discharged late tomorrow morning.

The evening visiting hours were ending when Sage stepped through the doors. The nun frowned until she recognized him. "I see you are back again. You best take the stairs to your friend's floor. I haven't exactly told the hospital superintendent about these late-hour visits and he's wandering about somewhere. He can't fire me but he sure could blister my ears and those of my Mother Superior."

"You are a jewel, Sister Joseph. I promise to be stealthy. Has anyone else entered recently who hasn't been visiting regularly?"

She shook her head and pursed her lips. "The only new person I've seen was a fellow delivering some medical supplies a few minutes ago."

Sage stiffened, alarm bells sounding, and he prodded. "Is it common to get a delivery this late?"

She shook her head. "I wondered about it so I asked him. He said a porter stowed it in the train station's storage room by mistake. He was wearing a porter's cap. Still, I thought that a bit strange since I've only seen negro porters at the train station and he was a white man."

"How tall was he?"

She put her finger to her chin and pondered his question. "I guess I would say he was about as tall as you but slender. What my mother would have called "a long drink of water.""

Now those alarm bells in his head were clanging so loud he was surprised the good sister didn't hear them. Horn was acting sooner than they expected. He turned toward the stairs and opened the door calmly. Once inside the stairwell, he raced upward, two steps at a time.

The third-floor hallway was quiet. No one was in sight. No guard sat outside St. Alban's room. "Damn it!" Sage exclaimed and ran down the hallway. Reaching the door, he encountered resistance when he pushed it open. Looking down he saw boots, then legs, then the torso of a man in police uniform. Leaping over him, Sage landed near the end of Vincent's bed. A figure stood at its head, his back to the door, his hand rising, a knife glittering in the faint light coming from the window. The unmoving patient lay on his side, his back to the door.

"No!" Sage shouted. He snatched up a chair and threw it at the figure. It didn't land hard enough to knock him over but it did distract. The attacker turned toward Sage and raised his knife. The man's face was shadowed but his clenched teeth gleamed in the faint light.

"Tom Horn, I presume," Sage said, causing Horn's steps to momentarily pause. Meanwhile, behind Horn, Charlie Siringo slithered out the bed's far side.

Horn's hesitation gave Sage time to set his feet in a bow stance and center, ready to defend against Horn's knife. Fong's oft-repeated pointers on how to defend against a knife-wielding attacker ran through his head.

Horn held the knife low. Sage felt a twinge of reassurance. Fong had made him practice defending against a gut stab maneuver at least a hundred times.

He bent slightly at the waist to protect his stomach just as the knife thrust was fully committed. Simultaneously, Sage clasped his hands together and slammed them onto the man's forearm, driving the knife-wielding arm downward.

Instantly, Sage slid his hands apart until one gripped the man's arm above the elbow and the other his wrist, forcing the knife point toward the floor. A vicious twist and the knife clattered onto the linoleum tiles.

Stepping closer, Sage twisted Horn's arm down, back, and then up, until it was high above the man's back. Having been on the receiving end of that particular move, Sage knew Horn had only one choice—he had to bend forward to prevent his shoulder and elbow from dislocating. Thanks to Fong's lessons, Sage knew the position was extraordinarily painful.

The second Horn bent double, Sage slammed his knee up, over and over, pounding it into the man's gut and face.

Putting all the force he could into the final jab, Sage kneed the man's gut again. He felt Horn's muscles and tendons slackened. Horn groaned as his legs gave way and he fell to the floor. For good measure, Sage kicked Horn's ribs but the man stayed limp and silent. He was out.

Hearing a shuffling sound behind him, Sage whirled, arm raised, leg drawn back ready to land a kick. He relaxed when he saw Meachum crawling onto his knees, holding out a pair of handcuffs. Sage grabbed the cuffs and quickly manacled the unconscious Horn.

Turning back to Meachum, Sage saw him struggling to speak. He said only, "He attacked me here in the room." Then his eyes rolled back in his head. Sage leaped forward, caught him, and eased him to the floor where he lay groaning. It was only then that Sage saw the blood.

A glance revealed that Siringo stood holding a porcelain bedpan in one hand.

"You okay?" he asked the cowboy.

Charlie nodded and asked, "What about Meachum? How bad is he hurt? I couldn't stop him from being clouted. It happened too fast."

Sage shook his head. "I don't know. He needs a doctor. He's losing blood. I'll get help."

Fortunately for Meachum, a doctor was on duty. Although the blood loss from the head bump was worrisome, the doctor said the skull was unbroken and Meachum was already coming around. The doctor said he'd prescribe some aspirin and opined that, while Meachum might have a headache, he'd still be able to take the next day's afternoon train.

The doctor escorted Meachum out, saying he would put him in a nearby room to spend the night being "observed".

Once the door swung shut, Sage turned to Siringo. "A bedpan?"

"Wahl, I was figuring to brain him with it until I saw you had things under control. That's some fancy fightin' you do. I ain't never seen the like. It's a right pretty thing to watch." Siringo carefully set the bed pan on the bedside table and added, "I had my six-shooter but I didn't want to cause a ruckus."

"Is that pan empty?"

"Well, I been stuck lying in that darn bed since visiting hours started."

Sage's eyebrows rose and he said, "Lord, I'm glad you didn't have to use it. Talk about a golden rain!" He began chuckling.

Hanke entered to find them both roaring with laughter. He waited for them to get it under control before saying, "I understand there's been a commotion."

He looked down at the unconscious man. "That Horn? What'd you use to knock him out? SSurely not that bedpan near Charlie's hand."

Neither man could answer because another round of laughter left them gasping, though whether it came from relief, humor, or both, the Sergeant couldn't tell. Shaking his head, Hanke left to call for reinforcements that soon arrived. Minutes later, they led a groggy and groaning Tom Horn away.

THIRTEEN

April 7 and 8, 1905

SAGE WAS STANDING ON THE train platform, saying his goodbyes to Vincent and Meachum when Vincent looked past him and grinned. Twisting to look, Sage saw Erskine Wood hurrying toward them, his grin a match for Vincent's.

Reaching them, Wood gave Vincent's hand a hearty shake and then Meachum's. "Bet you thought I wouldn't make it to see you off!"

Vincent laughed. "Well, I know how you like those late nights and loose women!"

Seeing Sage's puzzlement, Vincent explained, "Wood helped me with some of the legal particulars we needed in the bylaws for our one big union. Thanks to him, I have a decent bylaws draft to present at the convention," he said, patting his breast pocket.

Sage eyed the lawyer, surprise driving all words from his head. He knew Wood took up the cases of the wealthy and occasionally those of the downtrodden. Still, it was a surprise to learn he helped labor radicals as well.

For his part, Wood appeared equally surprised to see Sage because he cocked a questioning eyebrow in Vincent's direction. Vincent answered Wood's unspoken question. "Adair is a comrade from the Telluride fight. Since then, he's undertaken other tasks as well. He's the one who took my assassin down to the hospital floor last night. Because of Adair, the mine owners' thug is behind bars."

Sage quickly demurred. "It was a group effort, Meach and Charlie were just as important to the outcome."

Vincent's expression became serious as he spoke directly to Wood. "Erskine, I must ask that you keep Adair and his activities strictly secret. You tell anyone at all and you will jeopardize much. Not just regarding the assassination attempt on me, but many other things, now and in the future. Adair's my man and we need him doing what he does without folks knowing about it—especially those with whom you often associate."

Wood was silent for a moment then nodded. "I understand. No word regarding Adair will issue from my lips. Though, I may find it necessary to praise his rather fine restaurant."

Minutes later, the train pulled out, leaving Wood and Sage standing on the platform. Sage was the first to speak. "I'm glad you've been helping St. Alban but I am surprised."

Wood laughed. "Well Adair, you need to know that, despite all my highfalutin friends, I consider myself an anarchist. I follow Prince Kropotkin's philosophy. I believe this country desperately needs greater economic and social equality. Unions are one way to get that."

Of all that Wood could have said, Sage would never have imagined the prominent lawyer as someone supporting the Russian theoretical anarchist. "Kropotkin huh? Well, you've managed to surprise me yet again."

"No more than you have me. Someday we'll have to sit down for a drink and you can tell me of your adventures in Telluride. That was a helluva fight from what I've heard."

Wood slung an arm across Sage's shoulders and they began walking down the platform. "I'm glad you were here. Saves me a trip to Mozart's Table. I am happy to report that, this coming Monday your young police officer will start his undercover assignment in the North End's special police unit. As expected, Williams was eager to help young Dan Carter, my Republican friend's so-called nephew, start fresh in Portland. Though I hope he's smart and careful enough to keep his ears open and his lips shut. That particular group of officers are not men of the best caliber."

That night they closed Mozart's so Sage, Mae, Fong, Charlie, Lucinda, and Xenobia could attend Harry Lane's first major speech at the Burkhard Hall on East Burnside. His democratic opposition in the primary, George Thomas, would also be there. Harry often praised Thomas as a decent man who'd make a good mayor, but everyone knew Thomas lacked Harry's city-wide popularity. And that popularity was needed to boot the Williams machine out of office. Only Harry was beloved by Democrats and Republicans alike.

Still, they fretted that there'd be a low turnout at Harry's maiden rally because the *Gazette* derided Lane's candidacy in that morning's paper. Its editorial opined that Lane was not suited for the mayoral position because of his relative youth, claiming that, at 50 years of age, Harry would succumb to "youthful indiscretions" unlike Williams who it called an "experienced, venerable 82-year-old jurist." The Republican-controlled newspaper also predicted a huge loss for Lane should he receive the nomination, noting that any Democrat would lose since only 1,820 Democrats were registered to vote compared to 11,422 Republicans.

They soon saw that they needn't have worried about the turnout. Almost every person on the crowded streetcar disembarked when it reached the hall. All manner of people shuffled inside, their chatter excited, their garb varying from working duds to expensive, bespoke suits.

Although the speechifying wasn't due to start for another fifteen minutes, the hall was full, forcing Sage's group to split up. He sat with Lucinda and Mae, Charlie and Xenobia took seats in another row, while Fong stood against a side wall near the podium. Sage watched Sprig sidle up to Fong, exchange a few words, and settle against the wall beside him. The cabbie's presence meant Harry had arrived.

Gazing around and behind him, Sage spotted a few well-known Republican leaders in the crowd. Either those men were spies or they were part of the Albee faction. If the men in the hall were Albee's men, their presence was a good sign. Albee strongly opposed the Williams administration's political machine. He was one of three Republicans running against Williams in the primary and vowing to rid the city of its vice dens. The *Gazette* used a lot of ink castigating Albee as a Republican traitor.

Of course, Albee didn't stand a chance. Williams would win the Republican nomination. The Republican machine would see to it that Albee's supporters would be left with a choice: either vote for Williams or the Democrats' candidate. If Harry impressed them tonight, Albee's men might lead a Republican crossover to Harry's side in the general election.

A man came through a door behind the stage, trailed by two others and Harry. The first man went to stand before the podium while the others sat on the chairs behind him.

What followed were three long-winded speeches praising Harry Lane. The subject of their speeches looked uncomfortable during some of the praise but he smiled and laughed when the audience sounded their hearty approval. At last, Harry was summoned to the podium. After thanking his supporters and their kind words he launched into what was the shortest speech of the evening:

> As a candidate before the people for the office of Mayor of this city, it is but fair on my part to set forth plainly and with all candor what may be expected of me as a public servant, in the event I'm elected.
>
> I have my ideals as to how a public office should be conducted. I have held the same views all my life. It is easy to boast of what one will do if given a place of public trust. My guiding ideal, however, was tested when I was superintendent of the insane asylum. For every decision I asked myself, 'Is it in the best interests of the inmates and the citizens?' I remained true to that ideal.
>
> If a man can point to such a history, it is pretty fair evidence that he will do so again. If elected I will use but one rule and ask but one question, 'What is in the best interests of the city and is it right?'
>
> I will see that the people's money shall neither be stolen, squandered, nor frittered away if I can help it. I shall spare no effort on that behalf. No favoritism shall be indulged in by me. Nor will I sanction nor permit it at the hands of any subordinate. Neither blackmail nor kickbacks shall be collected by anyone from anyone.
>
> I guarantee that there shall be no Tanner Creek sewer scandal or such other ilk during my administration. A strict and careful investigation will be made of every contract before it is let and of every job of work before it is accepted or paid for.
>
> It is neither right nor gainful for a city to enter into partnership with any form of vice for the sake of revenue to be derived there from.
>
> No man who keeps his affairs within the rightful laws need fear me. No man who seeks to evade the law has anything to hope for in my election.

If I am to have this office, I want to come to it with clean hands and leave it with clean hands. I will remain free from all pledges or obligations to any individual or to any special interests. My time in office will be known for no more patronage, no more backroom deals, no more catering to special interests, no more scandals.

If any man can see in such an administration of the city's affairs anything which will interfere with his personal advantage or gain, he can safely mark me down as a man not to vote for.

I thank you for your time, your attention, and your kindness.

The crowd, at least 500 strong, jumped to their feet, clapping and cheering, while an overwhelmed Harry stood on the platform grinning and clapping with them. It was the most jubilant and exuberant crowd Sage had ever seen. When he glanced at the Albee Republicans he saw that they were also on their feet and enthusiastically clapping.

People pushed forward to shake Harry's hand as he descended from the stage. The People's Doctor basked in their warm-hearted affection. His smile was big, his laugh loud, and his gray eyes sparkling. Lola Lane stood beside her husband, her face shining with pride. Meanwhile, Fong and Sprig moved forward, taking up positions just behind Harry as their eyes scanned the crowd.

Speeches over, Mae, Lucinda, and Xenobia exited the hall seeking a bit of fresh spring air, Sage and Charlie lingered in the hall, only a little concerned there might be a killer in the crowd. That was because Solomon sent word that a porter remembered seeing a man who fit the description the week before. That man rode north to Seattle. The woman who worked in the Portland Club also remembered the man but said she hadn't seen him in the saloon for at least a week. They figured the porter's sighting and her report explained the failure of their searches.

They'd agreed that the killer wouldn't hang around Portland and risk being seen and remembered by even more people. They figured he'd stay away unless, or until, Harry won the May 5th primary. Solomon promised his porter friends were watching for his return.

At last, the hall emptied and Sprig left to drive Harry and Lola home. Sage and Charlie joined the others outside. Because of the huge number of Harry's supporters, it would be a while before there'd be room aboard a streetcar. While they waited, Charlie said, "So, I sure liked what Lane had to say, but how much of it was just politician blather? I've heard so much of it in my day and, been disappointed so often, that I am skeptical, no matter how likable the man seems."

Sage agreed but said, "Well, normally, I am skeptical myself. But Harry's a bird of a different feather. He's always been a servant first. When we've needed his help he's been quick to respond, with no hesitation, no questions asked. And, I know for a fact that he lost the asylum superintendent job because he was too honest. He rooted out all the kickback schemes, crooked contractors, and dishonest employees. He made sure the asylum's money went only to contractors who met the specifications. He saved the asylum and the taxpayers thousands of dollars and used those savings to greatly improve the inmates' living conditions. I saw that with my own eyes.

"More to the point, before taking the job, he warned the board of trustees that's exactly what he'd do. He told them he'd take the job only if every one of them promised to back his corrective actions. I've seen the letter. Still, the board of directors hired him. Then, when he did exactly as promised and rooted out the corruption, they and the governor refused to renew his tenure. It seems too many of their friends and donors lost money.

"Bottom line, what Harry said tonight is the truth. His honesty was tested and he passed with flying colors. I can say that I've never met a man I trusted more. He's not a politician. He's been the people's servant his entire life."

His mother tapped his arm, "Dear boy, time to step down from your soap box. Our streetcar's waiting." They stepped onto the streetcar, laughing as Sage looked chagrined.

The next morning Sage was again at the train station. This time he was on the covered platform saying goodbye to Charlie and Xenobia.

"Y'all sure do have lotsa rain in this here valley. While the greenery is mighty nice looking when the sun shines, all this gray and wet brings a man's spirits down, I'm a'thinking." Charlie doffed his hat and shook the drops from it. "I'll take the wide blue sky over that gray muck above any day," he added, pointing at the low gray mass beyond the platform's glass ceiling.

Sage laughed. "Yup, the weather here isn't for everyone. But, I love it. Having lived in the South, I grew to hate the infernal sunshine. I like stepping out into unknown weather every day. And, when it does shine, sprightly, smiling people are everywhere. Fact is, I find even dripping greenery invigorating and a delight to the eye."

Charlie shrugged, saying, "To each his own, as they say." He glanced at Xenobia and turned serious. "Me and Xennie talked it over. I'll be back with you come May 3rd or so. She's got to stay at the place to feed the animals. We can't be depending too much on our neighbor. He has to ride a far piece to help out."

Sage sighed. "Ah Charlie, you don't have to do that. You've done enough. I'm sure we can handle the problem."

Charlie shook his head. "Yeah, you folks probably could. But, me and Xennie like your Harry Lane. We'd hate to have anything bad happen to him. So, I'll be back."

Sage watched the train pull out, thinking, that there sure was a passel of fine, good-hearted, and brave people in the world.

FOURTEEN

April 26, 1905

TOGETHER THEY LIFTED THE MANHOLE cover and set it aside. Sage dangled the lantern in the hole and peered down. "Looks like the ledge below is dry enough. Hope it doesn't rain while we're down there." Sage's comment sent their eyes skyward. The stars, though obscured by wood and coal smoke, still glittered.

They'd talked to one of Leo's carpenters who'd worked on sewer projects before. He'd cautioned them to wait at least three days straight without rain before venturing underground. This night marked the end of a fourth rainless day. Both men were dressed as suggested by the man, in oil slicker coats and rubber duck boots. Each carried a tubular lantern.

It had been such a rainy April, they'd had to wait to explore the sewer. Seventeen days had passed since Charlie and his lady left on the train for Eastern Oregon. Meanwhile, Sage had worked at the construction site, eyes and ears open, trying to ascertain whether Riner was scheming to assassinate the one candidate promising to strictly enforce city contracts.

This interim period was a mix of excitement and fear for the crew: Excitement as they watched support for Lane's candidacy grow by leaps and bounds; fear because his win made an assassination attempt more likely. Until the primary, they could only wait. If Lane won it, they'd be going on full alert in just eight days.

Sage was tired of getting drenched at work—so the preceding three days of dry weather had been a blessing. Still, he found he enjoyed learning about carpentry. Emil was a patient teacher and liked to laugh.

There was also satisfaction in creating homes for people. The fair exposition had drawn in so many workers that there was a city-wide housing shortage. Even people with money couldn't find a place to buy or rent, which meant landlord price-gouging was everywhere.

He didn't learn much more about the Tanner sewer project. Periodically old man Riner and his son ventured onto the building site. Mostly, they stayed away. The foreman, Muckleroy, had reappeared but was still in a foul mood. Even Emil turned subdued around the dour man, telling Sage more than once that he wished he knew what had "gotten into Oscar."

During the Riners' rare visits, the city engineer, William Elliott appeared, looking grim and nervous, and huddled with them. Each time he left, they looked even more anxious. Muckleroy was never part of their discussions. Instead, he'd direct a hostile look at the engineer and disappear until after Elliott left.

Emil made a point of cautioning Sage not to ask Muckleroy about the sewer job. Said if he did, Sage would likely get fired or kicked in the butt.

His mother kept him up to date on what the newspapers were reporting about that scandal. She said the Riners weren't getting paid because the homeowners and the mayor were still arguing over the use of outside inspectors.

It was that delay now forcing them to undertake tonight's sewer escapade. At his request, Erskine Wood had met with him and provided a list of potential problems to look for in the sewer. Handing over the list, Wood said, "I'll be damned if I can figure out why the owner of a fancy restaurant wants to go down into a sewer. To quote Alice in Wonderland, your actions just get 'Couriouser and Couriouser.' Adair, like I said, I'm expecting an explanation over a whiskey or two in the near future."

After committing Wood's problem list and the contract specifications to memory, Sage and Eich felt prepared to take the next step. They were to look for bad or missing mortar between bricks and stone, insufficient numbers of bricks and stones, missing concrete flooring, sagging walls, and vault ceiling leaks.

Sage glanced around, seeing only dark windows and an empty street. "You trust what that cook told you—that no one would be watching this manhole?"

"She told me exactly where her boss sits. He likes to be comfortable. So, he's inside a saloon the next street over. He can watch the sewer's manhole through its window.

"She also said her boss and his friends are convinced that the mayor is delaying agreeing to the inspection to give the Riners a chance to cover up their mistakes. Consequently, they're taking turns watching the manhole, hoping to catch the Riners in the act."

"So why are they focused on that other manhole instead of this one? Is comfort their only consideration?" Sage wondered aloud.

Eich nodded. "I asked her that myself. She said that the manhole is right next to the Riners' tool shed. If they try to fix things, they'll want their tools handy."

Sage glanced around and seeing no one said, "Okay, that makes sense. We might as well get to it."

They started down the ladder, Eich going first. Once Sage was inside, he dragged the cover over to partially block the hole, hoping the gap wouldn't be spotted by a late-night stroller. They descended the iron rungs until they stood in the sewer's blackness with sewage stench filling their noses.

They quickly lit both lantern wicks and tied kerchiefs over their noses and mouths. There was no mistaking the function of the place. Still, the waste stream ran shallow and narrow, allowing them to edge alongside the slow-moving rivulet, rather than wade in it.

"Phew!" Sage exclaimed. "Let's get this over with." He took two small crowbars from inside the rucksack he carried. While Eich dug into the brick mortar, Sage levered up floor paver stones.

It was obvious to him that these were not the uniformly shaped, rectangular, closely-fitted, Belgian paver blocks the bid specification required. Instead, they were an uneven hodgepodge of ill-fitted, irregular cobbles. Worse, they'd been seated in dirt, rather than into the required concrete. Moreover, there was no mortar between them. Sage crept forward until about fifteen feet beyond the manhole. There he found only a dirt floor with a trough dug into its center. There was no stone flooring at all.

Water drips pattered his raincoat. Lifting his lantern he examined the roof and saw places where there was no, or little, mortar between the bricks. It seemed only the walls' inward pressure on the roof prevented the tunnel from collapsing.

That thought drew his eyes to the walls. Sure enough, even his inexperienced eye could see places where the walls already leaned inward. Once again there were problems. What mortar existed was crumbling. And, there was no underlying foundation beneath the walls. Instead of sitting on concrete sills, as specified, the walls sat atop narrow runs of crumbling brick.

Chills shot up his spine. The homeowners were right. This tunnel was certain to collapse. He fought the urge to retreat toward the safety above. What he saw was beginning to trigger his childhood claustrophobia. At nine years old, he'd been entombed by a methane explosion in a coal mine. He'd escaped but the experience left him fearful of enclosed spaces. It wasn't until a few years ago, that he'd finally learned how to control that fear. But this crumbling tunnel was challenging that control.

Just as he turned back toward Eich and the ladder up, a light flashed further down the tunnel. Quickly, he snuffed his lantern. They couldn't get caught down here. Given the thousands of dollars at stake, getting caught could have dire consequences.

He began backing toward their exit ladder, his alarm increasing as the light grew ever brighter. Someone was coming toward them. He heard voices, querulous and numerous. He paused, trying to discern what was being said. The light appeared to stop. He crept forward until the words were clear.

"I explained to you already. Slap some of that mortar into the gaps between the stones and the bricks. And, Oliver, you lay some of them stones farther down the tunnel floor. With luck, the damn inspectors will only snoop in the areas around the manholes."

It was clear these were Riners' men, doing precisely what the homeowners feared might happen—trying to cover up their inferior work. That voice sounded familiar. Sage tried to place where he'd heard it before.

A light suddenly flared behind him and Eich's voice called out, "Sage, are you alright?"

Sage whirled, put a finger across his lips, and signaled for Eich to douse the light. He did so with alacrity but it was too late. A curse sounded from further down the tunnel as that light was also extinguished. Sage cautiously retreated toward Eich, trailing his fingers along the damp wall as a guide. They had to escape the sewer before the Riner crew caught them.

Splashes sounded and boots thudded as light once again flared, snagging on the tunnel's uneven walls.

Sage didn't know how many were further down the tunnel but from the sounds, he and Eich were greatly outnumbered.

He bumped into Eich's soft bulk. "Hurry," he whispered, "We've got to get out of here." He continued toward the ladder, hoping Eich followed.

Behind them, the light strengthened and the footfalls sounded louder. It was iffy whether Sage and Eich would reach the ladder and climb up forty feet before getting caught.

His heart raced. If they got murdered down in this darkness, they'd never be found. The sewer's dirt floor would make it easy to bury their bodies. Dig holes, cover them with dirt and pavers, and no one would find them.

His groping hand finally touched cold iron. Eich came up beside him and Sage pushed him toward the ladder, commanding, "Climb! Get help!"

Seconds later the ladder vibrated beneath his hand as Eich hustled upward. But it was too late for Sage.

Lantern light rounded the sewer's slight bend, carried by men less than 40 feet away, If he started up now, they'd snatch him by the ankles and hurl him to the floor. He'd have to fight—disable them enough so he could escape or delay until Eich returned with help.

He turned, his feet seeking solid footing on the slippery floor. This was going to be tricky. Mr. Fong never taught him how to fight on slick cobbles wearing rubber boots. Despite narrowed eyes, the light prevented him from seeing the faces of the advancing men. He counted at least five of them. He'd have to get very lucky in his hits and kicks.

In that instant, a whistle shrilled down from the open manhole above. The attackers halted then turned back to quickly disappear behind the bend. Sage didn't hesitate. He jumped for the ladder and clambered up.

As he neared the manhole another, more distant, whistle sounded. This time it echoed down the sewer followed by an authoritative voice shouting, "You men keep coming this way. You're surrounded. I've got a man stationed at every manhole. I know you are in this sewer. I can see you moving. Riner, I know it's you and your men. I've been watching you! So far, you've committed no crime but if you don't return immediately, you'll be charged!" That voice Sage knew—Hanke!

Sage climbed out to find Eich waiting, whistle in hand. Quickly dropping the manhole cover in place, they stood atop it to cut off that exit.

Sage caught his breath before saying, "Sure glad you recruited Hanke into joining our little escapade." The cover beneath their feet wobbled as frantic hands tried to raise it but it stayed in place. That escape attempt stopped and the noises coming from beneath the cover ceased. They exchanged grins. Their would-be attackers had no choice but to face the music awaiting them at the tunnel's far end by the tool shed.

"We did it!" an elated Sage declared. "Does Hanke really have men stationed at every manhole cover?"

"Nope, it's just him and one officer together at the other end and us. Still, you are right. We did it," agreed Eich, "thanks to his invaluable and timely assistance."

The next morning, Wood expressed delight at their findings, declaring they'd proved his clients' contentions were valid. "Now they will never stop insisting on an inspection! Riner's son getting caught sneaking into the sewer is icing on the cake."

He found even more delightful the *Journal's* front page. Its reporter, armed with a flashbulb camera, had caught Riner's son and his men climbing out of the manhole under Hanke's watchful eye—proof positive that Riner tried to cover up the sewer's construction flaws.

The photo headline crowed, "Contractor's Sneak Attempt Fails!" Johnson's delight in exposing the fiasco imbued the story's every word. He'd also quoted the district attorney, Manning, who declared Riner's attempt justified a grand jury investigation. Manning vowed to indict all those found to be involved in the scandal and he joined the homeowners in demanding an independent inspection.

Hanke reported that the police chief was in a tizzy because the mayor demanded to know who'd ordered Hanke to watch the manholes. Hanke, of course, said he'd investigated after stumbling upon the open manhole.

The story had the desired effect. Mayor Williams had no choice but to announce that he'd agreed to let the homeowners' independent inspectors into the sewer. He also made a show of issuing Riner a stern warning not to make any more repair attempts.

When Hanke questioned Riner's son, he claimed the sewer workers had been bribed to sabotage the job. He said that the job's foreman would testify that someone, likely a competitor, tried to bribe him to short the job materials and work. He claimed some of the workers must have accepted bribes to ruin the job.

Riner stopped talking once Hanke informed him that it wasn't the police department's job to consider his excuses. Hanke also warned Riner he'd assigned the night patrol to keep a close watch on the sewer manholes to make sure there'd be no more attempts to enter the sewer until after an independent inspection took place.

❊ ❊ ❊

Tired as he was the next day, Sage returned to his construction site job. Once there, he watched the Riners and the city engineer engage in a fierce discussion that included angry arm gestures and jutting chins. It ended when the engineer stomped off in a huff, leaving the Riners looking more worried than ever.

Muckleroy noticed Sage watching the drama and angrily told him to "get back to work if you want to keep your job."

Sage was glad of the foreman's order because it gave his memory a sharp nudge. The night before, it had been Muckleroy's voice he'd overheard ordering a worker to extend the sewer's stone flooring.

So, there was no question now: Muckleroy was involved in the Tanner scheme. He was involved in the corruption and feared getting caught. Sage was certain the Riners planned to have Muckleroy swear that someone had tried to bribe him to sabotage the job. Of course, if Muckleroy complied, it would add perjury to the charges he might already face. That explained the foreman's recent bad mood.

Sage returned to work, toting, holding, and helping while whistling a merry tune, his cheeriness earning him a smile and headshake from Emil.

FIFTEEN

May 1, 1905

THE HOMEOWNERS' INSPECTORS ENTERED THE Tanner sewer on Friday, one day after Sage delivered their inspection results to Erskine Wood. Mayor Williams insisted the independent inspectors be accompanied by city engineer, William Elliott.

The inspectors must have labored mightily to produce their report because Wood messengered a copy to Sage early Sunday evening. He quickly scanned it. He saw enough that was eyebrow-raising to justify a Monday morning gathering of the crew. He also arranged to send word to Emil on the job site, stating that he couldn't work the following day because he had to meet his cousin's train and get him settled.

Then he left Mozart's with the report in hand. First, he stopped at the *Journal*, where Johnson read it, cackling as he scribbled notes. From there, Sage headed to Eich's lean-to at the edge of Marquam Gulch. Putting the report in Eich's hands, he asked him to analyze it and then describe its findings at the next morning's meeting.

It was early the next morning when Mae, Fong, Eich, Solomon, Lucinda, and Sage met. Breakfast over, all looked toward Herman. He nodded, swallowed the last bite of roll, gulped some coffee, and began. "The first thing you need to know is that this was essentially supposed to be a complete rebuild of the existing sewer that collapsed last January, causing that big flood. Contrary to the Riners' hopes, the inspectors evaluated the entire 1800-foot sewer. They report finding serious defects in five distinct categories along its entire length." He quickly scanned the list he'd compiled from the report. "I will address the five categories one at a time.

"First, it is clear that the city was charged for materials that never made it into the sewer. A typical example: The inspectors found that while the city was charged for 541 cubic yards of concrete at $15 per yard, they calculated Riner only used about 51 yards. The same with the Belgian floor stones. Just 1/3 of the Belgians Riner billed for, were used in the sewer. Same thing with the bricks—far fewer were used than Riner billed for.

"Second, the project specifications are explicit about requiring top-grade material. Riner charged the city according to those specs. However, it seems he actually used inferior, cheaper material throughout the project. The concrete is a good example. Instead of being made using a 2-parts cement to 1-part sand ratio, the inspectors found that Riner used 1-part cement to 4-parts sand to make the concrete. They predict that weak concrete will soon fail because it can't withstand sewage and rushing water. It's already crumbling in numerous spots according to the inspectors. Likewise, the inspectors found that Riner installed the lowest quality bricks. And, while the floor was supposed to be of tough, tight-fitting Belgian pavers, it is mostly ill-fitting irregular cobbles or dirt.

Eich paused a moment, a finger holding his place, sipped more coffee, cleared his throat, and continued, "In the third category, that of work-manship, the inspectors found it far below the standard required for a durable sewer. For example, even in those few places where the Belgian pavers were used, near the manholes, the stones are set in inferior con-crete or dirt. The inspectors also expressed alarm over the brick walls and roof. Both either lack mortar or, in those few places where mortar exists, it already crumbles at a touch. The inspectors assert that the shoddy workmanship means the walls and ceiling will likely collapse come the autumn rains.

"The inspectors found a host of other instances where the workman-ship deviated from the specs. The roof was supposed to be supported by substantial arches. But, instead of being three bricks wide, arranged on their edges, those arches are a single brick inserted flat into the ceil-ing. The arches and the walls are supposed to rest on sturdy concrete sills. Instead, they sit on inferior bricks or dirt. In some instances, the inspectors found bulging walls and sagging sections in the ceiling vault.

Eich glanced at each of them, heaved a sigh, and said, "Fourth, Riner failed to tamp earth around the sewer tunnel. You probably know that

Tanner Creek was named after a tannery that dumped its waste into it. Operated by Daniel Lownsdale, it was the city's and the West Coast's first tannery. The tannery is long gone but, for years, that gully was the dumping ground for all sorts of waste—big and small.

"In his final report, Riner certified that they'd removed all bulky waste and tamped the earth tight against the outside of the sewer as required by the specs. The purpose of tamping is to hold the sewer in place so it can't collapse outward into gaps caused by deteriorating waste.

"The homeowners' inspectors determined that no tamping whatsoever had occurred. Instead, their probes found great hollows surrounding the pipe. The gaps were created when the original waste material, like logs, household garbage, and appliances rotted into nothingness. What hasn't yet rotted will do so in the future, creating more gaps. Consequently, there is no outside support for the sewer. The inspectors state that is another reason why the defective walls and roof will soon give way."

Eich's finger jabbed at the bottom of the page. "The report states that the final area where Riner wrongfully increased his profits involves project add-ons. Riner seeks additional monies because of add-ons he claims were made. The inspectors found, however, that the claimed add-ons were never made or, that they were entirely unnecessary—one example being those two extra manholes Mae already told us about."

Eich laid his notes on the table saying, "That sums up the report. The homeowners are correct. The Tanner Creek sewer is a disaster in the offing."

Stunned silence followed Eich's final remarks until Mae breathed, "Them and the vice grafters are nothing but a passel of looters and leeches living off the rest of us. And, how did those idjits think they'd get away with it? The fall rains come and that sewer's sure to collapse."

Eich nodded in agreement. "As always Mae, you've summed things up with just a few well-chosen words. But you are right. The report concludes that the sewer won't last through the coming winter."

Sage addressed his mother's question. "Riner thought he'd get away with it because, in all likelihood, he already has countless times. The only difference is, this time, that sewer serves some of the wealthiest families in town who are taxed to pay for it. Those folks know how to hold on to their money and get what they want. Simple as that."

Solomon, who'd been scratching a pencil across paper spoke, "Well, one can see why the Riners might want Harry Lane out of the picture.

There is a considerable sum of money at stake. If he gets into office they could lose it all and go to jail. I calculate that just by shorting the concrete, Riner has gained $7350 in pure profit. It'll take me almost five years working at the hotel to earn that much. If you consider the rest of the material overcharges and shortages, we're talking about exceedingly high-dollar corruption. What puzzles me is why the city engineer allowed that to happen."

Lucinda laughed. "Oh Angus, you are too good for this world. That knave is getting a cut. He's probably been getting paid under the table on all the city's contracts for years."

Sage was bemused. "I saw in the *Gazette,* that the mayor already claims the independent inspectors falsified their findings. He's sending his inspector down into the sewer today. Evidently, he's certain his hand-picked fellow will refute the independents' report."

"That won't happen unless his inspector is also crooked as a barrel of fish hooks," Mae declared. "The *Journal* also says Williams ordered that the homeowners' report be kept secret. But, luckily, someone leaked the report. Much of what Herman just told us is on the front page of this morning's *Journal.* That's put Williams and his hand-picked inspector in a right, tight, box." She sent a knowing look at Sage.

He didn't refute her telling look, instead saying, "I understand that secrecy was the condition Williams demanded before he allowed the homeowners' inspectors to enter the sewer. I'm quite certain the home-owners and their lawyer didn't like that condition. However, I am also positive they can honestly state that none of them delivered the report into Johnston's eager hands last night."

Chuckles sounded as everyone caught his meaning.

Solomon's brow wrinkled. "What I do not understand is why Williams defends the city engineer and Riner's work."

Catching Lucinda's eye roll and gentle headshake, he laughed, "Alright. I guess I'm being naïve again. The mayor's in on it? That nice old man? You think he gets a portion of those ill-gotten gains as well?"

"You bet your boots he does!" declared Mae. "And, if the fingers start pointing toward that city engineer, who do you suppose Elliott will drop in the drink? Mayor Williams has no choice: He has to defend Engineer Elliott and the Riners."

Sage added his suspicions, "Solomon and Mae are both correct about Williams' motives. And, that leads us to the reason why Elliott and the Riners might be the ones scheming to eliminate Harry Lane from the mayoral race. He's the only candidate who can oust Williams. If he does, the whole kit and caboodle of them might end up in jail. We need to discover whether it's Williams, Elliott, Riner, or someone else who is planning to assassinate our Harry," he paused, adding, "but only if, and when, Harry wins that primary in four days."

Everyone around the table made scoffing noises, with Mae interjecting, "There's no 'if' about it. He's going to win. Even his opponent, George Thomas, says that. He promises to back Harry one hundred percent."

Sage raised a hand, saying, "I know, I know. Given huge turnouts for his speeches, Harry would have to do something profoundly stupid in the next three days to lose the democratic nomination."

"So that means we best get things in place before primary day," Mae said. "Does Hanke have any news?"

"I haven't had a chance to ask him. I'm supposed to see him today, mid-afternoon."

In the ensuing pause, he saw Mae and Lucinda exchange a long look. Mae gave Lucinda an almost imperceptible nod. Concern fizzed and he wondered what the two women were up to.

Lucinda cleared her throat. "Mae and I will be working at the Portland Club starting this coming Wednesday, two days before the primary. We figure that is the best way to spot the assassin fellow and his friends."

"Oh no! I never agreed you'd do that, either one of you!" Sage blurted, only to inwardly cringe at what was sure to come.

Mae glared before saying with sickening sweetness, "Well, dear boy, we never agreed to let you decide what we could or couldn't do. You best remember that I once changed your nappies."

Sage turned to Eich, "Herman, do you go along with their plan?"

Eich shrugged and said, "Not much choice. Mae's a grown woman with her own mind. So is Miss Lucinda."

He, Fong, and Angus turned expectant eyes toward Sage. They'd seen sparks fly between Mae and her son before.

Sage recognized he was in a situation where silence was the better part of valor. He was momentarily stumped until he thought of two sure-fire impediments to their plan, saying mildly, "There's no way you can both get a job there on such short notice. Besides, we don't even know if the fellow will ever again meet with his conspirators there."

Mae looked smug as she struck down the second impediment. "Actually Sage, we have a pretty good idea he'll turn up at the Portland Club. One of the barroom gals says he was a regular there until he disappeared.

And that's when Angus's train porter said the fellow left for Seattle. When he comes back, that's where he'll turn up."

Solomon spoke while directing an apologetic glance at Sage. "The porters are keeping an eye out for him. If he returns by train, we'll know right away. We can warn Mae and Lucinda."

Sage still resisted the idea. "Well, if he shows up there, Charlie will be there to see him."

"Yes and exactly what is Charlie's plan?" Mae asked, her expression mulish.

"Afternoons and evenings, he'll be there taking on comers in the saloon's shooting gallery. Peter Grant, the saloonkeeper has a shooting gallery in the saloon's alley. Gambling on the various shooters brings in a lot of money, and he takes a cut of every bet. Before he left, Charlie showed Grant that he's a damn fine shot who'll draw in boatloads of challengers. In between matches, he'll be able to check out the customers."

"Well, Charlie can only come up with so many excuses as to why he's hanging around that saloon when there aren't any challengers. As I understand it, the shooting gallery operates outside in the late afternoon and at night. So, someone needs to be there earlier in the day and inside the saloon. That's why, starting late mornings, Lucinda will barmaid and I'll cook."

"That's all fine and good but first you have to get hired just two days from now. That's not going to happen," Sage said, with a dismissive flip of his hand.

This time it was Lucinda who sounded smug. "That's where you are wrong, Sage dear. It's all set. Mae bribed the cook. She's going to have a sudden family emergency down in Medford. On the same day, the daytime bar gal simply will not show up. She's going to start working for a friend of mine. She's wanted to shift jobs for a long time."

"And, how will you…," Sage couldn't bring himself to ask the question aloud.

Her smile was saucy as she said, "Oh, I might have to put up with a fanny pinch or two but, for a while, that saloon is going to desperately need a barmaid to serve drinks and food. Besides, Grant will wait a while before he fires me. He'll figure I'll eventually give in and make him some money in his rooms upstairs. But we all know that won't happen. I think the assassin will turn up before he gets too pushy."

Sage raised his hands in surrender. They'd probably be safe enough. After all, the two women weren't going to capture the assassin, only set eyes on him, and more importantly, discover with whom he was meeting. He had to admit that it was a good plan that posed little danger to them.

Turning to Fong Kam Tong, Sage asked. "How's watching Harry going?"

While Fong had exclaimed and laughed along with the others, he'd otherwise said nothing. Sage could tell his friend was considering how best to answer Sage's question. Finally, he said, "Dr. Harry is difficult man to guard. No set schedule. Goes here, then there. I not see anyone watching or following. Sprig not see anyone either."

Sage smiled to himself. It seemed that Fong had made a new friend out of the cabbie. "What do you suggest we do to keep Harry safe?"

"Once Dr. Harry win election, I stick to him like shadow. Sprig say there room on cab perch because we both skinny. Sprig talk to Mrs. Harry. She okay if I stay in house too."

"What's Harry say about that?"

"He roll eyes, say we all crazy but not say no. Wife put foot down, I think."

Sage gazed around the dining room. "There is one little problem. With Mae working at the Portland Club, me working construction, and Fong attached to Harry like a barnacle, who will run Mozart's?"

Mae heaved a sigh. "Well, Ida, Matthew, and Homer could run the noon dinner hour and tea time with few problems. But, the supper hour would be much more difficult. So . . ." her words trailed off before she straightened and said firmly, "When the time comes, I propose we close Mozart's for at least a week, maybe longer. Ida and Homer have earned a rest from the restaurant and Matthew needs a break. He worked very hard to pass his school tests with high grades. I say we pay all three of them to take a vacation for a change."

Sage smiled at her. "What a great idea! They can sleep in and go for lazy strolls about town. It will be good for them. Meantime you, Lucinda, Mr. Fong, and I will get up at the crack of dawn and work our tails off finding the assassin and his employers."

SIXTEEN

April 2 1905

"SAGE, YOU CAN'T WORK ALL day in construction and then go gallivanting around all night," Mae admonished.

Sage was stripping the wax from his mustache so that it would droop. He wore his tattered and somewhat dirty John Miner canvas pants, flannel shirt, and stained coat. "Won't be all night, I promise. I'm meeting Hanke's young officer, Dan Carter, in the North End. We'll talk, and then I'll come back."

She sat at the alcove table, keeping him company while he transformed from John Adair, proprietor of a high-class restaurant, into John Miner, an itinerant worker from field and forest. He often roamed the North End as John Miner where he was known to be a friendly, often generous, fellow.

"Maybe you best tell me the place you're meeting. Just in case I have to send Fong to your rescue."

"Well, I hope that doesn't happen. He tells me I've practiced enough of the snake and crane to take care of myself in most situations."

"Be that as it may, there's no telling what you'll run into. That North End is a wicked place."

"Yeah, so says the woman who was down there selling soap to the crib ladies," he said with a fond smile. "I am supposed to meet Carter at the Rusty Bucket. He'll arrest me, take me outside. Once we're alone, I'll take him to a place Fong's set up so we can talk without fear of being overheard." He turned from the mirror to ask, "How do I look? See anything that will give me away?"

She studied him, her eyes dark with worry. "Well, you might muss the hair up a bit. It's too tidy. Straggle it down your forehead some," she advised.

Sage turned to the mirror and did as she suggested. Clapping a battered fedora onto his head, he said, "I'm off."

She followed him out into the hallway, watched him pull aside the tapestry, open the door to the hidden staircase, step inside, and pull the door shut behind him. She tidied the tapestry but left the concealing wheeled shelves to one side. If all went well, he'd be back within an hour or two. Once in the Miner getup, he always exited Mozart's through the hidden trap door in the neighboring alley.

A minute later, Sage carefully closed the trap door and slipped out onto the sidewalk to turn north. A few blocks later he crossed Burnside and entered the heart of the North End. As always, he found it disheartening to walk down the North End's Fourth Avenue. Lucinda had convinced him that prostitution could be a profession, but only when no coercion was involved and the profits were fairly shared.

Fourth Avenue, however, was a testament to the fact that most prostitution rarely reached such an equitable status. In between the saloons, it was lined on either side by shabby one- and two-story unpainted buildings with women's names crudely appearing over the doorways. Most cribs fronted the sidewalk from which women beckoned. It was a common sight throughout the North End. According to Lucinda, landlords, pimps, dope dealers, and the bribe-demanding special police kept these women in dire poverty.

Every North End block sported a mix of cribs, bawdy houses, gambling dens, and saloons. No wonder the police liked to call the area, 'White Chapel' after London's notorious vice district. And, no wonder the area's black citizens were moving across the river to start anew.

Reaching the Rusty Bucket after politely refusing countless entreaties, he pushed through its swinging door into thick smoke and the smell of stale beer. He made his way to the bar's brass foot rail. It was a meager place with only eight small tables and a scarred bar. Still, he preferred it because the saloonkeeper's wife forbade whoring within its walls and allowed only friendly wagers on card games. It was a safe place for a poor man, free of argumentative drunks, tricksters, jack rollers, and others scheming to take what little the customer might have.

Tonight, only the wife stood behind the bar. "Hey Belle!" he greeted. "Did that husband of yours leave you to work on your own?"

A big woman, she moved gracefully down the bar's length to stand before him. "Well, John Miner! What a happy day! Aren't you a sight for these sore eyes! It's been a while. Where you been?"

"Ah, hoboing around, seeing a bit of the country, working here and there." Her warm welcome was not unusual, though it seemed to carry a bit more intensity than usual.

The reason was immediately apparent because, after pouring him a draft, she nodded toward the far end of the bar. There a gaunt, old, shabbily dressed man slumped, his forearms holding him up while his head drooped.

"I see Curly Spencer's still with us. He already drunk tonight?" Sage asked.

She sighed. "Nah. He's as sober as he gets. He's pretty weak. I suspect all he's had to eat this past week has been the morning gruel they serve up at the city jail. He says that, given all this rain, that's where he's been bunking nights."

Sage got the message. "How about I buy him a couple beers so he can eat some of your sausages and bread?"

"That'd be right nice of you. That darn husband of mine has a hissy fit whenever I try to feed hungry sods on our dime. Says I start doing that and they'll overwhelm us like a troop of raccoons. You watch, when he gets back, he'll spot Curly eating and raise cane, accusing me of trying to send us to the poor farm."

"Where is Bubba anyway?"

"Oh, he's meeting with Mr. Weinhard—our landlord and silent partner in all that we do here." Her twisted lips telegraphed her thoughts about that arrangement.

Just then there was a rustling beside him. He glanced sideways to see the lithe frame of a young man leaning against the bar. He was dressed in the plain duds of the special police with a tin star on his suit coat and a billed cap on his head. Sergeant Hanke's undercover police officer was right on time.

Belle ambled down the counter toward the kitchen area to make Curly his sausage sandwiches. Sage was sure she'd add a little extra to it—she always did with the hungry ones. A low voice sounded beside him. "Good thing you wore that red kerchief like Hanke said. I might not have recognized you, Mr. Adair."

In a louder voice, Carter said, "You best tell me your name buddy. You fit the description of a head-thumping, jack roller running around these parts."

Belle swiftly interceded. "Hey! This is Mr. Miner, one of my best customers! He's no damn jack-roller!" she exclaimed.

Carter turned speechless at her unexpected opposition, finally declaring in a weak, but officious, voice, "Be that as it may, Mr. Miner had best come with me. Like I said, he fits the description."

"Goddamn special police! Yur always bothering people who ain't done a dadburn thing wrong!" Curly slurred loudly from his end of the bar, sausage in one hand, beer in the other. The saloon went dead silent before angry muttering swelled up.

Nonplused by how quickly things had gotten out of hand, young Carter was again at a loss for words. He hadn't anticipated needing to fend off barroom resistance. Sage jumped in. "Alright, officer. No need to get huffy. I'll come with you."

Without another word, the relieved Carter grabbed Sage by the elbow and steered him out the front door. A drunken shout followed them out. "Damned dirty, money-grubbing, bribe-taking copper!"

Once they reached the sidewalk, Sage quickly took the lead with Carter trotting behind. He led them into a dark alley half a block down the street. He turned to find the young man casting nervous glances about. Sage said, "Dan, you best put that badge and cap in your pocket. You can't look like a policeman where we are going."

Carter immediately obeyed, transforming into a young farmer out on the town, albeit one who'd lost his hat.

Sage moved deeper into the alley to stop before a narrow door. At three knocks, the peephole panel slid open and one dark eye peered out. Sage didn't hesitate, saying only, "Fong Kam Tong is a superior flute player." Sage felt silly saying it. He'd objected to using that as the password phrase but Fong had insisted, his eyes dancing. He knew that among his many skills, his flute playing was the only one Sage failed to admire.

The door opened and a Chinese man bowed in greeting. At Sage's nod, he opened the door just wide enough for them to slip in sideways. Once inside, Carter gave the place a wide-eyed survey. "What is this place?" he whispered.

"Hush," Sage said. "Just follow and say nothing."

The Chinese man set off down a narrow hallway toward what appeared to be a dead end. Reaching the wall, he pushed on something and it slid sideways. Soon they were trailing him up stairs, down stairs, and through hidden doors, some of them masquerading as cabinets and shelves, others as blank walls. Glances behind told Sage that Carter still followed, albeit with a nervously wrinkled forehead above wide eyes.

Finally, their guide opened a normal door and ushered them into a beautifully appointed room. Exquisite silk hangings decorated the walls, offering spare depictions of birds, trees, waterfalls, rivers, and flowers. The room's only furniture was a large, round, black-lacquered table and two chairs centered atop a crimson rug. A red lacquer tray, holding a small brown teapot and two cups waited on the table. Oil wall lamps shone dimly.

The Chinese man waved a slim hand toward the chairs and pointed at the teapot before silently bowing out of the room. Sage glanced around. He suspected this was where Fong held his mediation sessions between conflicting tongs. Yet another one of his friend and teacher's many intriguing activities. Besides teaching martial arts, Fong ran a provision shop with his wife, worked as a busboy at Mozart's, and was a well-respected flute musician among the local Chinese. Fong also served as the community's unofficial mediator, settling disputes among them. His high stature within the community was why Sage and Carter had been admitted into this inner sanctum.

Carter's whisper interrupted Sage's musings, "Whew, where are we? We wound around more than king snakes hunting barn mice," adding anxiously, "I'll never find my way out."

"Don't worry. These are friendly folk. Think of this as a learning experience. You now know why there's never been, and never will be, a successful raid on a Chinese gambling den. And, you haven't seen the half of it. Here, drink some tea. It'll calm your nerves," Sage advised, filling a tiny handle-less cup and sliding it toward the young policeman.

He continued, "We needed somewhere completely private to talk, a place where there was no chance that any of the special police or their buddies might see us together. My friend arranged this."

Carter swallowed some tea, made a face, and set the tiny cup down. "If it's all the same to you, I think I'll wait until I can find some coffee. Anyway, I can't be gone long."

"Okay, have you heard any rumbles from your cop colleagues or the vice folks about Harry Lane?'

"Well, yeah, tons. Boy, they sure do hate him. Especially after that speech he made last night. I never seen so many newspaper front pages being ripped up."

Sage wasn't surprised at the anger. Sage had attended last night's rally where Harry again promised a packed audience that he'd end the North End's vice and corruption if he was elected. Those building owners, saloonkeepers, brewers, cigar makers, madams, pimps, and even ladies of the night, all stood to lose some or most of their income if Lane followed through on his campaign promises.

Sage nodded. "Yeah, I heard him speak but didn't read the paper this morning, what's it say?"

Carter pulled a folded bit of newsprint from his inside pocket to read aloud the short article appearing below the headline, "Lane Targets North End Vice."

> Well-meaning citizens of our fair city, both Democrat and Republican, packed the Hibernian hall last night. There, they were heartened to hear the words of the city's most interesting mayoral candidate. This time, Dr. Harry Lane turned his wrath on vice and its accompanying corruption, stating the following with a firmness seldom used by today's politicians. He earned an enthusiastic standing ovation when he vowed, "The city will not engage in any partnership with any form of vice for the sake of revenues. If more revenue is needed then lawful and honorable methods will be employed, including raising taxes on this city's wealthy." One attendee was heard to remark that it was refreshing to hear someone who didn't talk out of both sides of his mouth. For sure, this will be a week of fired-up words, at least those coming from the Lane camp.

Carter finished reading, folded the paper carefully, and returned it to an inside pocket. "I've been asking questions, acting the part of a dumb newbie. Boy, have I heard stuff I never knew."

Sage chuckled inwardly. The kid didn't have to work very hard at playing the wide-eyed newbie role. It came naturally to him. "Go on," he urged.

"Well, of course, the special police don't like what Lane said. One told me half his income comes from payoffs. A person can't stay in business here unless he or she bribes the special police and even the regular police detectives. The cops have divvied up the North End into individual territories so that they all get payoffs."

Sage nodded encouragingly for the young man to continue. So far, he already knew everything Carter was saying. It was old information.

Then Carter leaned forward to say, "And, you know that Portland Club my sergeant is so interested in? Well, my partner and I were in there talking to the barkeep, Peter Grant. He supposedly owns the place but everybody knows a brewery fellow is the real owner. Not only does the owner get a cut of the alcohol sales but he also gets a piece of the other action as well." Carter paused, slurped some tea, made a face, and set it down again. "Forgot I don't like it. Tastes like boiled pasture grass," he said.

Sage thought it interesting that a brewery man owned the saloon. "Go on, Dan. This is interesting."

The young fellow puffed up a bit but his pride was soon overrun by his childlike eagerness to share. "Well, we got to talking and the bar-keep said the Portland Club pays out about seven thousand in fines and bribes every single month. When we said that was incredible, he said that it was nothing since every month, the saloon clears a profit of over twenty thousand after all the overhead, fines and bribes got paid." Carter shook his head in wonder, saying, "I guess all that boozing, gambling, and whoring adds up."

"It does, Dan. It also adds up to enormous human suffering. Every cent is taken from the pockets of those who can afford it least, often hungry families. The Portland Club's profit is a hidden tax on the poorest among us. It's their money that pays the bribes, and creates the profit. And, it's their money going into the city coffers as fines while the rich fight tooth and nail against any tax increase on them."

Red suffused Carter's face as he stuttered, "No, no, I don't . . . ," and then he straightened and his tone became adamant, "Let me tell you, Mr. Adair, I was raised up to be god-fearing and law-abiding. My ma always asks me what I am doing and learning. And, I can't lie to Ma. I've tried. I want to help end the vice. I feel awful seeing all this sadness," he swept his hand around as if encompassing the entire North End.

Sage felt kinship with the young fellow. He also found it hard to lie to his ma. He smiled and offered a hand to shake. "You are a good man, Dan Carter. Sergeant Hanke is right in his opinion of your character." This time, the young policeman's face turned red with pleasure.

After a few more comments, Carter declared he had to leave. So, Sage knocked on the door and the same Chinese man popped back in. Silently, he led them out the room's other door. After trailing him through the building, up and down, round and about, the man opened a door that deposited them just around the corner from where they'd started.

SEVENTEEN

May 2 and 3, 1905

"I GUESS THERE'S NO QUESTION but that he will win both the primary and the general," Lucinda said. She and Sage stood amidst a press of people, shoved so close together that her quiet words were said directly into his ear.

Sage, at six feet tall, towered over the heads of many in the crowd. Enough to see that the entire meeting hall overflowed with those who'd come to hear Harry Lane's final speech before the primary election, now just two days away. Even the overhead gallery seemed to be dangerously overcrowded. Vases of colorful flowers and fluttering flags edged the speakers' platform.

He bent to say into her ear, "I'm guessing there are more than six hundred people here. They expected no more than five hundred. They moved this gathering from the open-air plaza across from the courthouse because of the weather. It's a good thing they did. That plaza couldn't hold this many."

Sage felt joy and pride over Harry's success in attracting so many supporters wanting to see the city turn toward the good. Even Deputy Sheriff John Cordano, known as the king of Portland's "Little Italy," had cut short his Italian visit with his mother to return and campaign for Harry. Increasing numbers of Harry's supporters were filling every meeting hall, with many of those attending well-known Republicans. Meanwhile, William's meetings attendance was dwindling, forcing him to book into smaller and smaller meeting halls. The morning's *Journal* reported that Williams' meeting turnouts had dropped so low that his last few scheduled meetings were canceled. Evidently, he was counting on the *Gazette*'s strident endorsements, the wealthy men's money, and the illegally stuffed North End ballot box votes to keep him in office.

All of that was good news for Harry's campaign but it also strengthened Sage's fear for his safety. He summed up his joy and fear by saying, "I agree with you Lucinda. Harry Lane will be the democratic candidate. It's also beginning to look likely that he'll be our next mayor, but. . ." he added ominously, "only if he survives."

Indeed, Sage had never seen so many people gathered together in Portland, except maybe that one time when Theodore Roosevelt came to town. Around them, a chant of "Lane, Lane" started up to be followed by thunderous applause. A grinning Lucinda slapped gloved hands over her ears. The exuberant chants and applause continued until Sage wished Harry would appear and stop the noise.

The crowd finally quieted when two women and a pianist appeared. In quick succession, the refrains of the *Star Spangled Banner* and *Way Down Upon the Swanee River* floated out above the crowd that began singing along. Once that entertainment was over, Governor Chamberlain, followed by Harry Lane and a bevy of civic notables, mounted the platform midst enthusiastic cheers and waves of applause.

Harry Lane's campaign chairman and best friend, R. W. Montague, spoke first, discussing an issue that had everybody concerned: Election fraud. Historically most election fraud was carried out in the North End by the Republican political machine. As long as anyone could remember, wagon loads of drunks had been hauled from polling place to polling place—most voting repeatedly. Given Williams' low support and the adamant vice-lord opposition to Lane, people reasonably feared election fraud.

Montague sought to calm that concern. To nodding heads, he vividly described the problem. He next outlined the steps Harry's campaign was taking to prevent voter fraud's reoccurrence during the primary and the general elections, saying, "We consider the primary a good way to test our fraud prevention efforts before the general election. In recent days, we've uncovered evidence of countless false registrations on the Westside where Williams expects to win the most votes.

"Vice men, like Larry Sullivan, have taken tramps, sailors, and timber workers to the courthouse to register as voters—often registering at more than one precinct under assumed names. None of them are city residents. Our investigation shows that they are unknown at the addresses they used when registering. In just two examples, and there are many more, twenty-three men claimed to live in a boarding house that has only five rooms total—another fifty-one claimed they lived in a seven-room boarding house. The proprietors of both houses have signed affidavits stating that they know none of the named men.

"We have a list of those false registrants. That list will be supplied to the democratic poll watchers who will challenge them should they attempt to vote. Multnomah County's Sheriff Word will station deputies at the suspect precincts ready to arrest these men should they attempt to vote."

Sage and Lucinda exchanged worried looks. The assassination schemers would be even more desperate if the traditional fraud schemes couldn't be used to secure a Williams' election win.

Rousing cheers and applause greeted Montague's assurances and continued until Governor Chamberlain stepped up to the podium. His opening declaration that Harry Lane would win both the primary and general elections triggered more long minutes of applause and cheers.

Chamberlain was followed by State Senator Nottingham who simply vowed that, though he was a Republican, he would be voting for Harry Lane. Another five minutes of applause filled the hall.

Speeches, accompanied by enthusiastic claps, whoops, and cheers spooled out until finally Harry stepped to center stage where he had to wait through over ten minutes of cheers and applause. Once people quieted, a pin drop could have been heard. It seemed as if all were holding their breath. Harry ran a hand through his hair making it spring awry but his gaze was calm as he began:

> Tonight, you will not hear me speak ill of Mayor George Williams. I believe him to be a kind and honest man. Unfortunately, he has surrounded himself with men ruled only by their own self-interest. They have sadly misled him. His administration has raised issues that I must address. I owe that to myself and to you, the people of our beloved city.
>
> I promise, with all my heart and soul, that I will not allow corruption and that I will exercise my authority under the city charter to fire any employee who engages in it. There will be no more Tanner Creek-type scandals.
>
> Today the vice lords and those profiting from vice have too much power in this city. Men like Larry Sullivan, the Grant brothers, and their ilk, need to be reformed, not pulling the decision-levers of this city. There will be no licensing of vice. No turning of blind eyes.

Additionally, my appointments to the executive advisory committee and various offices will be irrespective of party affiliation or the donation the appointee makes to my campaign. Unlike today, neither a political machine nor an individual's wealth will impact any of my decisions.

I believe that my four years as superintendent of the state insane asylum have proven I am a man of my word. And, I am sure you read, in yesterday's *Journal*, the wonderful letter written by a former trustee of that institution verifying that I do exactly what I say I will do. Thank you for your support. With your help, we will make this city a showcase for all that is right and just.

Thunderous applause had punctuated Harry's every sentence. At his speech's conclusion, the cheers and applause went on and on, halting only when the Bricklayer's Union brass band marched down the aisle blasting ears with a rousing tune.

The rally over, it took a long while for the crowd to depart. Sage and Lucinda were the last to leave. They waited on either side of the exit door, looking for a stocky man with a grey streak at his temple. They never spotted him.

Early the next morning, Sage found his mother chortling over an open newspaper. Today was the first day of Mozart's closure. It felt odd to enter Mozart's kitchen and find no noon dinner preparations underway—only a perking coffee pot sat atop the coal-fired stove. He grabbed a cup, filled it, and sat down across from his still-chuckling mother. "What's so funny? And, why are you still here? I thought your cook job at the Portland Club started today."

"I told the saloonkeeper, that Peter Grant fellow, that I'd only work days, starting at ten o'clock and stopping at five. He didn't like it. I expect he'll fire my fanny as soon as he finds a replacement," she rubbed her thumb and forefinger together, "but I know how to deal with that."

"What have you and Lucinda planned for Grant?"

"Well, his barmaid's going to be mysteriously absent. So, if all goes as planned, I will be handing food to the most beautiful barmaid ever seen in that dive."

"She's pretty noteworthy, all right. I'm afraid she'll be recognized. You know how she and her women like to parade around in that fancy carriage."

"She's not worried. She says she'll be disguised. That sly Miss won't tell me how. Just says, 'You'll see.'"

Sage wondered about that for a bit then returned to his first question. "What *Journal* story got you laughing?"

"District Attorney Manning announced that he has begun proceedings before the grand jury over the Tanner Creek project. He says he is seeking indictments against George Williams, City Engineer William Elliott, and contractor Riner and his son who you're working for. He says Williams willfully failed to perform the duties of his office. He wants Elliott charged with failing to perform his duty, false certification of a project, and conspiring with Riner to defraud the city regarding the Tanner Creek sewer project charges."

"Talk about flinging the cat among the pigeons!" Sage exclaimed. "That's going to make the Williams supporters even more desperate to get rid of Harry."

She wrinkled her nose and said contemptuously, "As far as I'm concerned, the D.A. can't act soon enough to catch those crooks. Nothing would please me more than to see those three villains behind bars." Then her expression became perplexed. "By the way, why haven't you already left to work on Riner's latest construction project?"

Sage laughed. "I'm heading there this afternoon. I sent a message to my immediate boss, Emil, saying that I needed to meet my mother's train this morning. I told him that she's arriving from Seattle and is a harridan who will have my hide if I'm not on the station platform, flowers in hand when her train pulls in. He sent back an understanding message. Emil likes me and the exposition means there's a shortage of workers—so my job's safe."

Mae shook her head dolefully. "Oh my, I have raised such a fibber."

"Hey, not everything I said was a lie!" he said, before ducking the faux slap aimed at his ear.

Mae had to hand it to Lucinda. Her transformation was remarkable. It took a few seconds before Mae recognized her. First of all, the woman asking Peter Grant for a barmaid job was entirely too plump. Instead of golden hair, a dark wig, wrapped in a jaunty red headband, straggled beside a face so painted that it looked like a drunken hand had applied rouge, eyeliner, and skin cover with a trowel. Mae worried whether the effect was too slatternly even for a place as lowbrow as the Portland Club.

Seemingly not, since Grant immediately handed Lucinda a tray of beers and gave her fanny a shove toward a table of already drunk sailors. Lucinda shot him a glare from those cornflower blue eyes, one hot enough to make Grant step back and raise his hands in mock surrender. The scowl on his face, as he turned away, sent a shudder up Mae's spine. This wasn't a man to cross. She'd better warn Lucinda.

It was a day filled with drunken revelers and Mae's satisfaction at Lucinda's popularity—she knew how to flirt. Every time Mae spotted Grant eying his new barmaid with narrowed, speculative eyes, she interrupted him with whatever question that came to mind. By the end of their shift, it was clear that Grant realized he'd hired himself a feisty, though profit-generating barmaid, and a dimwitted cook.

When Grant descended into the cellar to fetch another beer barrel, Mae leaned over the counter to say, "If you'd sewed any more padding into the rump of that dress, you'd have trouble fitting through the door."

Lucinda laughed. "I told Elmira she was getting carried away adding so much padding but she insists sex-starved men like big-bottomed women. Besides, it makes the pinches less painful."

"Well, take care Grant doesn't get a handful. He's not a stupid man and his mean streak is a mile wide. He's watching you. You don't want him figuring out that you're a well-upholstered, bewigged phony. We best leave at the same time today."

Lucinda nodded. "I agree. Before I came, I got word from Sage that Charlie's arriving on the afternoon train. He should turn up about the time our shift ends. Once he does, we can leave. But, so far, I've seen no one fitting the description of the assassin. Have you?"

Mae shook her head. "Nope, but I figure he won't turn up until tomorrow, the day before the primary election returns come in."

Lucinda shook her head. "I'm not so sure. He could attack before that. Sage and I figure Harry's big rally forced them to see the handwriting on the wall. Sage figures the time has come for Mr. Fong to stick to our Harry like glue. He thinks they might strike even before the primary vote."

Just then, Grant appeared, spotted them together, frowned, and snarled. "You gals quit your gabbing and get back to work. I ain't running no social club for the likes of you two."

EIGHTEEN

May 3 and 4, 1905

"GLAD TO SEE YOU MADE it! I missed you this morning. I had to work twice as hard." Emil exclaimed with a smile when Sage appeared at his side. "How's your mother? She make the trip alright?"

Sage laughed and said, "She's ornery as ever! It takes more than a train trip to slow her down."

Emil laughed. "Had a mother like that myself. She's passed on. I miss her every day."

"I'm sorry to hear that, Emil. I know I'd miss my mother too. I've tried to get her to move here but she refuses." Only the last was a fib since Mae Clemens had jumped at the chance to live with her son.

"Well, we best get to work. One of the rooms is ready for lathe and plaster. That's our next job. But the good news is that we'll be working out of the rain for a change."

He turned away but halted when Riner and his son charged around the corner of the building, shouted Emil's name and beckoned. "I better go see what the top boss wants," he told Sage.

Sage roamed around picking up scrap lumber and tossing it on the burn pile while keeping his eye on the two. He was too far away to hear what was said but saw Emil shake his head repeatedly in response to Riner's questioning. Finally, he nodded, Riner left, and Emil returned to Sage.

"Seems like the plastering job will have to wait. The Riners want us to track down Oscar Muckleroy. He's gone missing and they're hot to find him." Emil shook his head. "Things sure have turned strange."

"What do you mean?"

"Well, the Riners' are on edge like I've never seen them. And, Oscar has always been a reliable foreman. He's never acted all 'here today, gone tomorrow' like he's been doing. It's worrisome. I can't figure out what's going on around here."

"When did it start?"

"Just in the past month or so."

Sage realized that Emil hadn't read the morning newspaper. He didn't know the district attorney was seeking an indictment against Riner and his son. He debated telling Emil but decided that it was best not to. Emil might volunteer more information if he didn't know what was at stake.

"Anyway, since I live near Oscar and we're friends, Mr. Riner wants me to go check on him. On the way back, we'll stop at the hardware store and pick up some things. Because I might need your help carrying stuff, he said it's okay to take you with me."

They hopped a south-running streetcar and rolled into the Buckman neighborhood, though some were starting to call it "Union Town" because many of the homeowners were union men. Their improved wages were driving the growth. Sage was surprised at how many new houses had sprung up on every side. Most were plan book houses, with the builder buying the plans and a materials list. That's why they looked similar.

They rode past the Lone Fir cemetery to step down at Morrison Street just as a streetcar rolled past, heading toward Mt. Tabor. That dormant volcano now had seven new drinking water reservoirs terraced onto its slopes, guaranteeing clear mountain drinking water for the entire city.

Minutes later, they reached Muckleroy's neat house. There a thin woman yanked the door open at their knock. Her lowered brow and compressed lips telegraphed irritation. Recognizing Emil, she smiled weakly before her face tightened with anxiety. "Has something bad happened to Oscar? Is he alright?" she asked.

"Nothing bad has happened, Betty. Far as I know, Oscar's fine. It's just that he didn't show up on the job this morning. Mr. Riner sent me to check on him. He's not here?"

She shook her head and gestured them inside. "Best you come through to the kitchen. I just made coffee. You look drenched to the skin. This spring weather has been lively."

For the first time, she noted Emil had not come alone. Emil caught her glance and said, "This is John Miner. He's my helper. I brought him along because we've got to stop at the hardware store on the way back. I need him to tote material."

She just nodded, briefly smiled in Sage's direction, and turned to walk down the hallway. They followed. Once she poured them coffee, Emil began gently questioning her. Sage didn't know whether he was asking for himself or Riner because he focused on Oscar's recent, unusual behavior.

Tears welled in Betty's eyes. She raised an apron corner to dab at them and said, "Emil, I swear I don't know what's gotten into Oscar lately. First, he came home with enough money to pay off our mortgage. That was a happy day even though he refused to say where he got it."

Her chin wobbled, she fought for control, and after a gulp, she said, "After that day, his spirits seemed to go downhill. He got quieter and quieter—and when he's not clammed up, he's snappish. I can't figure out what I could have done to get him so upset.

"Today was the worst. He said he wasn't going to work. He told me he was sick, but I didn't believe him. When I asked if he needed a doctor or medicine, he about bit my head off. I can't think what's the matter with him."

Sage eyed the kitchen. It was simple but clean. It had a coal-burning cookstove and what looked like a new icebox. The sink counter held two loaves of cooling bread and a plate of cookies. Beside them lay a folded newspaper.

Sage cleared his throat and gently asked, "Did Mr. Muckleroy see the newspaper this morning?"

"Why yes. That's the first thing he does of a morning. He fetches the newspaper off the front stoop before coming into the kitchen for his coffee. He reads it while I fix his breakfast. Come to think of it, he sat down at the table, took a sip of coffee, and right after told me that he'd be staying to home. He shucked his work boots and headed for the bedroom. He didn't even want the breakfast I'd fixed him. I had to feed it to the dog."

Emil's brow had wrinkled at Sage's question before he asked, "But after that, Oscar left? He's not here now?"

Betty looked even more anxious. "That's the funny thing. Two strange men knocked on the door about an hour ago. They didn't seem friendly. They asked for Oscar. I told them to wait on the porch while I fetched him.

"But, he wasn't in the bedroom or anywhere in the house. The bedroom window was wide open. He must have left the house that way. But I don't know why or when. He's never done anything so strange before. Oscar has always been my rock. You know that, right Emil? None of this is like my Oscar." Once again tears filled the woman's eyes.

Emil reached across the table to pat her hand. "First of all, Betty, it isn't anything you've done. Oscar's been strange at work too. Don't worry. I'm damn sure going to get to the bottom of what's going on with him. Too many weird things are happening here and on the job site. Maybe Oscar's gotten mixed up in something he shouldn't. That might explain where he got that extra money."

They soon left, but not before Emil again reassured Betty Muckleroy he'd get to the bottom of Oscar's strange behavior.

At the hardware store, Sage bought a *Journal*. Once the shopping was done, he persuaded Emil to take time for a coffee at a nearby café. After taking seats, Sage opened the newspaper to the front page and slid it across the table to Emil. "Maybe you best read this," he said.

It felt strange strolling the Exposition grounds without his cart. Herman Eich missed the satin feel of the worn oak handles and the forward lean needed to push the cart. Instead, he carried a tool bag because Leo had given him a card that allowed him onto the fairgrounds as a union carpenter.

All around, people were moving with a beehive's busyness, especially in this section the fair organizers called "The Trail." There were more bustling workers than he could count, all lugging the tools and materials of their various trades.

In a few days, at the fair's Monday opening, there'd be busyness of a different sort. Men in suits and ladies, with parasols aloft, would stare and exclaim over the fanciful frontages lining this wide avenue.

He pictured Mae Clemens with one of those frou-frou parasols and laughed aloud, catching a stare from a man painting a nearby booth. Eich sidled away until he found an empty, upturned nail barrel at the Trail's entrance. Situated at the fairground's main crossroads, it was the perfect observation post. Southward, a grand staircase led up to the exhibit buildings. East and west ran the lakeside promenade. And to the north, he had an unimpeded view down The Trail and across the lake causeway to the looming federal government building at its end.

The Trail was the fair's concession center. Twenty or so small buildings fronted it, with additional commercial outlets around the corner on the promenade. Colorful signs fronted every building, advertising wares and entertainment. Shopkeepers were creating table displays of eye-catching items and draping colorful pennants.

He scanned the signs. There was such a variety of establishments hoping to entice customers into spending their money: a charitable appeal for the Galveston flood victims, French, Japanese, and German restaurants, a bakery shop, and a collection of wondrous exhibits that promised educated horses, diving elks, exotic animals, and scary haunts. The largest building touted a Venetian experience complete with gondola rides on a canal.

Eich started when a dark-skinned man, wearing a caftan and fez, rounded the corner leading a big-eyed camel. The pair disappeared into the Cairo exhibit where the famous dancer, Little Egypt, was scheduled to appear once the fair opened.

An hour later, activity on The Trail ebbed without Eich spotting the would-be assassin. He swiveled on his barrel and eyed the stairway leading up to the exhibit buildings crowding the fair's south end. Those were impressive edifices, whitewashed plaster marvels doomed to only a few months of existence. Situated on a slight rise, they shimmered in sunlight now that the storm-battered sky had cleared.

He had to admit, the buildings were an elegant surprise given that Portland was a small city in a western state less than fifty years old. The Agricultural, Foreign, European, Oriental, Manufacturers, and Forestry buildings towered over the grounds. Except for the Forestry Building, all were constructed in the ornate, symmetrically proportioned Spanish Renaissance style, each with columns, baroque detailing, cupolas, domes, and arched openings.

But those megalithic decorative touches were not what impressed him the most. The most impressive thing was that every building, except for the Forestry one, was nothing more than a plaster skin over a wooden frame. They'd be torn down in less than a year. All of that work, all of that permanent-looking beauty, was illusionary. The idea brought to mind one of Mr. Fong's favorite sayings, "All that surrounds is temporary, only kindness in heart lasts forever."

He smiled at the truth of that homily. His friend, Fong Kam Tong said many useful things.

Only the Forestry building, sitting midst that artificial grandeur, was permanent. The enormous log cabin, with its barked log columns and cedar shingles, looked like a lumberjack mistakenly invited to a high-class tea party. It was his favorite building.

Turning away from the exhibit halls, he gazed northward, down The Trail toward the lake. A walking bridge crossed the once swampy water to what the promoters called 'Government Island'. Yet another grand, but temporary plaster building stood upon that spit of land. It was the federal government's contribution to the city's extravaganza.

He sighed, feeling inadequate to find the one man amongst hundreds of people scurrying around like frenzied ants. Somewhere among them might be the stocky assassin, that white blaze at his temple. He wasn't hopeful. His days spent lurking outside the gates had yielded no sight of the villain. And his effort today was so far, bereft of success. Still, if the assassin had gone to Seattle, he'd be returning soon, given that the primary election was tomorrow.

When Eich rose, his stiff knees signaled he should have stood sooner. These days, his joints froze if he stayed in one position for too long. Ambling west along the wooden esplanade, he planned to check around the American Inn even though it wasn't open for guests. The Inn was a long shot, but perhaps the assassin had worked there.

A few minutes later, he paused beside a fenced off field jutting into the lake. Four men were holding tie-down ropes encircling a floating, cigar-shaped dirigible. The metal frame dangling beneath the airship had a propeller at its nose, a pilot's seat, and a small huffing steam engine on its rear. Wires ran upward from the pilot's seat to a steering rudder beneath the airship's tail.

A young man ran forward and hopped into the pilot's seat. Once settled, he pulled on the wires, checking the rudder's movement. Grinning, he pulled down his eye mask and waved energetically. The motor revved and the men on the ground let go the ropes.

Engine huffing, the airship rose skyward. Although Eich had seen similar things on the East Coast, this dirigible was a first for Portland. A hundred feet above, the young man began hauling on the wires, turning the contraption south toward the central city. No doubt, the dirigible's flight was intended to stir up enthusiasm for the fair.

Despite earlier doubts, Eich had come to believe this Lewis & Clark Exposition would be a spectacle never before seen in the Pacific Northwest. It just might fulfill the fair organizers' dreams. They hoped it would increase the city's population permanently, bolstering Portland's status as the region's largest city. More important, they expected it to make them even wealthier. Even before the fair opened, the organizers were getting rich providing housing, food, and living essentials to the thousands who'd arrived looking for work. If they stayed and, if the fair attracted even more people and businesses, the fair organizers would become rich as the proverbial Croesus.

Eich watched the airship until it dwindled to a mere speck against the gray sky. With a sigh, he turned away and continued down the esplanade toward the red-and-white American Inn. It was reported to offer 585 rooms to fairgoers. Like the Forestry building, the Inn departed from the fair's predominate Renaissance architectural style. Instead, the Inn looked like a Berkshire Mountains resort hotel. One end abutted the promenade so that its long frontage stretched along the lake, supported by pilings in front and a boulder berm at its rear. Flat roofs separated its three gable peaks, while its water frontage sported a covered colonnade.

Eich approached a workman vigorously applying white paint to a colonnade pillar. Once the man noticed him, Eich said, "Excuse me, I wonder if you would be so kind to help me? I am looking for a man. I don't remember his name. I heard it too quickly."

"Oh boy, there be lots of men hereabouts. How might you expect to find him if you don't know his name?" The gentle Scottish lilt was faint, indicating this man had been some time in the country.

Eich described the suspected assassin and was elated, though he tried not to show it, when the man nodded.

"Aye, I know the man. You asking is a mite peculiar because we fellows were just chin-wagging about him."

"You were? Why is that?"

"Well, you know the hotel's not open for guests as of yet. They're still beautifying its bits. But that fellow you be asking about, Mrs. McCready gave him a room about a month ago."

"Why? Is he a relative of hers?"

"Nope. He's nobody she knows. I heard her argue about him with another fellow. She told him she didn't want some stranger underfoot. But, she still gave in. That fellow moved in just as we started painting the woodwork and such. Stayed a few weeks, then left."

"Oh, so he's gone now?" Eich felt disappointment stab. "Dagnabbit, I missed him," he muttered, only to have his informant respond, "Ah, but you didn't. That's why we were talking about him today. He's come back and Mrs. McCready raised another ruckus. Told him she didn't want some freeloader as her first guest. She likes things just so, does Mrs. McCready."

"Who insisted that the fellow stay here even though the Inn isn't open?"

The man gave a sly wink. "Well, doncha know it was one of her posh investors. Never knew his name but that's what our foreman said he was."

"Did you ever catch the name of this mysterious and unwelcome guest?" Eich asked.

"Don't know his first name, but I heard Mrs. McCready call him 'Mister Hess.' She hissed it—like he was dog dung on her shoe."

"Is he here at the hotel, right now?"

"Nah. He and Mrs. McCready got into a little argument on the front porch just this morning. I heard them going at it because, yah know, I was right here." He gestured at the freshly painted columns, then continued, "He told her she was supposed to fix him breakfast and she told him how the cow ate the cabbage . . . steam was near coming out her ears. Don't blame her none. She's been in charge of the construction and will manage the hotel once it opens. This close to opening day, she doesn't need to play wife to a fellow she don't want here in the first place."

"I take it that Mr. Hess did not eat his breakfast at the Inn?"

"Boy howdy, that's for sure. He practically ran down the boardwalk to get away from her. I thought maybe she was going brain him with that cane she uses." A smile lit the fellow's mug and he added, "That I woulda like to have seen. It'd make a better story."

Eich shared a chuckle with the painter before departing, eager to share the location of the assassin's hideout.

NINETEEN

May 4, 1905

FONG SLID INTO THE KITCHEN, dark pools beneath his eyes and a slump to his shoulders once he'd sat. "Good Lord," Mae exclaimed as she quickly poured and set coffee before him. "You must have had some night."

"Doctor Lane very busy man," Fong said after taking a sip. "Lucky he promise to stay in bed this morning, no matter what. His lady wife say she make sure of that."

"What happened?"

"I stick with him and Sprig all day. Everything normal. We go to office and wait. He next go to meeting and we wait. After, we go to TB hospital near Milwaukie and we wait. We go to his house. His lady wife feed me, Sprig, and Sprig's son, Brunch. She very good cook. After, because election tomorrow, I sleep on couch. Brunch, he stay on cot beside front door. Sprig go home. We all asleep until messenger come at midnight.

"All get up. Doc's lady wife, she used to it. We drink coffee then Doc Lane ready to go. He take coffee and bag to cab. "Poor Brunch, he ride out in the rain but he say he used to it. I start to climb up with him but Doc say to sit under cover beside him." Fong flashed a quick grin, "Fong Kam Tong not stupid. I not complain. Do what he say.

"Cab stop at Sullivan Gulch. Three of us slide down mud trail to shack at bottom. Woman inside going to have baby. Children in shack very scared. Doc tell me and Brunch, 'Make place warm, boil water.' It take many hours. Doc send Brunch out of gulch to get food. I cook for children. Finally, baby come out. But Doc Lane, he want to stay until sun come up."

"Good Lord. Have you ever helped with a birthing before?"

Fong rolled his eyes and shook his head. "Never. Hope never again. Much yelling." Fong stayed quiet for a bit before giving another head-shake, his expression now one of rueful admiration. "Heart of Doc Lane full of kindness. He not let lady pay. He pay for food basket Brunch buy when Brunch wake up storekeeper. When we go, Doc leave coins on table. He kind man, for sure."

"So, other than the pregnant lady, everything went okay?"

Fong heaved a sigh. "Not exactly. Me and Brunch, we pretty sure we see someone. He down street under tree with big leaf. He run away before I get close. Now I go sleep upstairs short time."

"You gals better not run Charlie off with all your chatter. He's making me a lot of money.," Grant warned before clapping on a hat and heading out the doors. The manager of the Portland Club was going to meet someone he called "the Boss."

Once the doors whapped shut behind him, Mae and Lucinda exchanged grins. Charlie stirred in the armchair where he'd been pretend-ing to sleep. He stretched his arms high before yawning and saying, "Yup, you women and your chit-chatter like to send me running for the hills."

Lucinda, who knew him best, landed a playful slug on his shoulder. "Charlie, you've got no room to talk. I remember spending many an hour listening to your jawing during our Prineville days."

The saloon was nearly empty of customers. Every table had been wiped clean, the counter too. Those who remained made no requests, so Mae and Lucinda joined Charlie Siringo at his table. He, with a lazy smile, drawled, "Why, aren't I the fortunate man? The two loveliest ladies in the room have chosen me for conversation."

Mae laughed, saying, "A fine compliment that is! We're the only women here, mister smooth-talker," she retorted before noting, "Grant is certainly pleased with you."

"And he should be. He sent runners out to say he's got someone at his shooting gallery that no one can outshoot. Fella comes in, pays Grant a buck for each shot, and the promise of a cash prize if he hits closer to the target's center than me. So, far no one has."

"What would happen if you weren't here?" Mae was unfamiliar with shooting galleries.

"Wahl, in that case, Grant runs just a target-hitting game. He's got marked-cards poker and Bunco dice games but the real money for Grant is the shooting. So, if I'm not here, the poor sap pays his buck to shoot at a paper target. If he hits the bullseye, ole Grant forgets he promised a big prize and instead pays the fellow a piddling amount. Since the fella's been guzzling Grant's beer, he don't usually notice. And, if he does complain, Grant calls in the special police and they chase him on down the road."

Lucinda glanced around the room. With a sigh, she turned back to Siringo. "We haven't seen the man with the streak in his hair. Have you?"

Charlie shook his head. "I'm betting tonight will be the night."

"Shoot, we don't even know if that galoot is back in town," Mae grumbled.

"Wahl, before I came here this afternoon, your friend Solomon sent me a message at my hotel. It said that a porter saw a man fitting the assassin's description riding the Seattle southbound train yesterday morning. So, I'm thinking maybe we'll spot him come this afternoon."

Mae and Lucinda exchanged looks. "How about we offer to stay a few hours later today if we haven't seen him by shift's end? If Charlie's out shooting targets in the alley, he might miss seeing the fellow," Lucinda suggested.

When Grant returned, he was delighted to accept their offer to work past the end of their shifts. "I'm expecting quite a crowd. People are het up about tomorrow's vote. I promised Sullivan and Turco that I'd keep them here overnight with free beer and a floor to sleep on. They'll drive them to the precinct polls first thing tomorrow. So, it'll be free booze until they pass out. Then coffee and breakfast in the morning so they'll be alert enough to make their mark."

Mae's forehead wrinkled. "Don't they have to be residents to register?"

Grant laughed. "Oh, Sullivan and Turco's got lotsa phony names registered. Once they get to the polling place they'll be told what name to use."

Lucinda snorted, drawing Grant's attention to her. He scowled and said, "What's so funny? Do you think that won't work? Let me tell you. That's the way things have been done in this town for years. Between my free beer and Sullivan's and Turco's wagon rides and payouts, Williams will win this primary and the general election. Don't think he won't!"

Siringo's prediction came true. About five o'clock, a stocky man stepped into the Portland Club and took the rearmost booth. When Lucinda hustled up to get his order, he removed his hat, revealing an unmistakable blaze.

Her momentary pause caught his attention but he mistook her reaction as an invitation. "I just want something to drink, honey. I ain't interested in nothing else." He looked her up and down. "But, maybe later. For now, just bring me a beer and two shots of your best whiskey. After that, don't come back. I'll wave atcha if I want more."

Lucinda nodded meekly, fetched the drinks, and returned to set them on the table. He took a swig of beer but moved the two whiskey shots to the other side of the table.

Lucinda hurried out the side door into the alley where Charlie was banging away. She waited until he'd taken yet another winning shot that sent a disappointed competitor hustling back into the Club to pay for another chance.

Stepping close, she said quietly, "He's here in the back booth and expecting company. Likely two of them. He's wearing a brown plaid coat and black fedora."

Grant stuck his head out the door, "What are you doing out here, gal? I ain't paying you to gab with the help."

An unsmiling Charlie cocked an eyebrow at Grant. "Help?"

Lucinda slipped back into the saloon past Grant who was saying soothingly, "No, no, Charlie. You and I are partners in this shooting gallery. You know what I meant. That gal ain't willing to provide full service upstairs so I can't have her dilly-dallying out here. I need her inside because the other barmaids are up there keeping busy. A lot of election dough landed in men's pockets today," Grant added as he rubbed his hands together in the universal gesture for making money before ducking back into the saloon.

Charlie turned to the next competitor in line. "I got to head out now so I'll have to forego this shoot'n match-up." The challengers lining the alley groaned—they'd made bets among themselves on the outcome of the next contest. Charlie looked at his competitor, saying. "How about I give you five bucks?"

The slack mouth of the young drinker formed an "O" and he raised his chin to look up at the much taller Siringo, "Wahl, how about that?" he crowed. "The best shooter in town is afraid to go up against me! Why, he's even paying me not to shoot!"

Charlie laughed, handed him some coins, clapped him on the shoulder, and trotted down the alley toward the street. Once there, he cast about for a good place, settling on a closed provision shop's darkened doorway half a block away. He touched his holstered handgun and felt reassured. His job was to follow the assassin back to his hidey-hole.

Grant was furious over Charlie's absence. Less than half an hour later, his face turned rage ugly when both his cook and barmaid tossed him their aprons before dashing out the front door. Here it was, the Club's busiest nights, and all three abandoned their jobs without a word. He'd be giving them a serious talking to tomorrow, especially that sassy cook.

It was after midnight when the crew met without Eich or Solomon present. Their smaller numbers meant they could meet away from Mozart's dining room. Instead, only Mae, Lucinda, Fong, Charlie, and Sage sat knee-to-knee around the alcove table in Sage's third-floor room. The street below was unusually quiet. It was as if the town was holding its breath in anticipation of the next day's election outcome.

"Harry tucked up for the night?" Sage asked Fong.

"He sleep until noon today. Get up, go to office. After dinner, he go to politic meeting. Now he promise stay in house. His lady wife say she tie him down if he try to leave."

There was admiration in his words. Fong respected strong women. He had to. These days, his capable wife was running their provision store without any help from him. "Sprig and Brunch sleep inside. I tell cousin watch outside." Fong called the members of his Tong, a Chinese fraternal organization, his "cousins."

"Good thing it stopped raining, otherwise your poor cousin would be uncomfortable," Lucinda said.

"Sprig put horse in barn but cab sit in front of house. He tell watching cousin stay in cab out of rain, wrap in blanket."

"What made you call in reinforcements?" she asked.

"Need cousin because, early today, I think someone outside house."

"Did you see if he was wearing a plaid coat?"

"I not see. More like felt." Fong responded, glancing at Sage who nodded. Fong strongly believed in intuition's veracity. Many times, he'd been proved right. Yet another something he tried to teach Sage—being aware of, and listening to, one's intuition.

"Well, I've got some good news," Sage said. "Eich discovered that the assassin has been staying at the American Inn on the fairgrounds. His last name is Hess."

"Wahl, danged if Herman didn't steal my thunder and then some," Charlie drawled. "I trailed him to the fairground gate. He went in but they wouldn't let me in. I didn't know where he went because I lost sight of him amidst all them big buildings."

"Well, now we know. We know where we might find him when we're ready," Sage said. "Your information confirms Eich's, Charlie. Confirmation is always valuable."

"Wahl I ain't smarting but a bit since I learned something else mighty helpful. Before he landed at the fairgrounds, he stopped at another place. I watched him go into that crib hotel down near the Slap Jack saloon. You know the one I mean?"

Shivers traveled up Sage's spine. Oh yes, he knew the place. It was a wren of second-floor cribs. Flimsy plywood walls topped by chicken wire stretching up to the ceiling above chopped-up rooms. But remembering the cribs wasn't what gave him the shivers. Instead, it was the memory of the young girl's body lying atop filthy sheets with her throat slit and the gold coin he'd given her clutched in her hand. As he nodded wordlessly, he caught his mother's sympathetic look. She knew exactly what he was re-seeing.

A puzzled Charlie caught their silent exchange but continued his report. "I learned something important. I paid the desk clerk to let me upstairs and found the crib where Hess was. Since there aren't doors, only curtains, I stood in the hallway and heard everything he said."

He paused, smiling as their anticipation peaked. "He asked his doxy of the evening if she'd like to move up to Seattle. He told her how, come the end of next week, he'd have money enough to set her up in a better house."

He fell silent, letting them work it out. Sage was the first to voice their surmise. "Charlie, you figure that, within the coming week, he expects to act against Lane, get paid, and skedaddle up north to set himself up as her pimp."

Charlie nodded. "Yup."

Sage steepled his hands, pointer fingers under his chin, and said thoughtfully, "Well, that's both scary and good to know. It means we better go on high alert if Harry wins the nomination tomorrow. It also tells us that, if we can catch the assassin and the money men behind him in the next week, we won't have to worry the whole thirty days between the primary and general elections."

Mae cleared her throat, breaking the ensuing silence. "If Charlie doesn't have more to say, I also had success. I followed one of the two men who met with Hess. He ended up at an address in South Portland. I watched the house until the downstairs lamps went out, so I think that's where he lives. It's a decent house but not wealthy. Tomorrow we can find out who lives there. Meantime, what's that city engineer fellow look like?"

Sage described the man Emil said was the city engineer, William Elliott.

Mae nodded. "Yup, that sure sounds like the fellow I followed."

"If he's Elliott, it means the Tanner Creek scandal is behind the plot," Sage said. "That makes sense. Harry keeps promising to investigate and punish everyone involved. So, the city engineer must be scared witless of Harry becoming mayor."

"Maybe, but I think we're looking at an unholy partnership. Charlie isn't the only one who roamed a whorehouse tonight," Lucinda declared, making all eyes snap toward her.

"What do you mean?" Sage asked.

"That second man, the other one who met with Hess, is what I mean. After Hess left, the two guys in suits he met with stayed on and talked a bit. I saw one of them come in through the back door beside the blocked-off stairway. Mae and I agreed he'd be the one I'd follow."

"Why stairs blocked off?" Fong asked.

"Oh, you know, the city council just gave in to those Municipal Association folks' fussing. They passed a new ordinance saying there can't be interior stairways to a saloon's second floor. They think it will prevent saloons from offering prostitution on the floors above."

Mae smirked and said, "Hah. All that ordinance did was force a bit of remodeling. Now the barmaids and their customers pop out the backdoor and climb up the new outside stairway."

Lucinda nodded. "Exactly. Anyway, once those two started winding up their conversation, me and Mae headed out. I ran around the block to the back of the Club. Sure enough, my fellow came out the door and climbed the outside stairs. I followed him but when I got up there, he was nowhere to be seen. I stood around until Maisie, one of Grant's barmaid moneymakers, trotted out to fetch whiskey for her client. She stopped and I asked her if she knew who the man was." Like Charlie, Lucinda paused for effect.

"Go on," Sage urged, "You've got us on tenterhooks. Besides, I got up at the crack of dawn to pound nails."

She relented. "Maisie said the man wasn't a client. He's got an office there because he does the saloon's bookwork. And, she also said he's the saloon's real owner, not Grant. Best of all, she told me his name. He's Jasper Helmut."

The name triggered gasps of recognition from Mae and Sage. "Yup, the fellow in cahoots with Hess and Elliott owns and operates one of the city's biggest breweries. Kind of surprised me too," Lucinda said.

Sage clapped his hands. "Wow! That means a fella involved in municipal corruption and a fella getting rich off vice corruption are the ones hatching the assassination plot. Our original guess was correct. Now, what do we do?"

Mae slapped her hands on the table and stood. "Right now, we best hit our beds. Come tomorrow morning, we need to meet with Eich and Solomon. Saving Harry is going to be tricky. It'll take all of us."

TWENTY

April 5, 1905, Primary Election Day

"SORRY FOR ROUSTING YOU OUT of bed so early," Harry said with his mischievous smile and gray-eyed twinkle.

Sage yawned and glanced outside at the morning dawning beyond Mozart's windows. "Not a problem. I had to get up soon, anyway. How are you doing?" Sage gratefully accepted the coffee Harry handed him.

"I'm tired. I couldn't sleep most of last night. I would have checked on my hospital patients but I didn't want to wake up my guardians. Lola just fed us all breakfast, and the three of us are on our way there now."

"I'm sure having two sidekicks feels like a burden."

Harry shook his head. "No, I enjoy their company. Your Mr. Fong is something else. He's been showing me some tricky moves to protect myself." He paused and sounded exasperated as he turned back to the issue of the assassination plot. "Good grief. Don't those fools realize I am just the leading edge? Change is coming to this city, this state, and this country. People are fed up with greedy scoundrels. They're sick and tired of just getting the dregs of the tremendous wealth their labor generates."

Sage raised a cautionary finger. "I don't think the plotters are looking at that big picture. If we're correct, their concerns are short-term and self-interested. You do ruffle a lot of wealthy feathers. Yet, the lack of laws and regulations lets most of them get filthy rich using legal ploys. Most of our so-called city fathers are confident that a majority Republican city council's vetoes will hold you in check if you become mayor."

Harry nodded. "Their hand-picked council probably will. I expect I'd get vetoed more than any other mayor in history. Even that's the short view. The long view, because of Oregon's new initiative and referendum law, is that I will use the mayor's office to offer people political solutions. As Teddy Roosevelt says, an office can be used as a bully pulpit to solicit popular support for an agenda. Bottom line, I trust that my fellow citizens will eventually pass into law those of my solutions they like and to hell with the rich bastards."

Gazing at Lane, Sage felt the same affectionate admiration that he felt toward Vincent St. John and Meachum. What rare and wondrous men they were.

Sage pushed those feelings aside and eyed Harry inquiringly. Harry delivered. "Well, much as I enjoy the excellent coffee and snacks provided by Mrs. Clemens, I am afraid I came seeking another favor. You've done so much that I'm embarrassed to ask for more."

"Harry, I want to help however I can. I also love this city." Sage said.

"You know Multnomah County Sheriff Tom Word?"

Sage shook his head. "Never met him. I've heard he's a straight shooter."

"That he is. Well, he's going to try a new poll-watching approach today. He thinks it will send a message and make the subsequent general election vote less corrupt than it has been."

"How so?"

"Well, as you know, in prior elections, most of the illegal votes were cast in the North End by paid-off drunks and itinerants. The sheriff wants a Democratic poll watcher paired with a deputy sheriff at each of the North End polling places. As we heard at the rally the other night, our folks have quite a list of phony registrations. The watcher will check the list and alert the deputy. He'll stop the vote and take the false voter into custody. Sheriff Word will have paddy wagons throughout the North End."

"Wow, that sounds like quite an operation. How do I fit in? I can't be a poll watcher. That's too public a role for Mozart's owner."

"We have a surplus of poll watchers. What Word needs is something different. I told him I knew someone excellent at working undercover in the North End saloons. We know that those two crimps, Sullivan and Turco, plan to round up the false voters from the various saloons and transport them to the polls.

"The sheriff needs someone in those saloons learning when they'll be taking the false voters to the polling place nearest to each saloon. That way, he'll be able to timely divert enough deputies and wagons to that polling place. They'll take the false voters into custody if they attempt to vote. If you agree, it would mean Sheriff Word seeing you in the John Miner getup. I didn't tell him your real name. I told him, Miner."

"Where's Word going to be? People will notice if they see me with him."

Harry raised a finger. "Now, that is an interesting turn of events. Your Mr. Fong has set it up. He says it's the same place you used recently."

Of course, Sage knew where Harry meant. He'd just been there with the young policeman, Dan Carter. He let his face show incredulity. "Are you telling me that Mr. Fong got the Chinese to agree to let the county sheriff operate out of their gambling den?"

Harry chuckled and swiped a hand through his thick hair, making it stand up straight as if he'd taken fright. "Well, I suspect it took some tricky maneuvering. Mr. Fong tells me that the Chinese hold me in high regard because I doctor so many of them without question or pay and without informing immigration. I warned him to tell them that, as mayor, I intend to stomp out their gambling and opium dens. He says they know that, but are cooperating anyway."

"Alright, I'll do it. Where will you go from here?"

"Me and my two guardians are heading to the hospital and then over to the Carpenter's hall to await the results. It's going to be a long darn day," he added ruefully, though his eyes sparkled with anticipation.

After Sage sent word to Emil that he wouldn't be showing up, he hit the streets an hour before the polls opened. He went first to the Portland Club. There he found a harried Grant rushing about, trying to cook breakfast for the many drunks who were just beginning to stir. Sage had to smile. Mae and Lucinda wouldn't be returning. They couldn't have picked a better morning than this to leave Grant in the lurch.

Grant noticed Sage in his John Miner duds and assumed he was one of the drunks who'd spent the night sleeping on the saloon's tables, chairs, and floor. "You look alert. Take these plates to those fellows at that far table. They've been raising a ruckus."

"Alright, but how long do we got to wait before we get paid?"

"You know how it works. Sullivan's wagon will swing by here as soon as the nearby poll opens. We're first on his list, thank God. All this free food and beer is costing me a fortune. Anyway, he'll be right outside the polling place to pay you when you come out. Don't think you can pretend to vote. He has people watching inside."

Sage gave a mental snicker. Sullivan's inside man wasn't the only one who'd be watching. Shrugging, he picked up the plates, deposited them on the table, and exited the side door as if heading for the alley privy. He needed to learn where that scoundrel Turco intended to start gathering up fraudulent voters.

Sage spent the day going from saloon to saloon, learning Sullivan and Turco's pick-up times. Once he got some of those, he met with Sheriff Word who was, indeed, running his operation out of the Chinese gambling den. Though, the Chinese were clever. They kept Word squeezed into the small entry room just inside the alley door. He'd never see their inner sanctum with its wren of hidden doorways and secret exits.

Sage paused in his saloon forays to meet Herman Eich in a nearby café. After he'd left Mozart's that morning, his mother had talked to the ragpicker and asked him to do two things. The first was to learn whether the man Mae followed from the Portland Club meeting was the city engineer, William Elliott. After answering that question, she asked the ragpicker to haul his cart across the river to the Buckman neighborhood and survey the situation outside Oscar Muckleroy's house. They wondered who the two strange men were that sent Muckleroy diving out his bedroom window. Was Riner's foreman afraid for his life? If so, maybe that created an opportunity to enlist his cooperation.

Sage was watching out the café's front window when he saw the ragpicker park his cart. Eich limped as he headed toward the table.

Sage stood. "What happened? Why are you limping?" he asked.

Eich waved aside the questions and said, "I'm fine. Don't tell Mae. She'll make a fuss."

"You greatly underestimate her powers of observation if you think she won't notice that limp. What happened?"

"Well first off, I tried to find out if Mae had followed the city engineer. He does live in the South Portland neighborhood. It's a lively mix of Italians, Jews, and other immigrants. That means a plentitude of bakeries and delicatessens to the dismay of my waistline." Eich patted that region, adding, "Still, I needed a reason to park myself for a chat."

"Good to know someone got to eat decent grub today. It sure wasn't me. But, did you learn anything?"

"Yup. The bloke Mae followed was indeed the city engineer, William Elliott. His neighbors aren't too fond of him. They consider him and his wife 'uppity.' She's let everyone know they're eager to leave their foreign neighbors behind. She's been bragging that they'll be moving up the hill to be among what she calls, 'more of their own kind.'"

"I imagine that's because Elliott expects he'll get a big payoff from the Tanner Creek scam. Wonder how his missus will handle that disappointment."

Eich just shook his head. "From what I gathered, she won't take it quietly. Anyway, once I learned all I could about Elliott, I headed across the river. Good thing I did."

"What do you mean?"

"Well, I never laid eyes on any fellow who looked like the Muckleroy you described. Still, I think I know where he's holed up. And, it's a good thing he wasn't at home."

"What do you mean?" Sage asked again.

"Two tough-looking fellows were sitting in a buggy down the road. Got snappish when I offered them some of my fine wares." Eich chuckled at the memory."

"What do you mean? Why do you think you know where Muckleroy is? Did you see him?"

'Nope. But his wife left their house and went to a house a few doors down. That house looked like the one you described as belonging to that Emil fellow. The first time, she carried a casserole dish. The second time, it was a laundry basket."

"Ah, you think Muckleroy is hiding out at my friend Emil's house? If you figured that out, those two men could also."

Eich nodded. "Yes, exactly. No 'could' about it. They did."

"Why do you say that?"

"Because when she was carrying the laundry basket, they came up behind her. One of them was trying to grab hold of her when he tangled with my cart."

"So, that's how you got the limp?"

"They didn't take kindly to being thwarted. They knocked me into the street and dumped the cart over. Some of my mended porcelains are beyond recovery—more's the pity."

"What did Betty Muckleroy do?"

"She screamed, hit him with the basket, skedaddled into Emil's house, and stayed there."

"Hmm. I bet Emil stayed home today. We better move the Muckleroys. They're in danger. So are Emil and his wife."

"That's my thought. So I've arranged for his escape."

"Tell me."

Sage spent the rest of the afternoon on pins and needles, as his mother would say. Eich's plan seemed flawless. Still, its execution would be tricky. Before Eich met Sage, he and Mae had gone to the Carpenter's hall where Harry awaited the election results. Because he was surrounded by scores of supporters, they figured he was safe from an attack.

Freed from their guard duty, Fong and Sprig picked up Mae and drove the cab across the river to Buckman. Eich had already determined that there was an escape route from Emil's backyard to the next street. Once Muckleroy and his wife reached the cab, Sprig would spirit them away over the Tabor hill. They'd hide out in a Montavilla boarding house run by Fong's Japanese friend.

The hardest part would be convincing the Muckleroys and Emil to go along with the plan. That's where Mae Clemens came into play. She would knock on the door, persuade Emil to let her in, and then gain everyone's cooperation. She'd use John Miner's name, claiming he'd overheard that Muckleroy was in danger and had sent the three of them, Eich, Mae, and Fong, to take the foreman and his wife to safety.

The Muckleroys were to slip into Emil's backyard. From there, Fong would lead them to Sprig's cab.

Meanwhile, soon as Emil opened the front door, Eich would push his covered cart to the door where he and Emil would create a diversion by making a show of loading Mae into it. She'd be dressed as a man. They figured the watchers would attack Eich and the cart once it traveled down the street a bit. As soon as the Muckleroys were safely away, Fong would run to defend Eich and Mae.

It sounded like a workable plan. Still, experience said the unexpected could happen. So, Sage pursued his undercover saloon work in an anxious state, his imagination fixed on events taking place across the river and every possible thing that could go wrong.

Seven o'clock came with Sage waiting beside Sheriff Word for the polls to close at eight. The deputies and paddy wagons had been highly successful at thwarting voting fraud. By late afternoon, Sullivan and Turco evidently gave up. No more wagonloads of phony voters showed up at the North End's polling places and the saloons were mostly empty since the phony voters were no longer drinking free booze.

Sheriff Word declared himself "tickled" by the result. Certainly the vote tallies were markedly lower in the North End compared to prior elections. Word told Sage to stand down saying his help had been "invaluable."

Sage remained with Word because that was where Fong was to report on the outcome of the Muckleroy mission. When a knock finally sounded at the door, Sage beat Word to the eyehole. Peering out, he saw Fong, his face somber. Dread washed through Sage as his fumbling fingers unbolted the door.

TWENTY ONE

April 5, 1905, Primary Election Day

THE 'WE'RE CLOSED" PLACARD REMAINED on Mozart's door, so Mae, Fong, Sprig, and Eich were already at the election night gathering when Sage turned up after the polls closed. The mission had been a complete success. The Muckleroys were safe and Fong had trounced the bad guys before they hurt Eich, Mae, or the cart.

Tonight, the Carpenter's hall was packed with Lane's supporters, all anxiously awaiting the ballot count results. Harry was a grinning whirlwind, shaking hands and clapping backs. Sage wasn't sure whether Harry's good humor was because he was confident of winning, because he'd be happy with either outcome or, because he just loved being surrounded by ardent supporters.

Various Democrats were observing the sealing and transportation of the precinct ballot boxes for the counting at the city clerk's office. Periodically, a runner would appear on the threshold, shout the current tally amount, and race back down the stairs. So far, the numbers looked good for Harry.

Eich, Fong, and Mae had snagged a table early on and stayed put because their activities had tuckered them out. "This is the most nerve-racking night I have spent in some time," Mae commented. "It's a good thing I trim my fingernails short because tonight is turning into a real nail-biter."

Eich reached over to pat her hand. "It'll soon be over my lady and we'll be celebrating."

Fong sat with a faint smile on his lips, his eyes missing nothing in the scene around them. Sage turned to him. "Mr. Fong, what do you think of this exercise in democracy?"

The Chinese man's lips twisted. "It messy but better than emperor."

Sage understood. Buddhist monks raised Fong after he was orphaned during the final days of the failed Taiping rebellion against the Manchu emperor. "'Messy' is the word, alright," Sage agreed.

He gazed around the room but saw no one with a blaze in his hair and the calculating eyes of a killer. All he saw was the hopeful faces of Harry's supporters. Returning his attention to his friends, he said. "Sure wish we would have found that guy before tonight."

Eich cleared his throat and leaned forward so his voice wouldn't carry. "Harry is going to win the nomination. Once he does, it will turn doubly dangerous, beginning tonight."

As if punctuating Eich's prediction, a flurry of activity erupted on the stairs outside as people rushed into the hall, whooping and hollering, "The count's over! Harry won!"

Everyone crowded around the messengers who said Doctor Harry Lane won over his Democratic opponent—683 to 289.

As the cheers died down, Harry climbed atop a table and patted the air for quiet. When the shuffle of feet was the only sound, he grinned and said, "I am appreciative beyond words for all your support. Despite the Republicans and their *Gazette* rag sheet's nonstop efforts, the people have voted for change." Loud cheers greeted that pronouncement.

Once the exuberance calmed, Harry continued, his face sober. "As you know, this was the easy part. From this night forward, we face an uphill fight. Numbers don't lie. Less than a thousand Democrats voted this day, while over 5000 Republicans cast their ballot.

"Now I know those numbers sound discouraging," he gazed across a crowd that nodded in agreement. "But, we can win this. Attendance at our town hall meetings has exceeded capacity every time. Many, many of those faces were Republicans. They are trying to decide whether to vote out a corrupt town or stay with the machine. We give them hope, and they will vote against corruption and cronyism because most of them are damn fine people."

Harry paused, got down from the table, and gestured for his wife, Lola, to join him. When she did, her face bright as all the others, he reached for her hand. "With the help of the most wonderful wife in the world, I promise I will work my tail off to give them, and you, that hope. I ask. No, I implore you to do the same. Not for me, but for you, for your family, and the future of our city." He raised his clenched fists high overhead in a boxer's victory gesture and roared, "We can, and we will, win this election!"

The crowd went crazy, stomping, cheering, shouting, and clapping. Sage gazed around, again searching for that one reaction that didn't fit. He didn't see it. Delight shone on every face.

It was nearly an hour before only Harry, Lola, Leo, Sage, and Mae remained. Eich and Fong slipped away; Fong to join Sprig Flowers on the cab that would carry the Lanes home and Eich to wheel his cart from the adjoining alley.

Sage, Mae, Lola, and Harry headed downstairs, leaving Leo to close up. Sage glanced at Harry and thought he saw satisfaction on the doctor's exhausted face.

Harry stepped through the outside doors first with Sage on his heels—the two women following. Directly opposite, Fong waited, holding the cab door open. Sage was amused at seeing Sprig had upgraded his hackney cab to a glass-enclosed hansom. He could charge a lot more for that weatherproof ride. It was gratifying to know that Sprig had put his hefty Lane campaign earnings to good use.

Sage breathed deep, the spring air light, sweet, and smokeless for a change. Behind him came the soft murmurs of his mother and Lola and the building door swinging shut. The sound of the cart's squeak and rattle issued from the alley as Eich maneuvered it toward the street. Normality shattered just as the front wheel of Eich's cart protruded from the alley opening at the same time a short man charged from behind the cab.

Fong must have sensed the sudden movement because he levitated to land in a wide bow stance facing the stranger.

For the first time, Fong wasn't fast enough. Just as his rear leg rose to land a roundhouse kick, a loud bang and spark spit from the attacker's midsection. Fong hit the ground.

Behind Sage, cries rang out. A glance showed Mae moving forward toward Fong, her hand outstretched. Sage grabbed her arm shouting, "Get the Lanes back inside!"

Harry froze, making an easy target for the next bullet. Gaslight glinted on the weapon in the stranger's hand as he turned it toward Harry. Sage leapt forward just as Eich yelled to distract the assassin. A second later, the cart's front wheel slammed into the man's legs. The gun banged again and, this time, Eich went down.

Beside Sage, Mae yanked Harry's arm and propelled him through the door Lola held open. Sage followed, using his body as a shield, giving the attacker no clear shot at Harry or the women. Harry's voice raised in angry protest. "Let me go! I've got to get to Mr. Fong. He's been shot."

"Harry Lane, you get your fanny this building! You can't help anyone if you get killed," Mae said with a firmness that tolerated no opposition. Harry must have given in because no more protests sounded before the door slammed shut.

Sage heard the exchange but kept his eyes locked on the killer. The gun began to rise and Sage tensed, readying to spring aside. The shot never came because a metal box shot through the air to crack against the attacker's head, sending him stumbling backward. The box crashed to the pavement, sprung open, and spilled wrapped sandwiches and an apple. Momentarily, Sage was mesmerized by the sight of that red apple slowly rolling toward the gutter.

Glancing up, he saw Sprig raise his arm, bend his elbow, and snap that arm forward, making a whip crack in the night air. It sent the gun flying from the shooter's hand and clattering across the sidewalk to disappear beneath Eich's cart.

That was enough to send the man fleeing. He turned and took off running. Sage started following only to pause. His two friends were shot. That was more important. He whirled toward Fong, who groaned as he tried to sit up, his front teeth clamped down on his lower lip.

Behind him, the door crashed open. Harry rushed out to shove Sage aside and kneel next to Fong. With a flurry of steps, Mae ran behind Sage toward Eich. Leaving Fong in the doctor's hands, Sage followed. Reaching the cart, he saw Eich sitting on the sidewalk between the cart shafts. Mae was beside him, her arms clasped around his torso.

"He's gone?" the ragpicker asked Sage. Then, softly he said, "Mae, dear, please don't fret, I'm perfectly fine."

Sage's mother wasn't the only one who needed reassurance. "Herman, are sure you're okay? Did that bullet hit you?"

Mae helped Herman to his feet. Once erect, the ragpicker dusted off his clothes, squeezed Mae, kissed her forehead, and gave Sage a steady look. "Not hurt even a little bit. Well, except maybe my elbow. It hit the ground hard. When I pushed the cart into him, I dropped just as he shot. The cretin's bullet passed overhead. I'm fine. But, how's Mr. Fong?"

All three looked toward the hansom. Fong was upright and on his feet. Sprig and Harry each gripped an elbow to help him into the hansom. Harry turned and said, "Mr. Adair, I leave my lady wife in your safe hands. Mr. Fong will be fine—it's just a crease. We're heading for my office. You can meet us there." He entered the cab and slammed its door shut as Sprig hawed his horse into a trot.

The four on the sidewalk watched mutely until the cab rounded the corner and disappeared.

"My goodness," Lola Lane declared in the quiet of the empty street, "That was a bit more excitement than I'm used to, even though I do live with Harry." She turned to look at the three of them and saw their faces. She smiled and said, "Don't you worry now. If Harry says he'll be fine, then he'll be fine." She turned to Mae. "How about you and I walk the few blocks to your restaurant and brew some tea? We can all meet up there. We have a lot to talk about. "

Eich cleared his throat. "If you ladies don't mind, I'll escort you back to Mozart's. My throat's parched and tea sounds wonderful."

Sage sent him a grateful look. Though Eich was a bit grizzled, he was strong as an ox and a quick thinker. Mae and Lola would be safe with him and his assassin-attacking cart.

They parted with Sage heading west toward Lane's office. There he found Sprig standing guard behind a locked, frosted glass door that didn't open until Sprig heard Sage's voice. Once inside, the cabbie snicked the lock shut and led the way to the examination room.

Sage noted the waiting room, hallway, and exam room were all wired with electricity. The light was harsh but Sage had to admit the light shone brighter than gas lamps.

Harry was wrapping a bandage around Fong's bare thigh. Sage seldom saw his friend's legs but had often experienced the painful thrust of those strong sinews, bones, and muscles.

Harry glanced up, saw Sage in the doorway, and said, "The women alright?"

"Eich's escorting them to the restaurant. They expect us to join them once we're through here."

He looked at Fong. His friend's smile was sheepish as he said, "I not fast enough."

Sage laughed. One of Fong's oft-repeated instructions on how to respond to an attacker with a gun was to run fast. "Well, it was dark.

I didn't see the gun until the last instant. You were already in the air when he pulled it out."

"Lucky for Mr. Fong that he was airborne," Harry said as he tied off the gauze and began packing away scissors and bandaging. "Because his leg was flying, it caught the bullet instead of his chest. And it didn't catch the bullet so much as deflect it. Your friend has a furrow down the side of his leg. I trimmed its edges and flushed it with sterile water. The groove is shallow and will heal quickly."

He patted Fong on the shoulder. "I'll give you a bit of laudanum Mr. Fong because that will be mighty painful for a few days."

Fong grimaced, shook his head, and said, "No thank you, Doc Lane. Opium and my people have bad history."

Sage turned to Sprig. "You saved the day with your lunch box and whip."

Sprig looked embarrassed and said. "Well, I admit I can throw a mean lunchbox. When I have the time, I sometimes pitch in baseball games at Union Park across the river. But my whip hitting the gun was dumb luck. First time I ever hit something that wasn't a tin can in the backyard. Fact is, I call it my 'show whip' because I'd toss it away before I'd ever use it on old Archie."

TWENTY TWO

April 6, 1905

DAWN STILL GLOWED FROM BEHIND the mountain when Sage knocked on Emil's door. The night before, once everyone was back at Mozart's, they'd discussed their next moves. After he vouched for Emil's discretion, they'd agreed Sage could tell Emil all that was going on. The best time to do that was before the Saturday work shift started.

Emil opened the door to cautiously to peer out. Seeing Sage, he swung the door wider. "Good Lord, what are you doing hoofing about this early in the morning? Come in, come in. The wife just put the coffee on and she can fry us up some breakfast."

Sage's stomach growled. He'd left Mozart's without eating. Once in the warm kitchen, Emil gestured for him to sit at the scarred maple table. Emil said, "This beautiful lady is my wife, Esther." The portly woman with the sweet face tsk-tsked at Emil and wiped wet hands on her apron. She reached to shake Sage's hand with one that was rough from hard work but firm in its grip.

Once they sat, Emil said, "Well, John Miner, I suspect you're here to say you're resigning. Hate to see you go. You've been a good helper." He looked genuinely unhappy at the loss.

"Well, maybe not today. Whether I need to come back depends on other things. I'm here to tell you something."

He glanced at Esther. She started to rise, clearly intending to give them privacy. Sage raised a hand. "No, no. Please don't go. From all Emil has said about you, I know you're trustworthy. Besides, he'd tell you anyway since you already know something is up after the whole Muckleroy ruckus."

Emil and Esther traded looks. After putting full coffee cups and a plate of biscuits on the table, she sat beside her husband. They stayed silent, waiting for him to continue.

Sage began by telling them what he knew about the Tanner Creek sewer corruption.

Emil sighed heavily and said, "Yup, that's pretty much what I figured after you showed me that news article and Oscar said he needed to hide out here. It ain't right what the Riners did. It's a gol darn shame Oscar got involved. He says he regrets it. I believe him. He's scared of the Riners and he's scared of going to jail."

"Well, we all make mistakes at one time or another in our lives," Sage said. "The Muckleroys are lucky they have you two as friends. Unfortunately, the problem is much worse than the sewer job scam." He went on to tell them about the assassination plot against Harry Lane.

Emil and Esther reacted with horrified exclamations. Emil swallowed hard and said, "My, Lord! I have nothing but good things to say about Doc Lane. Why, he's been in this house more than once. I voted for him yesterday and will do so in the general election. This town needs him!"

Esther spoke for the first time. "If the ignorant men allowed us women to vote, I surely would vote for Doctor Lane. Most women would."

Emil patted his wife's hand. "Now, Esther, this ain't the time to bring up women's suffrage." He turned to Sage and added, "Though I agree with Esther. Things would go a damn sight better if women like her got the vote."

Sage raised a hand. "No need to convince me, Emil. I also believe in women getting the vote. I think we'd be a better country. Why, women have led practically every improvement in this city—the last being their agitation for pure food regulation." He chuckled and added, "Besides, if I didn't, my mother and my lady friend would whack me with their frying pans."

That triggered laughter. Sage figured it was time to make his request. "Emil, I came here with two questions. First, I recall you saying you worked on the Tanner project." Emil nodded slowly and waited for Sage to continue.

"What exactly did you do on that project?" Sage queried.

"Mostly, I stayed up top nailing up timber braces to keep the tunnel from collapsing on folks. Every while, I had to go into the tunnel but I tried not to. I got a bit of that claustrophobia," he said, looking embarrassed. This time it was Esther who patted her husband's hand.

"I understand since I'm troubled by that condition myself," Sage confided. "But, I was wondering—while you were on that project, did you ever see the city engineer or the city inspector checking out the work?"

Emil snorted in response. "Oh, well, I saw the city engineer once or twice but he always stayed atop. The inspector too. That inspector seemed to be the engineer's buddy or relative. He'd turn up more regular and hang out in the work shed for a short bit. Then, off he'd trot. Some of the fellas said they usually saw him holding down a chair in a nearby saloon."

"He didn't go down into the sewer?"

"Yah know, not while I was there. I did overhear the city engineer tell him not to bother inspecting because the Riners always did a fine job. The inspector just nodded along. I sure never saw him go down the ladder. Of course, once I got them braces built, Riner moved me to another job. Oscar Muckleroy is the feller who knows for sure. But, we don't know where he is." As Emil said that, he sent a questioning look at Sage.

"I guess they told you I was behind the rescue of Muckleroy and his wife."

"Wahl, that's what that woman who came to the door and then crawled into the cart, told us. Now that we know what's been a'goin on, it makes sense."

"I can assure you that the Muckleroys are in a safe place. You needn't worry about them. But, that brings me to my next question: Would you be willing to talk to the district attorney about what you saw? I need to warn you—if the Riners get indicted, you'll probably be out of a job."

As Emil opened his mouth to reply, Esther surged to her feet and said briskly, "Come, my husband. You and I best have a talk." Turning to Sage she said, "We'll be right back. In the meantime, help yourself to more coffee and some of the biscuits and jam."

With that, the two of them exited the kitchen, shutting the door behind them. Sage wasn't optimistic. He knew he was asking a lot. The wall clock ticked, the wood cook stove snapped, and Sage waited impatiently, drumming his fingers on the table.

Finally, the husband and wife entered and sat once again. Emil looked relaxed and Esther determined. She spoke first, "My Emil is a good man. I've known him since we sat side by side in a one-room school house down Brownsville way. He's a darn fine carpenter," she paused as Sage nodded in agreement. "So, given that the Exposition is going on, we agree that he won't have any trouble getting hired somewhere else."

She paused, to send a look at Emil. "And I sure don't want him mixed up with the Riners anymore. But most of all, like I said, I know my Emil, maybe even better than he knows himself. I'm certain sure that he would not rest easy keeping mum about what happened on that sewer job."

Emil cleared his throat. "Esther's right. I'll talk to the district attorney fellow. Just tell me where and when."

Sage left the couple grateful for their decency and courage. He hoped that Oscar Muckleroy was made of the same sturdy stuff. However, that was questionable given that he'd taken bribes.

The electric streetcar to the Montavilla settlement slowly climbed atop Mt. Tabor's shoulder before swiftly dropping down the far side, brakes squealing. He tried not to think of the times runaway streetcars had jumped the tracks. When they reached the flat fields covered by Japanese truck gardens, a relieved Sage pulled the bell cord and got off.

A short walk later, he mounted wooden steps to knock on a boarding house door. The young Japanese woman answered his knock with an expression of cautious inquiry.

Sage was prepared. He handed her a piece of paper with his John Miner name and said, "Please give this message to Mr. Muckleroy."

She glanced at the name and surprised him by responding in perfect English. "Mr. Muckleroy and his wife are in the front parlor. I will inform him that you are here and learn whether he will see you."

She closed the door firmly, leaving a nonplussed Sage on the stoop. He should have known. The Japanese had been in Portland for decades. Of course, their children would speak fluent English. He waited on the porch feeling embarrassed. Just as he was about to knock again, the door swung open, and Muckleroy stood there.

"Mr. Miner, the cabbie told us to exspect you when he brought us here," the foreman said as he gestured Sage into the house. "Uh, please, come in."

Sage slipped past him into the entryway and then followed the man into the side parlor. Everything was neat as a pin, as his mother would say. Muckleroy gestured toward a woman sitting on a settee next to a warming fireplace, "This is my wife, Betty." He sat beside her.

Betty Muckleroy looked as drawn and exhausted as her husband. Sage couldn't believe the transformation in the man's face and posture. He wondered whether the couple had gotten any sleep since being spirited away from Emil and Esther's house.

Once Sage was seated, Muckleroy spoke, "I don't know how to thank you. The bastards attacked Betty. Had they gotten hold of her or me, bad things ccould have happened. Please convey our thanks to that ragpicker fellow and that woman who pretended to be me in the cart." His eyes filled with tears as he took his wife's hand.

Sage nodded. "I can't say what they intended to do had they grabbed either of you. But, I must tell you why my friends and I helped you." From there, he launched into the same story he told Emil, though the ending was different.

"Oscar, I not going to beat around the bush or try to entrap you. I am not with the police. My primary interest is to make sure no one murders Harry Lane.

"That said, I know you took money to look the other way on the Tanner sewer job. You went down into that sewer. As foreman, you had access to the specifications. You saw the substandard materials being used. You oversaw the shoddy workmanship."

A little cry escaped from Betty and she began quietly weeping. Muckleroy broke eye contact with Sage to cover his face with both hands as his shoulders shook. Sage waited, gazing out the window to give them privacy.

Once Muckleroy swiped his face with a handkerchief and raised his face, he said, "I'm going to prison. I admit took bribes. I admit I helped them cheat the city. They told me I had to testify that the workers and I were bribed to do a poor job. That just isn't true! I can't add perjury to the crimes I've already committed."

Sage was glad the man didn't deny his wrongdoing. That would have made the coming task harder. Gently he said, "Well, things do look serious for you. I can't tell you different. But, maybe, there is hope."

The man's face brightened as he parroted, "Hope? There's hope?"

"Oscar, have you ever heard of that lawyer, Erskine Wood?"

"Why sure. He's the town's most famous lawyer. I've never seen him but I've read about him in the newspaper."

"Well, I know him. He's a friend. And I think he'd be willing to help you."

"You think Wood can keep me out of prison?" Muckleroy looked dubious.

"I think Lawyer Wood can do something even better. I'm hoping he will keep you from being arrested in the first place."

Sage was aware that Betty Muckleroy had stopped crying and had slid forward to the settee's edge. A glance told him that her face had also turned hopeful.

"I don't want to mislead you. I'm not making any promises. Still, I believe that Attorney Wood will take the case and try to fix things for you but only on one condition."

The light in Muckleroy's face dimmed, "What? What's the condition?"

Sage made sure he looked at both husband and wife. After all, both their futures were on the line, not just Oscar's. "You'd have to agree to tell the district attorney everything and testify before the grand jury that has convened over the Tanner sewer affair. In exchange, I believe Wood can get the district attorney's agreement not to indict you. And, I think Harry Lane would second that idea. He's friends with the district attorney."

"Haa…Harry Lane would do that?"

"I'm pretty sure he would. He's a compassionate, understanding man. He hates corruption and he wants to see that the Riners, and whoever is behind that sewer project scheme, get what's coming to them. But, I think if you help bring down the real miscreants, the idea men and planners behind it all, he'll stick up for you."

Muckleroy drew a shaky breath and said, "I'll do it. I'll do whatever I need to do to stay out of prison."

Two hours later, Sage met with Erskine Wood. Once Sage said he'd be footing the bill, the lawyer readily agreed to try keeping Muckleroy's feet out of the fire. "I like the idea of getting Harry to intercede with District Attorney Manning. He's a Democrat who thinks the world of Harry. He can't wait for Harry to get elected so they can team up and start cleaning house."

Wood slapped a hand onto his highly polished desk. "So, let's get to it! I'm fairly certain I'll get leniency for Muckleroy provided he helps the district attorney indict the real scoundrels. My clients objecting to the Tanner sewer charges will support leniency for Muckleroy as well. I'm sure I don't have to tell you how much political clout they wield in this city."

Tasks completed, Sage went home to nap, satisfied with his morning's work.

TWENTY THREE

May 7 and 8, 1905

"It's WELL AND GOOD YOU found two witnesses against the city engineer. You've poked a stick between his wheel spokes. Knowing that Hess fellow is the hired assassin, that's a plus too. But us getting a'hold of Hess won't save Harry. The engineer and that brewery fellow could just hire another Hess. We got to figure out how to stop the two of them." It was a longish speech for Mae Clemens.

The group was much smaller than usual. Fong refused to leave Harry's side, Solomon had his work at the hotel, Lucinda was dealing with a parlor house emergency, and Charlie was at the Portland Club shooting gallery, keeping an eye peeled for Hess. That meant just Eich, Mae, and Sage were meeting to figure out their next step.

Sage huffed a frustrated sigh and said, "Well, the only thing that makes sense is for me to head out and find Hess and make him talk. First to us and then to Hanke. So far, we haven't had much luck finding him."

"Sage, he's a killer, I don't think you should try to get him all by yourself," Mae protested.

"I can be there to help," Eich interjected.

Mae reached over to pat her sweetheart's hand. "We know, dear. But Hess is a younger man and wrestling him down is a young man's game or, Mr. Fong's."

"That may be, Mae. But, Fong refuses to leave Harry and so does Sprig. I don't know Sprig's son well enough to know if he'd be a help. Besides, I agree with you that Sage needs help."

Mae turned to Sage. "How about asking Sergeant Hanke?"

He shook his head. "We don't have enough evidence for Hanke to arrest him. Besides, I might have to threaten a bit of physical persuasion. You know Hanke never wants to be part of that."

A knock sounded at the restaurant's front door. Mae jumped up to answer it and returned, followed by the answer to their dilemma. "Charlie!" Sage exclaimed, "You're a sight for sore eyes!"

Charlie's grin was lopsided as if he was unsure whether Sage's enthusiastic greeting boded well for his future.

Sage gestured for him to sit while Mae poured him a cup of coffee. "What are you doing here? I thought you planned to stay at the shooting gallery until late."

"Well, Sage, there was a raid by the special police. They closed us down."

"I would have thought Grant was all paid up with his protection fees."

Siringo chuckled. "Oh, he is. I got to listen to the conversation between the officers and Grant. Turns out Williams is running scared and sent word that the shooting galleries and other gambling businesses in the North End need to take a little vacation—apparently, just long enough to generate news reports saying the mayor is cracking down. Once that idea sticks in the public's mind, Grant will be back in business. In the meantime, I'm yours to do whatever needs doing."

"How did Grant react to that news?"

"He just shrugged. The regulars were playing cards with chips and all the doxy gals were downstairs serving drinks. Grant had already told me there'd be no shooting gallery gambling that night. I was nursing a beer, hoping to see that Hess fella, when the special police barged through the door, a'shouting and waving clubs. Grant didn't bat an eye. Someone already warned him about the raid because it went smooth as one of them pointy-toed ballet dances.

"The only fellows caught in the hullabaloo were two strangers playing cards with money on the table. Guess they were Grant's sacrificial lambs. He must have promised to bail them out because they didn't act too bothered about being arrested."

Charlie grinned and said, "So, whatever you 'all are cooking up, I'm in. Grant doesn't want me coming back to the Portland Club for at least three days."

Early Monday morning, Sage and Charlie climbed the carpenter hall stairs. As expected, Leo was already hard at work overseeing the dispatch of men to various projects. He waved and came forward to shake their hands. "Sure am glad you folks stopped that assassin Friday night. I'm sorry Mr. Fong got hurt. How is he doing?" he asked Sage.

"He says it's a mere scratch. I think his pride hurts worse than his leg."

Leo chuckled. "I've never seen him in action but you've told me enough that I can understand how he feels. By the way, I saw Emil at church yesterday. He's upset about losing you as his helper. Says he's never had a better one."

Sage flushed at the compliment. "He's an easy fellow to work with. I hope the regular guy appreciates him. But, enough of that. Is there any chance of me and Charlie getting into the Exposition today posing as two of your carpenters? We think the assassin is hiding out there."

"Shoot, anybody can get in with a 50-cent ticket. It's opening day."

Leo had a point, but Sage had a response. "We figure that as visitors, we might be restricted from looking behind the scenes, so to speak. As carpenters, carrying toolboxes, we'll be able to go anywhere. I understand the guards issue badges allowing access to everywhere on the grounds."

Leo's forehead wrinkled as he thought that over. "Hmm, okay that makes sense. We do have a few men on-site finishing up some last-minute details. I can give you a couple passes. You'll need to go in a side gate. Do you have toolboxes?"

Sage shook his head. "That's the other thing we need from you, if possible."

"Well, you're in luck for two reasons. Some of our itinerant members stash their boxes here for safekeeping. I can let you use them but you've got to bring them back."

"We'll do that or replace whatever we lose. What's the second thing?"

"I think there'll be fewer questions asked if I send the job foreman to the gate with you. He'll ease your way inside."

Leo called to a man sitting at a nearby table who was engaged in a lively discussion with some of the waiting men. "Hey, Finn, can I talk to you for a minute?"

The man got up and approached. Once he was close, Leo said, "Finn, I need to ask a favor. You know the exposition guards fairly well, right?"

"Yah, to be sure I do," the man said with a Scandinavian accent. "I've made friends with most of them."

"Okay, well, this will sound strange. I need you to escort Mr. Miner here, and his friend, Charlie, through the work gate and onto the grounds. They'll be pretending to be carpenters."

The other man hesitated and stared at Sage. "I guess I can do that. The guards might think it funny."

"They'll be posing as carpenters carrying toolboxes."

Finn looked less hesitant. "That should work fine, then." He waited, clearly hoping for an explanation.

Sage understood. The man was putting his credibility on the line should he and Charlie run into trouble. "Sir, we're going to look for the man who tried to shoot Dr. Lane Friday night when he left this hall."

Finn's startled look was genuine. "Tried to shoot?" he repeated. "I never read anything about that."

Sage nodded. "Yes, I know. We didn't tell anyone it happened. We didn't want a public outcry to scare the assassin into hiding. We need to catch him. We have reason to believe he's hiding out on the fairgrounds."

Finn's lips tightened and he looked determined as he said, "We best get a move on. The crew's already left and the streetcars will be full today. Folks are already lined up."

Sage grinned. "Boy, do I know that! We saw at least a dozen streetcars on Morrison between Third and Fourth. There were so many people trying to board that we barely got through on the sidewalk. So, I arranged for a coach. It's waiting at the curb outside."

As it turned out, the gate guards were overwhelmed by the crush of youngsters trying to sneak in through the work gate. It was Finn being recognized that enabled their entrance. The guards didn't even perform a cursory examination before tossing them two badges. Once inside, their escort left them, saying he had to check with the crew in one of the exhibit halls. He departed after shaking their hands and telling them to "stay out of trouble."

Seconds later, Finn was swallowed by the crowds, leaving them on their own. Sage and Charlie paused at one side of the entrance plaza to watch visitors pour into the fairgrounds between majestic pillars supporting graceful arches. Many entrants' steps stalled as they moved from beneath the arches, dumbstruck by the magnificence before them. Even Sage and Charlie momentarily halted at seeing the white exhibit halls looming above a newly created lake. The glistening white of the fair-ground buildings mirrored the perfect white of the distant Mt. St. Helens.

Their survey done, Sage got down to business. "I guess we'll be sticking together," he commented wryly.

Charlie chuckled. "Since that's what we promised Mae, we better. I hate to think how she'd react if we split up and one of us got hurt."

"You're right. And, she has a point. The fellow we're hunting likes to shoot guns. Did you bring a gun? I didn't."

Charlie nodded. "Growing up in rattlesnake country, you get so you never leave it behind. It's tucked into my boot. I'm ready to use it should a reptile give me no choice. I'd feel right naked without it."

"Well, that's reassuring. What do you say we go find the American Inn? That's where Hess has been staying. Maybe we'll get lucky."

It was a fairly long walk to the Inn. Once they reached it, Sage handed Charlie his toolbox and entered the lobby. It was full of people checking in and walking about. Approaching the desk he asked the harried clerk, "I have a message for Mr. Hess. Can you tell me his room?"

The clerk looked up from the guestbook entry and said, "I'm sorry, Sir. We are not allowed to divulge room numbers."

Sage didn't argue because it was a good policy. "Well, okay. I understand. Thank you anyway." His mild response did the trick because just as Sage turned to leave the clerk said, "Another reason I can't tell you the room number is because Mr. Hess checked out yesterday."

Sage paused. "I don't suppose he said where he was going?"

"No, Sir, he did not," the clerk said before turning his attention to the next guest.

When Sage exited, Charlie was nowhere in sight. He strolled to the far end of the covered veranda looking for his cowboy. There, a lone painter was slapping paint on the last column in the line. Charlie was talking to him, the man throwing comments over his shoulder while he painted without pause. Spotting Sage, Charlie said, "This here is Mr. Evans. He's seen our man Hess. Didn't like him much, ain't that right Evans?"

"Why is that?" Sage wondered aloud, not seeing why Hess would have interacted with the building painters.

The man lowered his brush and glanced up at Sage. "Wahl, there's been this little cat around. Some of us have been sharing our lunch with it. That Hess turned up here at the hotel in a snit and damned if he didn't kick that little cat right into the lake!" Outrage filled the man's voice and face.

"Oh, Lord. Did the cat drown?"

"Hell, no. Jimmy jumped right in after the poor thing and saved it. I wanted to slug Hess, but the fellows held me back." The man smiled slyly. "We still fixed his wagon, though."

"How's that?"

"We formed us a delegation and went to Mrs. McCready. We told her we were walking off the job if she didn't evict him."

"Did she?"

That triggered a big grin. "Sure enough, she did. It weren't but ten minutes later that he come storming out of the hotel, suitcase in hand. She likes that little cat too."

Charlie and Sage exchanged disappointed looks. Still, Sage had to try. "I don't suppose you have any idea where Hess might have headed?"

"Nah, your guess is as good as mine." He paused, giving them a squinty look. "You ain't friends of his, are you?"

Sage's laugh was genuine. "Far from it! He shot a good friend of ours and tried to shoot two others. We aim to make life uncomfortable for him."

"Wahl, in that case, if a fellow was looking for Hess, he might want to hang out around that Streets of Cairo concession on The Trail."

Charlie spoke, "And why is that? Something special about that place besides the camels?"

The man snickered. "You could say that. They got a dancer there called "Little Egypt." She does gyrations like you ain't never seen before. She's been practicing to music this past week. Some of us snuck in to see her." He smiled at the memory, before adding, "Boy howdy, don't tell our wives that!"

"And?" Sage nudged.

The man straightened and said, "That Hess fella has been hanging around Little Egypt like yellow jackets around chicken legs at a picnic. I suspect he'll keep coming back to see her."

TWENTY FOUR

May 8, 1905

Eɪᴄʜ ᴡɪsʜᴇᴅ ᴛʜᴇ ᴄᴏɴᴄʀᴇᴛᴇ ʙᴇɴᴇᴀᴛʜ his rear wasn't so hard. At least the rain was holding off. He'd been sitting across from City Brewery since early morning, early enough that he'd spotted its owner, Jasper Helmut when he arrived to start his day.

The brewery was bustling with casks and barrels being hand trucked in and out by fast moving workers. A heavy, yeasty smell layered the air. He wondered if those living around the brewery ever got used to it.

He hadn't brought his cart. Since his job was to keep an eye out for the assassin, they figured Hess would remember the cart that slammed into his legs just a few nights ago. So, Eich practiced his wood whittling. He was using a small knife to carve a small dog out of fir. He'd give it to the little girl who lived in the house attached to his lean-to. She loved dogs.

At every movement near the brewery's front door, he stopped carving to peer from beneath the brim of his floppy hat. He was admiring the elegant tail curl he'd just carved when he sensed someone coming toward him. Lowering his face, he waited until the man passed. Once the fellow was crossing the street, Eich studied him closely and felt excitement triggered by how the man moved but then, when he glimpsed the man's profile, he was sure. It was Hess.

Eich slipped knife and small carving into his coat pocket, making ready to follow, the second Hess reappeared. It was unlikely he would stay long with Helmut. Sage and Charlie were looking for Hess at the fairgrounds but the man could have changed abodes. So, Eich's task was to follow Hess until he entered the fair, or a hotel, or a rooming house.

After that, he was to return to the brewery and follow the brewery owner, Helmut, to see if he was up to something "fishy" as Mae put it. They hoped to catch Helmut doing something secretive and use it to force him into betraying the assassination attempt.

Eich leaned his head against the brick as if asleep, his slitted eyes riveted on the brewery's front door. Sure enough, Hess soon left the brewery, a frown on his face. Once again, Hess crossed the street, but instead of passing Eich again, he continued straight toward the commercial district. His stride was much longer and faster than when he'd arrived, as if he were angry. He soon vanished behind the building's corner.

Eich jumped up, hoping Hess wouldn't hail a cab because they were scarce in this area. Rounding the corner, Eich spotted his quarry disappearing around another corner. After turning that corner Eich stopped. Hess was nowhere in sight. Unless he'd taken off running, Hess must have entered a building on this block. That meant he had to figure out which building Hess had entered. Once he did, he could watch that entrance from across the street where an empty lot offered concealing blackberry bushes.

Eich dismissed the first entryway because when he looked in, he saw only a single man stitching a coach harness. The second entry was to a tailor shop. He peered in but couldn't see inside because the window display had a tall wooden backing. With a sigh, he walked to the third entry along the block. There he saw that the door opened onto a stairway leading to the second story. Wondering if it were locked, he reached for the door handle but never got to touch it.

A foot scuff sounded behind him just as a sudden piercing pain drove him to the pavement. Another pain exploded in his ribs and he heard a gravelly voice say, "You stupid old coot. You think I wouldn't remember you? My leg still aches from your fecking cart." Blackness descended before Eich could respond.

"I bet she don't even let him glance at that poster," Charlie drawled when a prim-looking woman and her meek-looking husband approached the Streets of Cairo concession. Sure enough, the instant her companion's eyes strayed toward the poster advertising Little Egypt's "exotic dance," the woman's hand tightened on his arm and she hurried him past.

Sage sighed. They'd been sitting at a small table under the Beef Sandwich's arcade for a couple of hours. They could remain there only because, whenever the concessionaire appeared to shoo them away, Sage fobbed him off with yet another coin. He and Charlie had been playing the observation game far too long. They'd already bet on which couples were married, whose shoes hurt, who would enter the Streets of Cairo, and now, whether the female of the couple would let her partner even look at the garish and somewhat salacious poster advertising Little Egypt's belly dance. Sage had lost interest in the game and only half-heartedly bothered to counter Charlie's imaginary bets.

"Heck, I'm going to go talk to Little Egypt herself. Maybe Hess told her where he was going," Sage declared. That decision made, he stood and picked up his toolbox, "Keep holding on to the table, pay whatever he wants for us to keep it, at least until I return." Charlie raised his soda bottle in salute, saying, "Will do. Good luck."

Sage paused at the avenue's edge waiting for an opening to cross. It would be like trying to wade across cattle streaming down a chute, only these animals were moving both ways. And, instead of a bovine smell, the pedestrians filled the air with perfumes and pomades.

Upon finally reaching the ticket booth, he paid his 15 cents rather than flash his carpenter's badge. That would come later. Entering beneath ornate arches, he found himself at the beginning of a busy indoor street and stopped to absorb what he was seeing. The enclosed space resembled a Middle Eastern street scene. Costumed characters manned booths lining both sides of the street, selling leather goods, rugs, brass vessels, and other exotic merchandise. Others wearing similarly strange garb mingled with the tourists.

A small donkey, led by a young boy trotted past. They were trailed by a two-hump camel. It carried a dark-skinned man in flowing robes wearing a flat-crowned hat. It was the first camel Sage had ever seen and he was surprised by the sedate grace of its steps. IIt placidly paced, not affected by the din of excited voices and musical instruments. Two actors were locked in fake mortal combat in a nearby corral. The clang of their sickle-shaped swords added to the cacophony.

He shook his head to end his goggling. He'd come back. Bring his mother and Lucinda. They'd like this place. Rising onto his toes, he peered down the artificial street toward the large stage across its end. That's where he'd find Little Egypt. He waded into the crowd, heading in that direction.

He didn't see her once he reached the elevated stage. Instead, dark-haired women in colorful, layered skirts cavorted in a peculiar dance with men outfitted in turbans, a variety of robes, vests, puffy pantaloons, and even short skirts. He was certain their dress came from all over the Middle East, not just Egypt. The shrieking music accompanying their dance was like nothing he'd ever heard before. Fong's flute playing sounded positively melodious in comparison.

He tore his attention away from the spectacle to find a way backstage. He started down a narrow passageway running beside the stage, only to have a burly individual block his way.

The man was polite. "I'm sorry Sir. This area is closed to guests."

Sage stayed relaxed and pulled the carpenter's admission badge from his pocket. He flashed it at the man and raised the toolbox. "I'm a carpenter. Got word there was a bulge in one of the dressing room walls. Seems some of the ladies fear it will fall on them."

The suspicion in the guard's face eased, but didn't disappear completely because he said, "Well, I haven't heard anything about a faulty wall. There's been a lot of men trying to get into that room so you won't mind if I take a look-see into that toolbox of yours will you?" Sage felt a momentary flash of gratitude toward Leo who'd made sure the toolbox contents were legit. He smiled agreeably, put it on the floor, undid the clasps, and lifted the lid.

The fellow bent over and peered in before saying, "Thank you." He gestured for Sage to close it up. Once Sage had the toolbox back in hand, the man reached to shake, adding, "Name's Laurence Emert but folks call me 'Larry'. Any problems, you let me know and I'll do what I can to help."

That hurdle surmounted, Sage continued along the passage. He hoped to spot the right dressing room without encountering any more challenges. In that, he was lucky. There were only two dressing rooms, one for the men and one for the ladies. The latter door was the farthest. He knocked softly. When a woman called, "enter" he stepped inside and closed it behind him.

She was surveying herself in a full length mirror. Startled, Sage back-pedaled toward the door, figuring he'd surprised her in a state of undress but then he paused at seeing her calm reaction.

It certainly was the most abbreviated costume to be seen in Portland. Even dancers in the bawdy theaters wore less revealing outfits. Her colorful, layered skirt hit her mid-calf and wasn't much different than that worn by the women outside on the stage. But above that, was something more risqué that showed her voluptuous body to good effect. Her pale belly was bare below a narrow strip of cloth stretching between puffy cap sleeves. It barely covered her breasts.

Before he could think of what to say, she whirled to say with exasperation in both words and tone, "Damn! Larry must have let another gawker through. Get the hell out of here before I scream."

Those words jarred Sage into raising a hand. "No, no, please. I only want to ask you a question or two about a man called, 'Hess.' I'm told he's a fan of yours."

She tilted her head to one side, curious. "What about him?" She nervously fingered a gold locket dangling around her neck but said, "That better be all. My husband doesn't take kindly to men bothering me and he carries a gun."

"Is Hess a friend of yours?"

She looked offended. "Most certainly not! He showered me with presents, thinking that gave him some kind of privilege if you know what I mean. My husband ran him off. I don't expect I'll see him again. And, good riddance."

"Why do you say that?"

"He has ice-cold, calculating eyes. He looked at me like I was prize beef on an auction block. Sent shivers up my spine, he did." She giggled, shimmied her upper torso, and declared, "It takes something to do that!"

Sage had to laugh. He decided the truth was the best approach. "Hess is threatening to kill a friend of mine. I'm trying to stop him. Did he say anything that told you where he might have gone once he left the American Inn here on the fairgrounds?"

She studied him thoughtfully. "Well, that explains something," she said.

Sage felt an expectant tingle. "What? What does it explain?"

Her lips pursed a moue of distaste. "Last time I saw him, he bragged about having rich friends and doing something for them. Said he'd be coming into a lot of money because of it. He even asked me to leave my husband for him." She grimaced, adding, "As if I would ever do such a thing!"

"Anything else? Anything that indicated where he might be holed up?"

She squinted in thought. "Well, I don't know if it means anything, but he said he'd rented a fine carriage from a stable near his hotel. He asked me to go for a ride. I know that isn't much but, there can't be many horse carriages stabled near hotels downtown."

"How do you know it was downtown?"

"Hmm," she thought again, "Now why did I think that?" Then she brightened, "I thought that his hotel was downtown because he complained that noise from the Exposition streetcars and boarding crowds never stopped until late at night. That could only be happening downtown."

Loud chattering voices were approaching the dressing room. Alarm crossed her face and she said, "Hurry. You need to leave. It will cause talk if the women find you here. And, my husband really won't like it." She moved toward a door in the back wall that he hadn't noticed.

She pulled it open. Beyond stood the elevated slides of the water chutes and further, the visitor-packed esplanade along the lakeshore. He crossed the threshold only to turn back and say, "If Larry asks, tell him I checked the wall and found nothing wrong."

She glanced down at the toolbox in his hand, "Oh, you are a clever man, aren't you?" She shut the door in his face before he replied.

Charlie was waiting, his face expectant when he saw Sage. "Any luck?" he asked.

"Well, she said I was a 'clever man,'" Sage replied with a grin. Charlie's forehead wrinkled, uncertain whether to believe him.

Sage swept a hand to take in the table and arcade, "And, sad to say, we'll have to leave this all behind us. The fairgrounds are a dead end."

They spent the next two hours visiting downtown hotels situated near stables. One hotel clerk thought he might remember Hess, but wasn't sure. Saying, if it had been Hess, he'd already checked out. The nearby stable owner had a stronger memory. "That scalawag done run off with my horse and carriage. He best bring them back soon along with a pocket full of money or I'll get the coppers after him. I needed that carriage this morning."

TWENTY FIVE

May 9, 1905

"HE'S GOING TO BE OKAY?" Sage asked his mother. Her face was the picture of fatigue: droopy eyelids, dark circles below, and every line in her too-pale skin deeper. She'd spent the night at Herman Eich's hospital bedside.

She nodded wearily. "He finally came to around 4 a.m." Tears filled her tired eyes. "He would be dead if that police officer hadn't seen the man kicking him and run him off. Doc Lane says Herman's lucky. He's just got a bad bump on the head and a few broken ribs. But Harry says he has to stay in the hospital for a few days to make sure he doesn't have internal injuries."

"Did Herman say it was Hess for certain?"

"Well, he woke up with a terrible headache. Harry told me not to excite him, so I didn't ask."

Charlie cleared his throat and said, "I think we best assume it was Hess. So, what do we do now?" He looked at each of them, Sage, Lucinda, Mae, and Solomon. "Our numbers are shrinking and, if we hope to catch Hess at the Portland Club, it must be from the outside. Grant will never hire the ladies back since they walked out on him, and the shooting gallery is temporarily closed. So, I have no excuse for hanging around."

Sage looked at his mother. "Ma, you are dead on your feet. Head to bed. I'll tell you what we decide when you wake up."

For once, she didn't bristle or object. She nodded wearily, dragged herself to her feet, and headed to the staircase. Once there, she turned,

"I told the hospital to send word if Herman takes a turn for the worse. You wake me up if that message comes."

"Absolutely," Sage said and meant it. She nodded and disappeared up the stairs. Glancing around the empty dining room, he remarked, "Darn good thing we decided to close the restaurant. There'd be no one to run it. Matthew and Ida are visiting his folks in Marshfield. Ida's husband, Ike, works long days at the shingle mill, and Fong's on twenty-four-hour Harry Lane guard duty."

"I wish I could help more, but I'm tied to the dining room podium ten hours a day," Solomon said.

"I'm afraid there's not much I can do, either," Lucinda said. "Charlie's right. Grant won't hire us back at the Portland Club, not after we walked out on him." She paused, her eyes narrowing as a thought crossed her mind. She looked at the others. "I know it's a long shot, but Hess could have moved to a whorehouse. We've looked in the boarding houses, but not the whorehouses. But really, all it would take is money to rent an empty room in one of those."

"That's a good idea. We've got to try everything. As long as Hess roams the streets, Harry is in danger."

"Right now, I'm thinking our best luck at finding him would be to watch and follow the city engineer, Elliot, and the brewery owner, Helmut," Charlie suggested.

Sage could only agree. "I best take Helmut because Elliott probably saw me at the work site when he met the Riners there."

"Do you think the Riners know about the assassination plan?" Solomon asked.

"Hard telling. They might know of it. Still, I can't see them as being involved in the planning. At this point, they're acting too nervous to be trusted."

"I guess it doesn't matter since we haven't anyone to cover them too," Solomon said and stood. "Well, I best be on my way. If I hear anything at all, I'll let you know. Oh, by the way, I received word from one of my porter friends that St. Alban and Meachum arrived safe and sound in Chicago. A contingent of union men met their train. I think they'll be hard to get at again."

"Huh. So much has happened since they left that I forgot to be worried about them. I'm glad to hear they're okay."

Solomon's smile lit his brown eyes. "Yes, I know. But Mrs. Clemens remembered and made a special trip to visit me in the dining room before they got on the train. She asked if I could have the train porter take extra special care of your two friends."

"That Ma of yours sure don't miss much, does she?" Charlie observed.

Sage first went to the hospital. There he found a frustrated Eich. "Good to see you! I hope you came to get me out of here," he said as soon as he saw Sage.

"Sorry, my friend. I can't do that. Ma would kill me if I went against Dr. Lane's orders. Besides, once she wakes up, she plans to come see you."

Eich shifted, squinting with pain as he struggled to sit up. Sage grabbed a pillow off the neighboring empty bed and slid it behind the ragpicker.

"Thank you, Sage, I don't know how long I'll stay awake but I'll try."

"I am sorry to bother you with this but I am about to head over to the brewery to watch for Hess. If he's the fellow who attacked you, I'll need to be extra cautious."

Eich's hand gently rubbed his side. "My lord, but these ribs feel like they're stabbing my innards every which way." He went silent and then said. "I am certain it was Hess."

"What makes you say that?"

"Three things. First, I didn't see who hit me but I trailed Hess after he left the brewery. I turned a corner and couldn't see him anywhere. I'm certain he ducked into a shop. Then, I got attacked from behind. Also, I remember that Mr. Meachum said Hess's voice sounded rough and gravelly. So was my attacker's voice. Finally, it was what he said that cinched that conclusion."

"What? He spoke to you?"

"Sure did. He said his leg still hurt from my cart. Since I don't make a practice of ramming people, I have to believe it was Hess."

The window was dirty and the slats on the crate were deadening his rear end. Sage heaved a sigh. He'd been looking out the second-story window for over three hours. Of course, it was better than sitting in a doorway like Herman had. Safer too. Neither Hess nor Helmut would see him perched up here.

He'd been lucky in two regards. The ground floor business also owned the building. Its second story was empty save for a scattering of boxes and bins. One five-dollar gold half-eagle and Sage was "welcome to use the space for the entire day." And, because Helmut was a frequent Mozart customer, Sage would recognize him.

So far, no sign of Hess. He was starting to think that Hess wouldn't show his face on the street below. Eich's presence had alerted him. Besides, the brewery occupied an entire block. There had to be more than one entrance. If Hess wanted to alert Helmut, it would be easy to sneak inside by another door. He probably did so right after he attacked Herman.

Across the street, the brewery's front door swung open and Helmut hurriedly stepped out. He had a frown on his face and carried a briefcase. He raised a hand and vigorously waved at a carriage waiting down the street. The driver straightened, shook the reins, and the carriage rolled forward.

Sage jumped up. Where was Helmut going in such a hurry? He raced for the stairs, waving at the shopkeeper on his way to the street. Just as he reached it, the carriage pulled away from the curb. Fortunately, an empty cab was traveling in the same direction. Sage leapt into the street and stopped it. Seconds later he was aboard, shouting for the cabbie to "follow that carriage." Shrugging, the man obeyed.

Helmut's carriage cornered at the next block to head north. Sage knew that Helmut had a fancy house in the Nob Hill neighborhood. Sure enough, a few blocks more and the carriage stopped before a large, elaborate house. Its façade was busy as a fairytale castle, sporting spindled and gabled balconies clad in decorative shingles. A conical tower at one corner anchored the pile.

The cabbie drove past and pulled to the curb in the next block. Sage leaned out to watch as Helmut quickly exited the carriage and ran up the front steps. Interestingly, the carriage didn't pull around the house to the rear stables. Instead, it stayed waiting at the curb.

A few minutes later, Helmut reappeared, carrying the briefcase and a small satchel. Hmm, wonder what he's up to? Sage thought. Could he be fleeing the city? If so, Sage's suspicion was correct. Hess had found a way to enter the brewery through another door.

Once Helmut was aboard, his carriage pulled away from the curb and soon passed Sage's cab. The cabbie leaned over the side and said, "Still want me to follow?"

Sage said "Yes" and, with a jerk, they were again rattling over the cobblestones following close behind Helmut's carriage. Their little parade turned east, heading toward the river. Some blocks later, after no deviation in direction, Sage was certain that Helmut's destination was the train station. Sure enough, his carriage headed straight for the station's 150-foot clock tower ahead.

As they neared the station drive, Sage's cabbie flicked the reins and sped up the horse so that they parked directly behind Helmut's carriage. The second it halted the brewery owner jumped down and trotted toward the station's brass-handled doors. Sage jumped down and followed, after tossing the cabbie a ten-dollar gold eagle. When the cabbie's amazed gratitude sounded at his back Sage waved a dismissive hand but kept his eyes riveted on Helmut who disappeared inside. He needed to know where Helmut was headed.

Entering the echoing, marbled lobby, Sage spotted Helmut standing in a nearby ticket line. Sage quickly crossed to stand behind him. The man didn't seem to notice. Instead, his gaze kept flicking between the huge wall clock and the entrance doors. Sage wondered if the man feared someone might try to prevent his escape. Hess maybe?

When Helmut reached the clerk's counter, Sage stepped close enough to hear him brusquely ask for a one-way ticket to San Francisco. Sage glanced at the departure board, noting that the train was leaving in five minutes. No wonder He'd left home in such a hurry. Ticket in hand, Helmut strode toward the platform. Sage left the line and followed.

Unfortunately, a guard stopped him from entering the platform area. From the lobby, he watched Helmut reach the train just as the conductor began raising the steps. Helmut disappeared inside. The train blew its whistle and made its stately exit from the station. Sage felt frustrated at losing his chance to corner the man and force him to confess his role in the assassination plot. And, more importantly, reveal its details.

On the other hand, Helmut's hurried departure suggested that something bad was going to happen soon. Otherwise, why would he be so desperate to flee town? As his mother would say, the man had "run off like rats from a burning barn."

Overhead clouds, looking dense as granite, rolled in from the west, raining black streaks to the ground. Sage hailed an empty cab, and once again he was bouncing along, heading back the way he'd just come. When they drew up outside Helmut's fanciful residence, Sage told the cabbie to wait. He jumped down, strolled up the walk, and climbed the steps onto the curved porch. A maid answered his knock. He doffed his hat and said, politely, "Hello, Miss. May I speak to Mr. Helmut? I have an appointment."

The maid looked nonplused, glanced over her shoulder, and said, "I'm sorry, Sir. The mister isn't here right now."

Sage made a show of wrinkling his forehead in dismay. "But, I had an appointment with him at this exact hour."

"I'm sorry, Sir, but Mr. Helmut was suddenly called away."

"Can I speak with your mistress? My appointment was about an urgent matter. I need to know how to find him."

She gave a vigorous headshake. "Oh no, she can't speak to you right now. She's most upset."

"Oh my, I'm sorry to hear that," Sage said and let the silence lengthen until the young woman felt the need to augment her reply. "He just come running in here, threw clothes in a satchel all higgledy-piggledy, and ran out the door. The mistress was chasing after him asking where he was going and why. He never told her. He just skedaddled out the door like a ghost was chasing him."

"My goodness that sounds like quite a ruckus. Does he do things like that often?"

Another vehement headshake was her first response, followed by, "He's never acted like that before. My mistress didn't know what to do. She's taken to her bed, she's so upset."

As the cab carried him away, Sage looked back at the ornate house built by vice profits and the suffering of many. He figured the time had come for Sergeant Hanke to be brought up to date. Accordingly, he asked the cabbie to take him to the police station.

Reaching the station, Sage learned Hanke wasn't there so he settled for leaving a note. Shortly after nine that evening, the big sergeant rapped on Mozart's kitchen door. He entered a kitchen filled with the enticing smell of Mae Clemens' beef stew. Sage had warned her that the policeman might turn up. So, she fixed a hot supper saying, that Sergeant Hanke always brought an empty stomach, adding "Poor dear man."

While they ate, Mae reported that Herman Eich had recovered enough that Dr. Lane said he could go home in the morning. After that, Sage began to tell the sergeant what they thought was going on. He hadn't got far into his tale before a pounding on Mozart's front door interrupted and a key turned its lock. The door burst open and Fong stepped aside, key in hand, as a frantic Harry Lane brushed past him. The doctor's eyes were wide and staring. His hair stood straight up as if he'd been raking his fingers through it. Charging toward their table he shouted, "Those bastards grabbed Lola!"

TWENTY SIX

May 9 and 10, 1905

SAGE JUMPED UP TO GRAB the agitated man's arm and guide him to a chair. Mae went to the buffet and returned with a glass of whiskey before Lane gathered his words to speak. Sage glanced at Fong who looked grim, his eyebrows lowered.

"Harry, drink this, then tell us what's happened," Sage urged.

With a trembling hand, Harry tossed back the whiskey, swallowing it all in one gulp. From his inside coat pocket, he withdrew a piece of paper. It was wrinkled as if it had been wadded into a ball and then flattened again. He tossed it on the table.

Hanke grabbed it, turned it about, and read aloud, "At tomorrow night's rally you will announce you are dropping out of the race or you will never see your wife alive. If you tell the police or anyone else, your wife will die. That's a promise."

Following a moment of stunned silence, Mae laid a hand on Harry's forearm and said, "Don't you worry about Lola. We'll find her." She glanced at the others who responded with murmurs of agreement.

Harry's voice was dull as he aimed his words at his white-knuckled hands gripping the table edge. "We got back to the house late. I had meetings, my rounds, and a sick baby to tend. Lola was gone. I recalled she told me that she needed to go shopping. I thought maybe, afterward, she visited friends because I told her I might be late. About half an hour later, there was a knock at the door. A boy on the stoop handed me this note. It was in a sealed envelope. By the time I read it, the boy had disappeared. Mr. Fong ran after him but he didn't catch him."

Sage glanced at Fong who nodded and said, quietly, "I think boy hop on streetcar. I missed it."

"No matter. It's unlikely that he could have told us anything useful," Sage soothed, certain his friend keenly felt that failure.

Harry looked up. With trembling lips, he said, "I'll do what they ask. I can't lose Lola. We have been married for nearly twenty-three years. She's put up with my long and late hours, the uncertainty of our life, and my rants. She's my anchor. The center pole of my life." His chin trembled and he looked away.

"What time is the rally tomorrow?" Mae asked.

"It starts at 7 p.m.," Harry mumbled.

She looked at Herman and Sage and seeing only determination, she said, "Don't worry, Harry. We'll find Lola before you have to say that you're dropping out."

Harry looked hopeful before shaking his head disconsolately. "We've less than 24 hours before the rally. This town's too big. How could you possibly find her in such a short time? All these days and we still haven't found that Hess fellow." Putting his elbows on the table, he dropped his face into his hands, and his shoulders shook.

Sage put his hand on Harry's back. "Harry, we're going to try. But, you must promise that you will stay here while we look. Right now, I am leaving to send messages to the whole crew. I'll tell them it's an emergency and get them here tonight so we can strategize on how to find her."

"I've got to be out there looking," Harry protested, shaking off Sage's hand and starting to rise.

Sage gently pushed him down again. "No, you've got to be safe. While we look, you need to stay here. We can't be looking for Lola and worrying about you at the same time. We need Fong and Sprig Flowers free to look. They can't do that and watch over you too."

Lane narrowed his gray eyes at Sage before nodding. "Okay, I'll wait here but only because I wouldn't know where to start looking."

"Fortunately, we do," Sage told him. "If the kidnappers are the same people involved, we already know who they are and where to find them. If it's not them, then you might have to make the announcement they told you to make."

Sage left for the Hasty Messenger Company, leaving an agitated Harry Lane pacing Sage's third-floor room. After dropping off the summonses,

Sage had Sprig drive him to R.W. Montague's house because Harry's closest friend was the person best able to keep the doctor calm and remaining inside. Within the hour, everyone had arrived at Mozart's. Soon all were sitting and planning, with only Eich absent. He'd learn of the situation in the morning. They, along with Montague and Harry, discussed and planned. They resolved to act come dawn.

Sage was outside the Carpenters' hall when the doors opened. Lane was once again at Mozart's with his best friend by his side. Learning of the situation, Leo immediately sent three burly union men to stand guard. Sage left the hall feeling that Harry would be safe inside Mozart's.

Before dawn, Fong had left to get his 'cousins' searching. They'd look for Lola Lane in the underground and ask other Chinese whether they'd noticed a respectable white woman being manhandled or abducted.

Hanke and his trainee, Dan Carter, would roam the North End streets and saloons, trying to spot and follow Hess.

Sage and Charlie would first search the Tanner Creek sewer. They knew it was unlikely Lola Lane would be stashed down there, but they couldn't take the chance. It was abhorrent to think of her being imprisoned in that stinking dark.

Once they finished that unpleasant task, Sage would stop by Lucinda's. She had left the night before to visit the bawdy houses near Helmut's brewery and in the North End. Since she'd sent no word, he figured she hadn't found Hess or Lola but he had to make sure she was safe.

Once he saw Lucinda, Sage would meet up with Mae and Herman. Meanwhile, Charlie would join in the North End search.

Sprig's first task was to collect Herman Eich from the hospital, tell him of Lola's kidnapping and their plans, before driving him home to his lean-to beside the Marquam ravine. Mae would meet him there and they'd then find a place in South Portland from which they could watch the City Engineer's front door. If he left, they would follow.

Once Eich was home, Sprig Flowers, atop his cab, would rove the streets, looking for the assassin and the city engineer—the latter being someone he'd transported before and knew on sight. If he spotted either man, he'd follow.

They hoped one of the miscreants would lead them to Lola. Regardless, everyone agreed to meet back at Mozart's by 5:30 p.m.

When Mae Clemons stepped from Mozart's she paused to admire the blue vault overhead. The air was hazy with the smell and smoke of coal and wood fires burning away the morning's chill and cooking breakfasts. Spotting a cab rattling toward her over the cobbles, she raised a hand and was soon entering South Portland.

As always, she relished the neighborhood's vitality. It was already bustling with an industrious and voluble mix of its Italian, Irish, Greek, and Jewish inhabitants. Most were greeting each other with nods, waves, and shouts.

Some people were heading to work carrying the tools of their trade. Others were mothers shepherding children to school. Swift-moving men were loading produce and junk wagons. On every side, delicatessen, bakery, and grocery proprietors were raising awnings, sweeping sidewalks, and watering the dirt street before their shops. Thanks to Mae's acquaintance with Herman, she'd come to love the neighborhood. She knew if she ever moved from Mozart's, this was where she'd want to live.

She rapped on the cab roof to make it pull to the curb. She would walk the last two blocks to Herman's. But first, she entered an Italian bakery to buy his favorite jelly cannolos to go with the hot coffee he'd have brewed.

Minutes later, Herman greeted her with a hug, a sweet kiss, and a grin of delight. "Wonderful! Might these be cannolos from my favorite bakery?" he asked as he took the paper-wrapped package. They ate swiftly, both of them eager to take up a post outside Engineer Elliott's house.

"Can you imagine," Eich said as he wiped jelly from his neatly trimmed mustache and beard, "The folks tell me that Elliott's wife refuses to shop in the neighborhood. She won't eat anything bought from those she calls 'nasty foreigners.'" Eich chuckled and added, "Apparently, she doesn't know that half the purchases in those 'foreign' shops are made by maids and cooks sent by Miz Elliott's social 'betters' who live up on the hill."

As they left the lean-to, she asked how they'd find a spot from which to watch Elliott's door. Eich said confidently, "I'm a friend of Abramo and Giuseppina Cereghino. A very nice couple. They're unusual because he comes from Italy's north, while she's from its south like most of the Italians here. Anyway, they run a boarding house across the street and down one house from the Elliott's. I stayed with them when I first got to town. I'm positive they'll let us park our fannies in their parlor for as long as it takes. Though, I have to warn you to be careful of Mrs. Cereghino."

Mae looked at him and saw the smile on his face. "Why? Is she easy to offend?"

Eich chuckled. "I've never seen that. But, she's Sicilian and a wonderful cook. If you're not eating, she thinks you're starving. So, whatever she feeds you, and she will certainly feed you, take small bites and eat slowly." He patted his small paunch and added, "I admit, sometimes, I take advantage of her generosity."

When they reached Elliott's street, he led them to the modest boarding house. It was a wooden clapboard with a two-story addition on one side. The porch was covered, its roof held up by simple two-by-four posts. Three double-hung windows, and a single four-paneled door, fronted the porch. Mae smiled when she saw that whoever built the porch had encircled a tree rather than chop it down.

A small, rotund woman sat on the porch, shelling a basket of peas. When she saw Eich, she shouted, hurriedly put the basket on the floor, and rushed forward to hug and kiss him on each cheek. She looked at Mae and stepped forward to hug her, saying as she did, "This must be the wonderful lady friend, Mae, who you've been telling me about!"

"This stinks worse than a stock corral. Cow shit smells a lot better," Charlie complained as he lifted his rubber boot from black muck that didn't want to let go.

They were in the Tanner Creek sewer having already sloshed down about half of its 1800 feet. Kerchiefs were tied over their noses and mouths. Goodyear galoshes covered their shoes and legs up to their knees. It smelled more fetid than the last time Sage had entered it— probably because it hadn't rained for a few days.

Trudging the entire length wasn't something Sage relished doing, but he couldn't take the chance there was an alcove along its route big enough to hold Lola Baldwin. The thought of that kind, gracious woman being frightened and alone in this stinking dark made his blood boil and quickened his steps. Charlie grumbled but he didn't protest against Sage's insistence they walk the sewer's entire length.

Half an hour later they were at the end and climbing out a manhole. Fortunately, it was possible to lift it from underneath so they hadn't needed to backtrack. Once atop, they tried to scrape the muck off their galoshes but it was hopeless. "No way we can wear these into Mozart's. I think they're a lost cause. If we had time, we'd take them to Mozart's alley and rinse them off. But we don't," Sage said.

Charlie agreed and after carefully peeling the galoshes off their shoes, they left them lying on a grass verge. Maybe someone would find and use them.

Sage glanced around and saw Riner's tool shed a few yards away. He wandered over and tugged at the padlock. No sound came from inside when he knocked. Charlie motioned him aside. Big brick in hand, Charlie stepped up and slammed the brick onto the hasp. It tore loose, the padlock still attached. Charlie pushed the door open and stuck his head inside. "She ain't here. Just a few broke tools is all."

Elmira let Sage in and asked him to wait, saying, "Miss Lucinda just drug herself in the door not two hours ago, looking tired as a dog that ran ten miles. She was up all night searching." When Elmira came back downstairs, she told him to go up as Miss Lucinda wanted to speak with him in her bedroom.

She was in bed, sleepy-eyed but smiling. "I am sorry to wake you," he said sitting beside her and kissing her cheek. "I needed to know you were safe and wondered whether all your visits last night gave us any information."

Her nose wrinkled. "Whew, what's that awful smell that followed you in?"

Sage glanced down at his pant leg. "Uh-oh, I best stop by home and change my pants." He told her about his and Charlie's sewer excursion. She laughed and said, "Well, as bad as you smell, I'm glad you didn't find Lola down there. That would have been a nightmare for her."

Sage had to agree. "Well, you're right. A mixed blessing, I guess. But it's eight in the morning and we have less than ten hours to find her. And, although I never said this to Harry, there's no guarantee that if he drops out of the race, he'll get his Lola back. If she's seen their faces they won't take the risk."

She sighed and patted his hand. "Harry Lane's a very smart man. I'm sure he's figured that out for himself."

TWENTY SEVEN

May 10, 1905

WHEN A WELL-DRESSED MAN STEPPED out of the Elliott's house, Mae put down her pastry and leaned forward to peer out the window. "That's him! That's the fellow I followed! He's the one who met with Hess in the Portland Club!"

Eich stood. "We best get ready to chase him" He turned in the direction of the kitchen where Mrs. Cegrighino was fetching coffee to go with the pastries she'd just delivered, calling, "Giuseppina, I'm sorry! We have to leave! Elliott is on the move!"

During their two hours of waiting, Giuseppina kept them company—feeding them words and food nonstop. In return, Eich told her of Elliott's sewer contract corruption and of their determination to bring him to justice. She said she knew all about the Tanner Creek scandal because she read the *Italian Tribune* every day, like most Italians in South Portland. The paper reported the story in great detail.

Across the street, Elliott donned his hat and walked to the curb. They watched through the lace curtains, ready to follow once he took off walking. He didn't move. Instead, he stood at the curb and pulled out his pocket watch to eye the time.

"Well, darn it all to heck," Mae muttered. "That lazy dog. He's waiting to be picked up. He gets in a buggy, we'll never be able to follow him on foot!"

Eich scanned the street both ways and, as if summoned by Mae's words, a cab turned the corner and rolled to a stop before Elliott. Seconds later, the cabbie sent his horse into a trot, and the cab rolled away.

"Come on!" Eich urged. He pulled Mae out the door and onto the porch. The street was empty except for a scrap metal wagon standing curbside next door. Eich turned to Mae. "You too proud to ride on that wagon?"

She looked offended. "I'll have you know I grew up riding three on a mule. What do you think?"

Holding her hand, he led them off the porch and to the wagon. Just then, an old man with a gray beard exited a small outbuilding. He tossed a rusted bit onto the full wagon bed. Spotting Eich he exclaimed, "Why Herman Eich, it is a pleasure to see you!" and held out his hand.

Eich shook it quickly and said, "Vetter Fox, I have a tremendous favor to ask. Do you see that cab, a couple blocks down the street?"

The man looked and nodded.

"We need to follow him and see where he goes. It is very important! Truly a matter of life or death!"

Without a word, Vetter Fox scrambled onto his wagon with a speed that belied his age. Once seated, he reached a hand down to Mae and pulled her up beside him. The wagon began to roll as Eich clambered aboard.

The horse just beyond their boots was a magnificent creature, much stronger and healthier than the one pulling Elliott's cab. Soon, Fox was slowing his wagon a few yards behind Elliott.

Eich breathed a sigh of relief. "That was close," he declared. "We were about to lose him. Thank you, Vetter!" He leaned forward to look at Mae on the other side of Fox, "Mrs. Clemens, I would like to introduce you to this fine and generous gentleman, Mr. Fuchs. Everyone calls him 'Vetter Fox.'"

At her cocked eyebrow, he explained, "Fuchs means 'fox' in English. Vetter is 'uncle' in Yiddish . . . hence 'Vetter Fox.'"

Switching his attention to Fuchs, Eich said. "We believe your neighbor, William Elliott, is part of a gang that has kidnapped a friend's wife."

"Oy vey!" Fuchs exclaimed. "That he would do so does not surprise me. He is a nasty man. We've talked about him at Shabbat dinners. But he has an important city job. Why would he do such a thing?"

Mae couldn't hold back. "He's greedy, that's why. He's up to his nose in corruption. And, now we think he's involved in a kidnapping to save his job!"

The old Jewish man looked at her, shook his head, and flicked the reins to trot his horse. "Don't worry, we won't lose the rascal!"

As expected, Eich's lean-to stood empty. However, as promised, there was a slip of paper stuffed in the door crack. Unfolding it, Sage recognized Eich's elegant script and read, "You can find us at the Cegrighino's boarding house, 326 Front Street."

When Sage knocked on the boarding house door, he was greeted by a smiling Italian woman who pulled him inside, saying, "Allo! You musta be Mista Miner, Mista Herman's friend? You are handsome like Miz Mae said."

When Sage acknowledged he was Miner, she patted his arm and said, "Herman lefta a nota for you." She left him in the entry, entered the nearby parlor, and returned with a note. This time, Eich's message said, "If we're not here, we're following E. See you at M's, 5:30."

Sage thanked Mrs. Cereghino and turned to leave. She stopped him, saying, "You see Mista Herman soon?"

He shrugged, raised his eyebrows and both hands, palms up in one of the few Italian gestures he knew. She nodded her understanding, patted his arm again, and handed him something wrapped in grease-stained paper, "Thisa for him and his lady. Good cassatina. He lika it very much. You not see him soon, you eat."

Sage thanked her for the note and package. The fragrance wafting from the paper-wrapped bundle made him wish he wouldn't encounter Eich soon. The ragpicker often lauded this woman's baking.

Once aboard the trolley, heading toward the central city, he had second thoughts and decided Eich and his mother were probably already stuffed with Mrs. Cegrighino's pastries. He unwrapped the small cake and moaned at its heavenly taste.

Charlie leaned against the building across the street from Halloran's cribs. He'd cruised through the downtown saloons without ever spotting Hess. Now, he was outside Halloran's in the North End and dragging his feet about entering. He delayed partly because he hoped to spot Hess, coming or going. And, partly he delayed because he hated places like Halloran's.

As a young whippersnapper, he'd visited a whorehouse. He still shrank from the memory. Today, his hesitation sprang more from knowing

Xenobia and Lucinda. During the long days of the Prineville smallpox quarantine he'd learned of how, as young girls, both had been sold to whorehouses. Sage had told him all about Halloran's. It was an evil place that specialized in very young girls.

Finally, he straightened. "Might as well get it over," he muttered. Once the wheeled traffic cleared, he charged across the street and stepped across the establishment's threshold.

Inside, it was just as he remembered. A fat man, Halloran he presumed, sat behind the counter. He was stuffing his face with fried chicken, his chin and hands shining greasily in the light coming through the front window. Seeing Charlie, he dropped the chicken leg onto the plate and licked his fingers before drying them on his shirt front.

"Hey, there Cowboy. What can I interest you in this fine afternoon?"

Charlie resisted the urge to clout the man's phony smiling face and said, "Mmm. Wahl last time I come here I liked one gal pretty much."

"Ah, that must have been when my son was manning the desk. I sure don't remember you, and I would. We don't often see cowboys in here all duded up in buckles and boots."

"Wahl, I don't come here much. Don't really like the city. Too many people, too much noise. A man can't think."

"So, do you remember the gal's name?"

Charlie shook his head, paused, and said, "I'm thinking the number over the curtain was nine. Do you keep them staying in the same stall?"

"Usually, I do. It helps with repeat customers. Anyway, I know just who you mean! She's been working outta that crib all this last year. Her name's Alma Belle."

Charlie nodded eagerly. "Yup, that sure does sound like the name. Is she available?"

Halloran made a show of pulling out and squinting at his pocket watch. "Her guest should be fixing to leave any minute now. 'Course, if you're in a hurry, I have other gals ready to make you happy, if you know what I mean." This time, he leered.

Charlie fought to keep his face looking 'aw shucks' embarrassed as he said, "Naw, I'll just wait on Alma Belle. Don't want to chance nobody else."

Five minutes later a logger-looking fellow came down the stairs, buttoning his trousers on the way. He nodded at Charlie and pushed out the front doors without saying anything to Halloran.

"That was her customer who just left." The crib owner said. He took Charlie's money and gestured toward the stairs. "Go ahead on up."

The stairs were narrow, the walls on either side grimy from decades of filthy hands. Charlie tried not to touch anything. At the top, a long hallway ran parallel to the street outside. Charlie knew it well since he'd lurked in it, trying to overhear what Hess said during his visit with Alma Belle.

There was no privacy. Every room, on each side of the hall, had been split into small cubicles. Their doorways were split into two narrow cubicle openings, a curtain covering each opening. A tin number was nailed above each curtain.

He walked down the hallway until he reached number nine. A weary "come in" answered his soft knock on the doorframe.

Inside, flimsy boards formed walls six feet tall, topped by chicken wire. An iron bedstead took up most of the space. An iron bedstead took up most of the room. A woman stood at a corner basin, using a rag to clean herself. Charlie started backing out.

She turned, saw his embarrassed retreat, and laughed. "Sorry, I should have told you to wait." When she dropped the rag in the basin he heard a small splash. She stepped forward and asked, "You want me to light the candle or do you like it in the dark?"

"Light would be good," he said, finding his equilibrium.

She lit a small candle, lifted the holder, and said. "My but you are a big handsome cowpoke! You just ride into town? I ain't never seen you before."

Charlie took the candle from her and gestured to the bed. "How about we sit awhile?"

She plopped down, stretched out, and patted the mattress beside her, saying, "I like a man who don't dilly-dally."

He studied her in the dim light: No more than eighteen, maybe younger. Already her face was drawn with disappointment and maybe despair, so guessing her age was hard. She had curly auburn hair, a wide mouth, and up-tilted eyes of some indiscernible color. There was intelligence in those eyes and she was just short of what his ma would call "comely."

He sat at the bottom of the bed near her feet. She frowned and her face turned suspicious. "You're not one of them special coppers are you—looking for a free time? 'Cause, if you are, you need to work that out with Halloran, not me. Only he can okay me not charging. He gets part of my take as well as the room rental he charged you downstairs."

Charlie reached into his pocket and pulled out a twenty-dollar gold piece. He raised the candle so that the coin glinted. In reaction, she used her palms to push up into a sitting position. Her eyes on the money, her face still suspicious, she asked, "What exactly are you buying? I'm choosy about what I'm willing to do, not like some other girls here at Halloran's."

"Just talk Alma Belle, nothing more."

"About what?" Suspicion replaced the practiced warmth.

"Some days back, you had a customer. His last name is Hess. He's stocky and has a light-colored blaze in his hair. Have you seen him lately?"

Her nose wrinkled with distaste. "Oh, him. I know who you mean. I don't like him much."

"When did you see him last?"

When she said, "Yesterday," he felt a spark of excitement shoot up from his boots.

"What did he talk about?"

"Same thing he always does. About me moving up to Seattle with him," she snorted, "As if I would. He gives me the crawlies."

"Why is that?"

"He's got eyes like a snake. Icy cold. I bet he'd murder me in a second if I back-talked him. When he left yesterday, I hoped he wouldn't come back."

"Tell me what he talked about."

"Hmm, wahl," she stalled, trying to recall. "He bragged, saying he'd be getting lots of money soon. He says that every time. I figured he was just chest puffing as usual. Men like to do that." She gave Charlie a sideways glance.

"Anything else? Did he say anything else? Try to remember. It's real important," Charlie urged.

She was silent and then said, "Well, it was kinda funny. When he first came in, he said he was late because he had to build a nest for a sweet little bird." She shivered. "He laughed after he said that bit about the 'nest'. It were an ugly, evil laugh."

TWENTY EIGHT

May 10, 1905

SERGEANT HANKE ORDERED A BEER and used the bar mirror to survey the saloon's patrons. He didn't see Hess. Sipping, he mulled over his failed search of twenty saloons. He'd divided up the North End saloons between himself and young Dan Carter. Hanke was to look for Hess west of Broadway, while Carter was to search those saloons east of that street.

Because of his large size, Hanke wore a logger disguise: suspenders buttoned to canvas trousers, flannel shirt over itchy woolen underwear, high-top boots, and a wide-brimmed crush hat. So far, no one had called him out as one of Portland's top cops.

He worried they wouldn't find Hess and Lola Lane in time. It'd be a loss for the city if Lane dropped out of the mayoral race. Even worse, Hanke dreaded disappointing Sage and the crew. Last year, they'd done so much to help him and his friend, Ura Stahl, when Ura's boy got kidnapped.

Casually, he turned so that his back was against the bar, lifting the beer stein to hide his face. The afternoon patrons were a subdued lot. He scanned their faces and froze, locking eyes with a special police officer he knew.

It was Knapp, a man who hated Hanke because the sergeant had gotten him booted off the regular police force for being unnecessarily rough with the blacks and Chinese he encountered. It had been a bitter day when he learned Knapp had been rehired as a special police officer in the North End.

Knapp broke eye contact and leaned forward to speak with his two companions. Hanke turned to face the bar and hunched his shoulders. Maybe Knapp hadn't seen through his disguise. Maybe he'd think Hanke looked somewhat familiar without putting a name to his face. Still, a cold sensation traveled up his back. It was best to leave before trouble came calling. Pulling his crush hat low, Hanke pushed his nearly full beer glass aside. As he turned to leave, he saw Knapp and his special police companions rising, donning hats and coats. Seconds later, they'd exited the saloon.

Hanke breathed a sigh of relief. He'd wait a few minutes before leaving since Hess wasn't here either.

Once outside he headed toward the next drinking establishment. As he passed an alley entrance, someone stepped out and said, "Hanke, what the hell are you doing on our turf?"

"Ah, so you did recognize me, Knapp," Hanke responded. He moved back when the other two men from the saloon emerged from the alley to stand shoulder-to-shoulder with Knapp, blocking Hanke from moving forward.

Knapp snarled, "You're down here checking on us special police, aren't you? We all know you don't like us none."

Hanke shook his head. "No, I'm here for reasons that have nothing to do with you."

"Bet you're eying the chief's job if that Lane fellow gets in."

Hanke again shook his head. "Nah, Knapp. Not interested. I like getting out on the street. Besides, I'd hate the politics of the chief's job. I'd be awful at it."

"But you'd like to see the mayor do away with our jobs, wouldn't yah?" asked one of the men behind Knapp. "We heard you have Harry Lane's ear. You've been seen at his meetings, clapping and carrying on."

Though he knew he shouldn't, Hanke said it anyway, "Harry Lane's ears are his own. That said, you are correct. I think the special police unit is a carbuncle on the rear end of this town and a disgrace to the policing profession. So, yes, I hope Lane wins the election and that the first thing he does is get rid of the unit and the three of you."

"You son-of-a . . ." the man next to Knapp moved forward.

Hanke stepped back and raised his hands, "You don't want to do that," he cautioned.

The three exchanged looks and he caught the moment they reached a silent agreement. They wanted to teach him a lesson.

He glanced at his scarred knuckles. He'd grown up near Chicago's stockyards where bare-knuckle fights were the order of the day. Being a big fellow, he'd encountered plenty of boys hoping to prove their manhood. With a sigh, he calmly tucked his chin, raised his fists before his face, and widened his stance. He was ready when the first man, the largest, charged, swinging wildly, like someone who'd always won fisticuffs because of his size.

Hanke's rear uppercut connected solidly with the man's chin, knocking him backward to be caught by his two companions. The man shook off their hands and charged. Once again, he stepped too close. He raised his fists before his chin, expecting to block the same blow. It was a bad move because Hanke's big fist came from the left, high up, in a lead hook that snapped the man's head sideways, driving him down onto his knees before he toppled over. Flat on the ground, he didn't move.

The second man stepped over his friend on the ground, raised his fists, and cautiously moved forward. Those raised fists were only chest high, telegraphing his inexperience.

Hanke didn't have time for this nonsense. Rotating his hips and shoulders, he delivered a powerful right cross to his attacker's chin. The man staggered backward, his eyes rolled upward, and he crumpled to the ground and didn't move.

Only Knapp remained. With part of his mind, Hanke had been aware of Knapp studying Hanke's moves. He'd be the toughest opponent.

And he was. Unlike the other two, Knapp didn't move close in. Instead, he raised his fists and held them before his face ready to block any knockout blow. His advance was deliberate, slow. When Knapp got within punching distance, his right hand shot out, quick as a snake's strike, trying to land an uppercut on Hanke's solar plexus.

The sergeant only had time to tighten his muscles and twist slightly to the side before Knapp's fist connected. The punch didn't reach his stomach but it hurt enough to make Hanke grunt and gulp air.

Stepping back, Hanke studied Knapp and decided the time had come to end things. He'd use the moves that had always worked for him. As his trainer said, the time had come "to throw punches in bunches." He grinned and hit Knapp with a double jab from his left hand before swiftly pivoting to slam Knapp's chin with a right cross. He pulled his punch just enough—knocking Knapp off balance but not out.

As Knapp staggered back, Hanke stepped forward to grab the man's arm. He whirled him around and shoved him at the building until

Knapp's right cheek smashed against the brick wall. At the same time, he pulled Knapp's arm up and pushed it against his back. Knapp squealed. Putting his mouth against the man's ear, Hanke asked, "Enough?"

"Uh. You bastard Hanke," growled Knapp.

"I asked, have you had enough?"

"Yeah, you . . . "

A jerk on his twisted arm cut off the insult. Hanke said, "Like I told you, Knapp. I'm not here to spy on you. I just need information. You tell me what I need to know, and I'll let you go. Maybe before your two friends wake up so you can brag you got the best of the fight and ran me off."

Knapp stayed silent, so Hanke jerked the man's arm higher.

"Ow! Stop! What, what do you want to know."

"Are you going to answer my questions?"

"Yes, but let go of the arm, will you?"

"First, tell me: Have you seen a short, stocky man from out of town? He has a white blaze on the left front side of his hair."

"Huh? What you want that fella for?"

"Never mind why I want him. Where did you see him, and when did you see him?" Hanke gave the twisted arm another jerk.

"Stop, damnit. I'll tell you! He's been around. I saw him yesterday, early."

"Did you talk to him?"

"A bit."

"Think real careful before you answer. What exactly did he talk about?"

"It was nothing special. He was talking about the fair. Said he'd already toured the grounds. Said that Egyptian dancer was something to see."

"Anything else? Anything at all?"

Knapp was silent before whining, "Come on, Hanke. Leave go my arm. You're breaking my shoulder."

"Think real hard, Knapp. What else did that man talk about? Did he ask about anything?"

"Ask about?"

Knapp went silent and Hanke got the sense he'd thought of something in particular. "What?" he demanded.

"Well, he did want to know what streetcar lines crossed to the eastside."

"Which streetcar line?" Hanke eased up on the arm twist, let go, and turned Knapp to face him.

Knapp rubbed his shoulder and said, "Well, he asked about the streetcars running across both bridges. But, it seemed like he was more interested in the one that crosses the Steel Bridge into the Albina district. He asked where to catch it."

Officer Dan Carter was discouraged. More than anything, he wanted to show Sergeant Hanke that he could be a good police officer. If he found that fellow, Hess, Hanke would think better of him. Though the sergeant hadn't yelled or acted disappointed, Dan still flushed at how he'd left that man in the hospital unguarded. If that Miner fellow hadn't turned up, Mr. St. Alban would have died.

As the day wore on, his feet began aching, and his spirits dove lower and lower. He checked his pocket watch. He was supposed to meet the sergeant on a downtown corner at 5:15 p.m. He had only half an hour left to find Hess before he'd have to give up. He was a failure.

He began walking southward, toward downtown. The boardwalk was crowded, so he wasn't surprised when someone, hurrying past, knocked into his shoulder. Dan glanced at the man who began rapidly crossing the street.

Dan started to continue straight, then looked again. Amazement rooted him to the spot. Their collision had knocked the man's hat back on his head so that the white streak above his left temple caught the late afternoon sun. Not only did he have the streak, but he was also short and stocky.

"Holy Cripes Almighty! It's him!" Dan declared aloud before following across the street, almost getting flattened by an empty produce wagon.

Hanke paced up and down the sidewalk, irritated and worried in equal mix. Carter was fifteen minutes late. He was irritated because they were already late for the meeting. He was worried because he'd sent a raw recruit after an experienced killer.

Finally, two blocks distant, he spotted Carter running toward him. Hanke strode to meet the young man. "Where the heck have you been, Carter? Don't you have a pocket watch?" His tone was sharp from pent-up frustration and worry.

Carter gulped air, then said, "Sarge! I saw him! I was heading here when I saw him."

"Where is he?"

The young police officer looked shamefaced. "Well, I lost him too."

Hanke sighed. "Whereabouts did you lose him?" That fellow Hess was proving 'harder to catch than ghost lights over a marsh'—one of his dad's sayings.

"He got on a streetcar heading over to the east side. There were so many streetcars lined up and so many people waiting to board that I couldn't get on. It was like I was bucking the wrong way up a cattle chute. Hess's car pulled away before I could jump on, otherwise, I would have stuck with him."

"Did you see which streetcar he boarded?"

Carter's head nodded and he said with pride, "Sure did. It was the one that goes across the Steel Bridge, over to Albina."

Hanke clapped Carter on his shoulder. "It's too bad you weren't able to follow him but what you saw is helpful. It confirms what I learned. Together, our information might be a solid lead on the part of town where they're holding Mrs. Lane."

Hanke turned and started trotting back the way he'd come. "We're late," he called over his shoulder. "We best hurry. We didn't capture the fellow, but at least we can contribute a bit of information."

Halfway down the block, Hanke stopped abruptly to clutch at Carter's shoulder and halt him. Once he had the young officer's attention, Hanke said, "Look, Dan, you are about to hear things and see people meant to be kept secret. You can't tell anyone about them or about what you hear—not even your blessed mother. You also mustn't ask questions or speak until I tell you to. Do you understand?"

Carter's wrinkled forehead said he was perplexed, but he only nodded and clamped his lips firmly over whatever questions he had.

Hanke loosened his grip and clapped him on the shoulder and exclaimed, "Good man! Let's get cracking."

A block later, Carter's eyes widened when his sergeant ignored the closed sign on a fancy restaurant, opened its door, and beckoned for Carter to follow him inside.

TWENTY NINE

ONCE INSIDE THE CLOSED RESTAURANT, Dan saw people sitting around a big table. The man he knew as John Miner, savior of Vincent St. Alban in the hospital, rose from the table and crossed the room to greet them. "Sergeant Hanke, Officer Carter, glad you're here. We were growing concerned about you!"

He shepherded them toward two empty seats at the table.

After they sat, Sergeant Hanke said to everyone, "Folks, this young man is Officer Dan Carter. I asked him to help search the North End."

They greeted that announcement with nods and subdued smiles but no one spoke.

An older woman appeared, poured them coffee, set sandwiches before them, and then took a seat herself. Dan sipped his coffee while looking at the people. It was a strange mix. The older woman and an older man, maybe husband and wife, sat beside each other.

A sharply dressed, dignified black man, who looked familiar, sat on the other side of the older woman. The man next to him wore a snap-button shirt and had a weathered face. He looked like those drifter cowpokes who sometimes worked the roundup on his folks' ranch.

Then came Mr. Miner. At his elbow sat a beautiful, richly dressed, honey-haired woman. Next to her was the oddest member of this group, a Chinese man. He looked at Dan, his dark eyes seeming to stare into his soul.

The next man at the table wore an expensive suit. He looked like a businessman or a lawyer. But, it was the man next to the stranger who caused Dan to gape in surprise. This was a man Dan knew, Dr. Harry Lane—his very own doctor.

It was a Harry Lane Dan had never seen before. His brow was deeply furrowed. Black smudges darkened skin beneath anxious gray eyes that Dan had only seen show mirth or compassion. And those hands, ones Dan had felt gently bandage or console, were aimlessly twisting and turning.

What the heck was going on? It was only after his mind formed this question that Dan realized the older woman had begun talking. He stopped staring and began listening.

"Herman and I watched for a few hours, and finally Elliott came out. We hitched a ride on a scrap metal wagon and followed his cab. He went straight to his office in City Hall. Because the building has two doors, we had to split up. Lucky for us, there were cafes across from both the doors so we kept watch in comfort.

"Unfortunately, it was a wasted day. Elliott never came out of City Hall. We finally left to make this meeting."

While she spoke, the older man beside her nodded along. Dan surmised he was the "Herman," she mentioned. However, that left Dan wondering who the fellow Elliott was. He didn't ask because the sergeant had told him to stay quiet.

The sergeant must have read his mind because he leaned over to whisper in Dan's ear, "Lola Lane's been kidnapped. Elliott is the city engineer. He's involved. So is the Hess fellow we were hunting today. These folks are trying to find her. Sorry, I couldn't tell you before."

Dan struggled to wrap his mind around the enormity of what Hanke had just said. Why would someone kidnap the doctor's wife? Then he got it. Someone wanted to pressure Lane into doing something.

The Black man spoke next, in a low, cultured voice. Dan started, he remembered him. He was the maitre'd at that fancy Portland Hotel. He swallowed his surprise and listened to the man explain, "I enlisted the aid of numerous porters. They are adamant that no woman matching Mrs. Lane's description rode as a train passenger in the last twenty-four hours. Of course, the railway porters don't work on the suburban lines. But, the luggage porters working the station lobby are certain she didn't board a suburban line. Neither did any fellow with a white blaze in his hair. I fear we must conclude that, if they took Mrs. Lane from the city, it was not by train. I am fairly certain of that."

Silence fell until the cowboy cleared his throat and took his turn. He spoke in the slow drawl of the open prairie. "Wahl, I managed to haul my carcass into every downtown saloon. Lord a'mercy, I swear you folks must surely love to swill beer. You got a watering hole on every corner. I looked in every darn one, but I never caught sight of that snake, Hess. The whole day was a dry hole, despite all the beer I swallowed."

So, the man was not a local and likely a genuine cowboy. Dan thought it peculiar he'd be in the city helping to search for Lola Lane.

The cowboy spoke again. "One of Halloran's gals saw Hess yesterday. He told her he'd built a "little nest" for a bird. I take that to mean he does have Mrs. Lane."

Mr. Miner began speaking. "Well, this morning, Charlie and I slogged down the entire length of the Tanner Creek sewer. She's not being held there. Afterward, I roamed the streets and saw no sign of her or Hess." He looked at Dr. Lane who had grown ever more agitated as each person spoke of their failure to find Lola. "Harry, we will keep looking. At least we know some of the places she isn't."

The beautiful woman took a sip of water and looked straight at Dan with bright blue eyes. His heart skipped and his face reddened. After flashing him a faint smile, she looked at Dr. Lane and said, "Harry, I looked, and I sent out runners. My women colleagues did the same. We are fairly certain she's not imprisoned in a whorehouse. There were easily twenty people out looking and asking. I'm so sorry."

Dr. Lane nodded, his lips a tight, white line. He cleared his throat to say, "I thank you for taking the trouble, Miz Lucinda." The doctor had struggled to speak.

The Chinese man spoke softly, saying, "My news not better. The cousins search the underground. They also look on every street. Never see man with white streak in hair. Never see doctor's lady wife."

When Dr. Lane dropped his face into his hands, the suited man beside him reached an arm around his shoulders and leaned to murmur into his ear.

Beside him, Hanke cleared his throat, startling Dan. The sergeant said, "Well, when searching the saloons I also experienced nothing but "dry holes" like Charlie. I'd assigned myself the west side of the North End. After searching every street and saloon, I found nothing. No Hess. No Mrs. Lane.

"However, unexpectedly and with a little bit of effort," he held up a bunched right fist, "I got a bit of information from one of the special police. I don't know how helpful it will be. He talked to Hess yesterday. All he could tell me was that Hess said he'd been on the fairgrounds, liked seeing Little Egypt dance, and wanted to know which streetcar would take him to Albina. My informant told him to take the streetcar that crosses the Steel Bridge."

Dr. Lane groaned again. Hanke rushed to add, "But, we learned something that reinforces the idea they might be holding Mrs. Lane over in Albina. Officer Carter, here, did spot Hess." All eyes turned on Dan as Hanke urged, "Go ahead, Carter. Tell them what happened."

Dan straightened in his seat and shot a glance toward Dr. Lane. He was dismayed to see hope on the doctor's face. It hurt, knowing he would disappoint. "I'm sorry Dr. Lane. I'm near certain I saw Hess but I lost him when he jumped aboard a streetcar. There were so many people pushing to get on the fairground cars that I couldn't reach his streetcar in time. But, he didn't get on a fairground car. He got on the one that goes to the east side, across the Steel Bridge, and ends up in Albina."

"But, there are hundreds of places in Albina where they could be hiding her!" cried Lane.

Dan was horrified to see tears spill out and run down the doctor's face.

Mr. Miner spoke up, "Harry, we will keep looking. You go to that rally. If we find her, we will bring her there. If we don't find her before it is time for you to speak, go ahead and announce you're dropping your candidacy. You don't have a choice. But know that, no matter what, we will be looking for Lola throughout the night. We will keep searching until we find her!"

The Chinese man spoke again, his voice calm as he directed his words at Dan, "Officer Carter, please to tell us exactly what man Hess look like—top to bottom. Close eyes. Make picture."

Dan closed his eyes and thought, trying to recall exactly what he had seen. He started at the top. "He wore a brown crush hat. You know, the kind that keeps its shape even if you stuff it in a pocket. Kinda like what the sergeant is wearing right now. I only saw that streak in his hair because Hess was near running and the hat almost flew off his head. He shot up a hand to catch it."

Dan let his memory drift lower. "His coat was also brown. It had a plaid pattern—dark brown with black stripes and hung below his butt."

Dan's eyes flew open, and he shot an embarrassed look at the two women. "Sorry, ma'ams, I forgot my manners." Both women smiled at him.

He shut his eyes again to picture the man's pants. "His trousers were light brown. Maybe they were canvas or they could'a been wool. I'm not sure. His boots were also light brown, I think. But maybe that was the mud."

An exclamation came from the far end of the table. Dan opened his eyes to see Mr. Miner leaning forward, his eyes intent. "Did you say 'mud'?" His tone was sharp.

Dan hesitated, "Why, yes, I just remembered that. There was mud on his trouser cuffs and thick mud on his boots. All caked. That's why I'm unsure whether his boots were brown or black. I only saw the muddy heels. He was moving fast."

Miner jumped up, knocking his chair over. His voice allowed no opposition as he ordered, "Harry, you and Montague must stay here until it's time for the rally. Go, if we're not back by then.

Mr. Solomon and Lucinda my dear, I'm afraid, neither of you is dressed for the next part of our search. So, please stick with Dr. Lane. Help keep him safe.

"Everyone else, except for Mr. Fong, head over to Albina. Meet us in front of the Albina School on Russell between Williams and Vancouver. You might have to wait a bit for us to get there."

By this time, all were on their feet, every face wearing an expression of mixed hope and perplexity. Dan also wondered what got Miner so excited. A partial answer came when Miner turned to Dr. Lane and said, "Harry, I'm pretty certain I know where they're holding your wife."

The doctor looked stunned until he grinned and declared, "Thank the blessed Lord. I'll do what you say. Godspeed, my dear friends!"

Miner nodded and looked at everyone else. "Okay, folks. Let's get our fannies in a'movin', as Ma likes to say!"

Seconds later, coats were donned and people rushed out the door. Once they reached the sidewalk, Sergeant Hanke gave Dan a stout cuff on the shoulder and said heartily, "You did a mighty fine job observing, Officer Carter."

Prideful pleasure, and the cuff, nearly toppled Dan before he picked up his heels and trotted after his swift-moving sergeant.

THIRTY

May 10, 1905

WITH THE LEWIS AND CLARK exposition extravaganza underway, the sidewalks were crowded with people eager to board the fairground streetcars. It being late afternoon, they likely hoped to see the electric lights turn the exposition grounds into a sparkling fairyland.

Sage thought that would be something to see, despite the lights being a blatant promotion by the electric company. Every year brought more electrified buildings and more fires since all those hot wires were unregulated.

Today, the dense crowds on sidewalks and streetcars meant Sage couldn't talk to Fong because it would be noticed and they'd be overheard.

Once they'd stepped off the streetcar at the Buckman stop, and were walking deeper into the neighborhood, Sage said, "I vaguely remember Emil telling me that, on one of the days when I wasn't working, Riner sent him to build a tool shed at a construction site in Albina. I've learned that construction sites are very muddy this time of year. All the tromping around in the rain turns a worksite into muck underfoot."

"Ah," Fong nodded, "You think mud on Hess boots come from there?"

"Yup. Anyway, it's the best lead we've got."

"Where we go now?"

"We have to ask Emil where to find that Albina construction site. Maybe have him show us if he'll go."

"We maybe rescue Lola by ourselves. Others not get hurt that way."

"I'm not happy about them helping but we don't know how many men are guarding her. And besides, we don't want any of them to get away. Hanke needs to be there to make the arrests."

"Surprise you take me with you to Emil's house."

"We might run into a fight there. Elliott and Riner are desperate to find the foreman, Muckleroy. They need his testimony to support their fabricated story of bribery and sabotage. Those two galoots might still be watching Emil's house."

"You need me when only two galoots?"

"Well, thank you for thinking I can tackle them on my own, Teacher. But time is short. We've got to handle this quickly with no delays. We both know you can make that happen faster than me."

Reaching Emil's front door, Sage knocked loudly and glanced around. He saw no one watching the house.

When Emil opened the door, he blinked at seeing Sage. "Well, my goodness. Here you are again." He peered around Sage to see Fong. His face registered surprise but he said, "Come on in, the both of you. The wife has just brewed a pot of coffee. You're most welcome."

Sage held up a hand, saying, "Sorry Emil, but we can't come in. No time. It's an urgent matter. We're hoping you'll guide us to the Riners' Albina construction site—the one where you built the shed. I'll explain why on the way."

Emil nodded and turned to holler, "Esther, I need to leave with John Miner!" Quickly donning a coat and clapping on a cap, he stepped out, shut the door behind him, and led them to the sidewalk.

As they strolled rapidly toward the streetcar line, Sage told Emil about Lola Lane's kidnapping, the demand made by the kidnappers, and Harry Lane's intention to comply. "If she isn't rescued before he has to speak at tonight's rally, he will announce his withdrawal as a candidate."

"Criminy!" was Emil's response as he picked up the pace.

Minutes later, they jumped on a streetcar heading west. When it reached the river's east bank, they switched to a northbound streetcar. They rode down Williams Avenue until getting off at a stop three blocks past Russell Street.

Emil led them toward a construction site. He said it would be best to survey the site from inside an adjacent grove of Douglas fir trees. Entering the grove's north side, they carefully made their way toward its far side.

Heavy undergrowth, a clutter of downed branches, ferns, and Oregon grape, made for slow going. They also had to step carefully because no rain patters covered the sound of their advance. Nor did the air ring with the normal job site sounds of hammers pounding or workers shouting. Sage ducked behind the foremost tree and peered around it, while Emil and Fong took up posts behind nearby trees.

No one was working on the half-built house. Nothing moved. All was still. That silence was worrying. Did it mean Lola wasn't here? Was he wrong? He saw only a vacant building site and heard only bird twitter and a distant train whistle.

Dismayed, Sage stared at the tool shed. He sighed, only to start at a light tap on his shoulder. He turned to see Fong crouched behind him. His friend pointed at the farthest corner of the shed. Sage squinted. There was a trickle of smoke wafting out from behind the shed's hidden side.

Sage grinned with relief and beckoned for Emil to advance. Once he joined them, Sage whispered, "What's on the shed's far side?'

"Riner had me attach an overhang to it. It extends about six feet wide and runs the whole end of the shed. That's where we store the lumber and wire. And, that's where the men sit to eat their lunch."

Sage thought. "So, we better see who is sitting there smoking a cigarette."

Fong nodded and slipped away toward the far end of the grove. A few anxious minutes later he returned and held up five fingers. "Not all carpenters. No tools on belts."

That's great, Sage thought. It meant Lola Lane was inside that shed. He considered the odds. It wasn't just his and Fong's ability to overcome five men. They could do it. They'd done it before. But this time, there was Lola Lane's safety to consider. A single captor could end her life. Prudence required more rescuers. He turned to Fong. "I think Emil should fetch the others. He can lead them to us."

Fong didn't hesitate. "Best idea," he said.

Sage quickly described the where and who of their reinforcements. Emil immediately retreated into the grove. Once he reached the street, he'd fetch the others from in front of the Russell Street school. He'd cover six blocks coming and going. It would take a while.

Their wait felt endless and full of worry. If Lola Lane wasn't in that shed, they were wasting precious time. Worse, he had no idea where to look next. Sage couldn't remember ever feeling this anxious.

At last, the sound of sticks snapping beneath footfalls sounded from behind them. Sage and Fong retreated to the grove's interior where they found Emil, Hanke, Carter, Mae, Herman, and Charlie waiting. It was a relief to see their somber faces.

Quickly, he laid out the plan he and Fong had settled on. "There's likely to be fisticuffs, so we have to divide our force. Mr. Fong, Sergeant Hanke, Charlie, and I will start a fight. Emil, you know this construction worksite. Do you think you can find something to break that padlock off the shed door?"

The carpenter nodded. "No problem. I'll come up with something."

Sage looked at each of them in turn before he got to the heart of the plan. "First, six of us will get to the door-side of the shed. If that goes well, Emil will look for something to break the padlock. "Emil, you and Officer Carter will run across with us. Emil, once we get there, stick close to the shed wall. We don't want those fellows to see you wandering around."

He turned to the young policeman, "Officer Carter, you'll protect Emil."

He turned to Mae and Herman. "Once Emil is ready to bust the lock, he'll motion for you to run over as fast as you can." They both nodded silently.

Sage continued. "The next part is tricky. We four men will sneak up on those hanging out under the overhang. We'll make noise and distract them.

"When that ruckus starts, Emil will break the padlock off with Officer Carter standing guard. Once the door is open, the three of you, Mae, Herman, and Emil, grab Mrs. Lane and get her into the trees. Don't stop for anything. Keep going. Hail a cab, wagon, streetcar, or whatever you can and get her away. Take her to the restaurant."

Sage turned to Officer Carter. "As soon as they make the trees, Carter, you run to help us on the other side of the shed. Arrests will need to be made."

Sage turned to Emil. "Look, I know you'd like to be part of the dustup but there are two reasons why you can't be. First, those men might recognize you. We don't know what the future holds, and they know where you live. We can't put you and your wife in jeopardy. Second, we need you to lead and protect the other three once Officer Carter stops guarding. One of the bad guys might chase you. You know how to get away because you know this area best."

Emil's determined nod made agreement with the plan unanimous. Sage turned and led the seven others toward the grove's edge. Soon everyone stood concealed behind a tree.

❀ ❀ ❀

Mae watched Sage, Charlie, Hanke, Fong, Carter, and Emil quickly cross the thirty yards of thick mud to hide behind the shed. No one appeared around the building's far corner. She sighed with relief as Emil started searching the ground while Carter guarded his back.

Emil picked something up, straightened, looked toward the fir trees, and beckoned. She and Eich exchanged glances before heading across the muck. Once they reached the shed, Sage's hand squeezed Mae's shoulder before motioning for the four fighters to split up. Seconds later, they began creeping alongside the shed toward the overhang, two to each side.

Lola's remaining rescuers waited beside the shed door, straining to hear the start of a ruckus. Soon, shouts and cries filled the air.

Emil jammed a length of metal into the gap between hasp and wood. Next, he laid his weight atop the metal lever until the hasp ripped free with the muted screech of screws releasing their grip. The hasp, still carrying the locked padlock, swung loose.

Emil opened the door slowly. They all peered inside. The only light inside came from the open doorway. At first, Mae saw nothing. But then, she breathed a sigh of relief. In the far corner, Lola Lane sat bolt upright on a cot, her eyes blinking at the sudden light, her hands gripping a short length of 2x4.

"Lola!" Mae whispered urgently. "It's Mae Clemens and others come to rescue you! Are you tied up?"

The woman jumped up. "No," she whispered back, "They figured the padlock was enough."

It was hard to hear her because the noise beyond the shed wall was increasing, meaning a free-for-all was underway.

Worry twinged through Mae until she remembered that Mr. Fong was with him. She quickly stepped to Lola's side. "Hurry, we must get out of here," she said, wrapping her arm around Lola to guide her from the shed.

Lola Lane didn't resist nor did she need help. Her step was sure.

Outside, a vigilant Carter was scanning the surroundings. At his nod, the four of them began their run toward the fir grove. A few steps into the tree line, Mae glanced over her shoulder but couldn't see the fighting men though she did see Carter running toward the fray.

Taking a final look, her gaze lighted on a young man. He was rounding the corner of the half-built house, loaded down with lunch tins. He must have seen them entering the trees because he halted and stared in their direction. Dropping the tins, he shouted and began running toward the grove.

At first, Mae ran after Lola and the others. Then she paused. Their most important task was to get Lola Lane to her husband. That meant she needed to slow the man down. Fortunately, Sage and his buddies were keeping the other captors busy. They couldn't be giving chase.

Ahead, Lola was disappearing, sandwiched between Eich and Emil who each held an elbow. They were lifting her over the undergrowth and fallen logs, making a speedy escape.

As she followed, Mae's skirts kept snaring on the sticks and plants. Cursing, she lifted the skirt to her thighs. "Damnable skirts. Don't know why women can't wear trousers," she muttered.

A jolt of fear popped that thought as if it were a soap bubble. Close behind her, twigs were snapping beneath hurrying feet. The rascal was in the woods.

A few steps ahead loomed a grandfather fir. Reaching it, she jumped to its backside and swished her damnable skirt out of sight. A frantic search, and she silently whooped. A stout branch lay at her feet. She snatched it up, squeezed its rough bark in a two-handed grip, and waited.

Gasping breath and heavy footsteps approached. She sent a prayer skyward and tightened her hold. She'd only have one chance.

As the man lumbered past her, he must have sensed a movement. Yet, he turned too late to dodge the heavy stick swinging at his head like a baseball bat. It was a lucky blow that sent him pitching forward onto his knees.

She didn't hesitate. She gave his head another clout. He stopped trying to get up. However, Mae was relieved when he moved and started groaning. Dropping the tree limb, she quickly unlaced his boots, tugged them off, and flung them in opposite directions. Then she lifted her skirt and ran.

Sage charged toward the man who had a streak in his hair—Hess—finally! Charlie, Hanke, and Fong were already attacking, even as Hanke shouted "police" at the top of his lungs.

Hanke's shouts made no difference. Not one of the five raised his hands in surrender. Nor did any man try to run away. Instead, they advanced, each holding either a length of two-by-four or a glinting knife.

Turning back to Hess, Sage noted that the assassin's stocky body looked to be all muscle. For a brief moment, Sage was glad his training had always been with the similarly short Fong. Sage studied the cold black eyes and the sneer on his opponent's face. The way Hess held the knife in his right hand meant he was experienced. But of course, he was—being a paid assassin and all, Sage thought wryly.

According to Fong, run was the first response to any knife-wielding attacker. Not possible in this situation. His mother and the others needed time to rescue Lola and get away. Besides, these five belonged in jail—especially Hess.

Sage backed away, his eyes fixed on the knife as Fong had instructed. His foot encountered a length of lumber. Eyes still on the knife, Sage snatched it up. Now things were a bit more equal. Fong had been teaching him the saber form of the snake and crane martial art. He hoped he remembered the moves. Or, maybe he'd feint a jab with the wood as a distraction. What he did would depend on Hess's moves.

Sage stepped into a wide stance, his right foot back, his knees slightly bent, with his side turned toward Hess. His right hand held the lumber, ready to swing it forward to strike or feint.

Hess grinned, his brown, broken teeth ugly in his face before he lunged, leading with his knife hand. Sage instinctively dropped the wood and sidestepped. He grabbed Hess's arm, sending the knife streaking past, narrowly missing his hip.

Instantly, Sage's rear leg snapped forward, his knee jamming Hess in the gut even as his hands twisted Hess's stabbing arm and jerked his shoulder in a painful direction. The knife dropped into the mud. Sage heel-kicked it behind him.

Hess wasn't finished. He used his forward momentum to slam into Sage, knocking him off balance. Sage didn't fall, but it broke his power stance. He backed away. As he regained his center, he heard the smack of flesh hitting flesh and cries of pain.

He glanced sideways and saw Fong fighting two attackers. Of course. Those were Fong's favorite odds.

Having regained his balance, Hess advanced again with his fists raised before his face. It was time to end this. They had arrests to make.

And, a rally they couldn't miss. Certainly, by now, the other four were safely on their way.

He waited until Hess moved within striking distance before stepping back again. Confidence bloomed on Hess's face as he advanced once more. Sage took a single step back and pretended to stumble and fall to the ground. Using his elbows to prop himself up, he stared up into Hess's face, hoping he looked defeated. The man sneered as he shifted his weight onto his front foot, ready to deliver a rib or head kick.

A lightning-fast Sage jammed his left foot onto Hess's forward foot to hold it in place. In the same instant, Sage brought his right foot up to slam against the back of Hess's knee.

That combination of moves sent Hess falling into the dirt. Before Hess could recover, Sage was atop his back, grabbing his hands, and yanking them high. He gave Hess's arms a violent jerk and heard the pop of shoulders dislocating. Hess screamed. Through gritted teeth, Sage hissed, "That should teach you not to kick old men in the ribs!"

Sage cast about for the electrical wire Emil said was stored beneath the overhang. A coil of it lay nearby. Stretching, Sage managed to grab it and soon had Hess hog-tied, his wrists and ankles bound together. Charlie will be impressed, Sage thought.

Once Hess was secure, Sage looked to see how his friends fared. Hanke was delivering a powerful right cross to his opponent's jaw. It was a knockout punch, having started from down low. Once his man was down, the Sergeant bent over, hands on his knees, to catch his breath. His eyes met Sage's and they exchanged grins.

Just then, Hanke's opponent got to his feet, grabbed up a board, and charged the sergeant. He never reached him because Dan Carter flew at least five feet through the air to knock him off his feet. Seconds later, Carter had the man on his stomach, a pair of handcuffs cinched around his wrists.

In the other direction, Fong's two opponents were also kissing the mud. One lay curled on his side, hands clutching his middle. The other was silently holding his head. Both were done.

Sage grabbed up Hess's knife, He cut through the wire still connected to Hess. He tossed the coil to Fong, who caught it and quickly bound his captives' hands.

That left only Charlie. His fight had moved at least twenty feet from the shed. Charlie was making the most of it. The other man was big. He was built like what Mae called a 'brick shithouse.' He looked to be at least half a foot taller and twice as wide as the cowboy.

But, years of range riding and horse breaking had served Charlie well. He was nimble, wiry, and deceptively strong. His snapped punches left the big guy reeling every time he lurched toward the cowboy, staggering like a drunk, throwing weak punches that didn't connect.

Meanwhile, Charlie darted and danced around in his pointy cowboy boots; his leather-covered fists unerringly finding the man's vital parts.

Though it was satisfying to watch, Sage finally hollered, "Fun's over, Charlie! We got to get going." Even as those words issued from his mouth, Charlie swung a brutal uppercut into the other man's jaw. Head snapping back, his body following, the man hit the ground. He wouldn't be getting up for a while.

Hanke strode over to Sage, hauling his groggy, handcuffed captive along. He looked at Hess and shook his head before saying, "We best get moving. We need to get these felons jailed and Mrs. Lane delivered to her husband."

THIRTY ONE

SAGE, CHARLIE, AND FONG ENTERED through the kitchen. They found only Eich and Emil waiting in Mozart's empty dining room. Sage looked around. "Where are Harry, Lola, Mae, Montague, and the others?"

Eich smiled. "I guess you don't have a pocket watch. It's after 6:30. The rally will soon start. Harry, Montague, and the carpenter guards were gone when we got here.

"Mae and Lola are upstairs. Mrs. Lane says there's no way she's appearing before all those people in a filthy, torn dress. She put up a fight when they grabbed her. She says she gave one of them a bloody nose."

Minutes later, footsteps descended the stairs. Mae appeared, followed by Lola Lane wearing his mother's best dress. It was a bit tight but presentable. Mae grabbed two coats off the rack and gave one to Lola who donned it hurriedly.

Lola started for the door and then paused. "Did you get all the rascals?" adding in a firm voice, "Aren't you coming?"

"Yes to both questions," Sage said, jumping up. Outside Mozart's front door, a big carriage waited. No doubt an example of Eich's foresight. Seven was a tight fit but no one minded. They were too ecstatic.

Once underway to the Armory, he told of the fight to capture the five men, ending with, "Somehow, we ended up with a sixth bad guy. He staggered out of the woods, holding his head. Didn't even try to resist. Once all six were tied up, we hauled them over to Williams Avenue and enlisted the aid of a Jewish vegetable peddler. He'd sold all of his produce

LOOTERS & LEECHES | 203

and was heading home to South Portland. Turns out, he knows Herman. Anyway, eleven of us climbed aboard his empty wagon.

The peddler drove us to police headquarters. After hearing about Lola's abduction he refused to take our money.

"Hanke and Carter herded them into the station. The sergeant said he'd put them in separate jail cells. He hopes one of them will spill the beans."

His tale finished, Sage looked at his mother. "I don't suppose you know what, to quote that sixth fellow, 'blankety-blank woman' hit him with a tree limb and stole his boots?"

The noise in the armory was rising. Harry checked his pocket watch for the umpteenth time. Seven-thirty. The rally had started promptly at seven. They had no choice. Increasingly restless supporters filled the auditorium. Many had already been standing for at least an hour.

Harry's speech was to follow those of three introductory speakers. He had insisted that his friend, Dick, speak just before himself. Montague didn't relish public speaking. Consequently, he was the master of brief speeches. So, he'd blanched when Harry begged him to talk as long as he possibly could.

Harry was stalling, hoping that his Lola would walk in through the doors at the back of the auditorium before he had to take the podium.

Poor Dick Montague was doing his best, sweat now trickling down his face. His words were faltering and his voice so hoarse that his throat must hurt. Worse, folks were becoming rudely restive, moving around and talking loudly. Harry crossed to the podium and laid a gentle hand on his friend's sleeve. Dick stopped speaking mid-sentence, grimaced an apology, and stepped aside. His face went crimson at the crowd's relieved whoops and hollers.

Now it was up to Harry to stall things for as long as he could. He had already decided he'd start with family history and go on from there. Poor souls.

Opening his mouth he began, "I'm going to start by talking about my grandfather, General Joseph Lane." This was going to be difficult. He wasn't proud of his grandfather who'd led brutal army campaigns first against Mexicans, and then against American Indian tribes. The general had openly joked about "taking a turn with the squaws." That brutality had won Lane the appointment as Oregon's first territorial governor. Worse, in later years he'd been vocally pro-slavery, running for vice president on the pro-slavery ticket against Lincoln. His grandfather was everything Harry despised.

He might as well start there. Before announcing he was dropping out of the race, they'd get to hear how his values differed greatly from those of his illustrious ancestor. Maybe the evolution of Lane family values toward a more compassionate sensibility would stick in their minds and give them hope that society could and did change.

As their carriage rolled to a stop, they saw that the armory doors and windows were propped open. People filled the sidewalk and spilled into the street. All were silent as they strained to hear the campaign speeches coming from inside. That mass of folks blocked their way.

Then there was a stirring amongst the crowd as Hanke and Dan Carter, with the help of four burly officers, began clearing a path from the carriage to the door. The officers, along with the four men from the carriage, quickly formed a wedge with Mae and Lola walking in the middle. Hanke took the apex position, elbowing people aside while proclaiming loudly, "Make way for Mrs. Harry Lane!"

Initially grumbling resistance met his efforts. But when those at the back of the crowd saw Lola, they gave way. Astonished murmurs replaced their initial irritation: "Why isn't she already inside next to her husband? Why does she have so much police protection?" But even as they questioned, they joined the effort to get Harry's wife inside.

When he entered the auditorium, Sage heard Harry's voice. As always, the doctor held the audience in the palm of his hand. Scattered titters and outright laughter broke the otherwise deathly silence of the crowd.

Hanke and his officers continued to edge forward, quietly moving people aside, clearing a passage for Mrs. Lane. Once people saw the police officers, they quickly obeyed. Sage and everyone else brought up the rear.

Harry must have noticed the commotion because he suddenly stopped talking. Sage finally spied him. Lane stood on tiptoe at the edge of the elevated stage, straining to see. When the crowd finally parted sufficiently, wonder transformed his face. With a shout, he jumped off the stage and ran towards Lola, his eyes shiny with tears. The crowd silenced at the sight.

Lola strode rapidly forward with greater dignity and a radiant face. Seconds later, her husband's fervent embrace lifted her off her feet.

For a few moments, they held each other, exchanging whispers, alone in the crowd. When they stepped apart, Harry looked at Sage and the others with gratitude suffusing his face. He opened his mouth but closed it when Sage put a single finger before his lips. Harry nodded in understanding. Sage pointed at Hanke and Dan Carter, motioning toward the stage.

Harry took Lola's hand, grabbed Sergeant Hanke by the elbow, and gestured with his head for Officer Carter to follow. He led all three toward the stage. Once on it, Harry again took the podium, with Lola on one side, and Hanke and Carter on the other side. He turned and beckoned a reluctant Dick Montague to join them.

Harry grinned at the crowd. "Boy howdy, this has been one helluva day! Do I have a story to tell you!" he exclaimed. He wrapped an arm around Lola's shoulders and pulled her close. "For those of you who don't know, this lovely lady is my wife, Mrs. Lola Bailey Lane."

That triggered loud clapping. Once it settled, he continued, "Yesterday, Lola was kidnapped. The kidnappers didn't want money. They wanted me to stand before you tonight and tell you I was dropping out of the mayoral race. They said if I didn't, they would end her life." Angry cries and shouts greeted his words.

Once quiet returned, Harry continued, "I know you felt restless having to listen to Dick Montague here," he gestured at his friend, "yammer on endlessly. Believe me; he hated it more than you did!" Roaring laughter greeted that declaration.

"But, he was doing me and Lola a tremendous favor. We had to buy time. We needed sufficient time for some very hard-working, wonderful people to find my Lola."

He turned to Hanke standing by his side. "Sergeant Hanke, of the Portland Police, was one of her rescuers." He pointed at Dan Carter, "And so was Officer Carter. Tell us, gentlemen, did you capture the miscreants?"

When Hanke nodded, Lane clapped him on the shoulder. "Tell us, who were they? And, where are they now?"

Hanke cleared his throat and reported, in his most official voice, "We currently hold six men in custody. We believe one of them is a paid assassin brought into town to kill Dr. Lane. All six were captured outside the structure where Mrs. Lane was imprisoned." Cheers resounded and stomping feet thundered.

Harry asked Hanke the foremost question. "Do you suspect Mayor Williams masterminded this attempt to interfere with the election?"

Hanke didn't hesitate. "No, we have no evidence that Mayor Williams knew anything about either plot."

Harry felt compelled to underscore Hanke's answer. He turned to the audience and declared, "I consider George Williams to be a good-hearted, decent fellow. His only failing, unfortunately, is that he doesn't stand up to powerful men. But I believe, with head and heart, that George Williams had nothing to do with any plots."

Lane turned back to Hanke, asking, "Have you identified and captured the people who directed the assassination plot and my wife's kidnapping?"

"Well, we have some leads. We're looking at two individuals, in particular. One has fled the city. We will be talking to the other one very soon."

The crowd erupted, many demanding to know who the masterminds were.

Hanke raised a hand to halt the noise and said, "Sorry, I can't tell you that. We're still gathering evidence. And, we still have to interrogate the six men we just captured."

Protests broke out that Lane quickly quieted by raising his hand. He turned to Hanke and said, "Sergeant please escort Mrs. Lane to a chair."

Turning back to his rapt audience, he said, "Now, dear friends, I want to tell you what I intend to do should I win this election."

The six jailed men were glum. Each was locked into his cell, kept as far from each other as possible. When one of them attempted to confer, the police guard raised his baton, hit the cell bars, and told him to shut up or get clubbed. After that, all was silent except for the town drunks' snores and mumbles.

Hanke returned to the station elated. The armory hadn't cleared out until after nine. He'd sent two of his best men, and Dan Carter, home with Lane and his wife. Fong had also gone with them. Hanke suspected the Chinese man would stay by Lane's side for the duration of the campaign.

He paced before the cells, peering at his prisoners, looking for the most nervous man among the six. The man he settled on was the bootless one Mae Clemens hit with a tree branch. Hanke ordered him escorted to the interrogation room.

It was a dirty-walled, gray space, calculated to depress and dishearten even the merriest soul. Tonight that effect was unnecessary since this fellow, who said his name was Dougie Dinsmore, looked thoroughly crushed. He kept his eyes downcast, while his rough hands trembled and his fleshy lower lip quivered. He kept fingering a lump on the side of his closely shaved head.

Hanke cleared his throat. "I guess I needn't tell you that you're in a lot of trouble," he said, giving his voice sympathetic warmth.

The young man nodded. "No, Sir. I surely know I'm in big trouble. But we weren't going to hurt that lady. He said we'd just keep her a few days and then let her go."

"Did he tell you why?"

"Wahl, he said her husband owed some rich man money and we took her so he'd pay up. We weren't going to hurt her!"

"Why did you think she wouldn't get hurt?"

"Because some of us asked. He promised we wouldn't hurt her. I never woulda had nothing to do with it otherwise."

"What do you think he planned to do about the fact she'd seen all your faces? That she could identify every one of you, including him?"

Dinsmore's face blanched. He looked down at his hands and then up at Hanke, his mouth gaping. Horrified he asked, "You think he planned to kill her, no matter what?"

"I'm afraid so, Dougie. Who told you that she'd be released after only a few days and that her husband owed money? Who was in charge?"

"That fellow Hess. He paid us fifteen dollars apiece for just two days work. The job was supposed to end tomorrow."

"Well, Dougie, every single thing he told you was a lie." Then, Hanke told him what Hess was really up to. As he told the barebones story, Dinsmore initially shrank down in his chair but by the end, he was upright with anger.

"You're right. Everything that Hess told us was a lie—beginning to end. He never said none of that. He's a low-down, dirty bastard."

Hanke believed Dinsmore was genuinely outraged and telling the truth.

He could use that anger. "Well, I can't speak for the prosecutor but, if you help us convict Hess and the men behind him, I'll put in a good word for you with the prosecutor. He might go easy on you."

Dinsmore straightened and said, "I'll do it, Sergeant. What do you want to know?"

Hanke smiled. "Let me get you some coffee and food. We're going to be here a while." He left the room and came back with two coffee mugs, a sandwich, and an officer who settled down in a corner, notepad and pencil in hand.

Hanke was encouraged. Dinsmore looked eager and determined. He wanted to tell his story. After setting the mug and food in front of the man, Hanke said, "Okay, Dougie, start from the beginning. Tell me everything that happened."

EPILOGUE

Mid-June, 1905

SAGE BREATHED DEEPLY, SAVORING THE mix of wood smoke, sweet summer air, and Lucinda's perfume. He sat on the log, his arm around her, and felt contentment. Westward, the setting sun touched the western ridge with shimmering gold and blackened the river. The distant murmur of the busy city drifted across the water. "What a perfect place!" he said, loud enough for all to hear.

Smiles and nods greeted his declaration. Looking at their faces, he felt such tenderness. It wasn't bonfire smoke stinging his eyes.

His mother, Mae, was holding hands with Herman. Sergeant Hanke was sharing a joke with Angus Solomon. Fong and Sprig Flowers were regaling Emil and his wife Esther, with their Harry Lane guarding adventures, while Charlie Siringo and his wife, Xenobia, were updating Lucinda on their hilarious goat-raising efforts.

These people had worked as a team to accomplish the near impossible. They'd thwarted two assassinations and a kidnapping. In doing so, they were directly responsible for the election of a mayor who would shepherd the city into a brighter future. That newly elected mayor was stepping from the woodsy shade, his arms carrying wood for the fire he'd just built.

This was an odd place for their traditional celebratory gathering. Usually everyone met at Mozart's immediately after a mission to recount their adventure and its ending. But, this time, Harry had insisted that they wait until after the general election to gather here on Ross Island.

So, here they were, in the middle of the Willamette River, butts on peeled logs, having just shared a long and detailed recounting of all that had happened since that March night when Meachum and St. Vincent came to town.

Harry and Hanke imparted mostly good news about the aftermath. The city engineer and both Riners, father and son, had been indicted for the Tanner Creek sewer scandal. The elder Riner had fled to San Francisco, leaving his son to face trial. The Tanner sewer was being redone and the Riners wouldn't be paid a penny.

Engineer Elliott was talking to the prosecutor, hoping to trade bribery information for his freedom. He'd probably succeed. Still, he hadn't gotten off scot-free. With Williams voted out of office, Elliott resigned from city employment. From Eich came the report that, to the neighborhood's delight, Elliot's wife had packed her bags and left him.

The Lane kidnappers were still in jail awaiting trial—all except Dougie Dinsmore. He'd returned to the family farm, chastened, and vowing to stay there. The assassin, Hess, was being extradited to Los Angeles where he was certain to be hung for murder. They believed Elliott and brewer, Jasper Helmut, were the masterminds behind the Lane debacle. But, Hess wasn't talking. And, he was the only one who knew.

Once their mission wrap-up concluded, Harry and Lola voiced profuse thanks. A comfortable silence followed until Harry stood and announced he would gather more firewood.

Now that he had returned, Harry added small logs to the fire, took his seat on the log next to Lola, and remarked, "Never any shortage of wood because of all the log rafts tied round the island."

Lola laughed and told them, "Harry loves this island almost as much as he loves building bonfires. He says it's the one place in the city where he revisits his childhood. You know, as a youngster, he spent many days with the Indian tribe living near Corvallis. I think that experience is why my Harry is such a good man."

Harry hugged her to him as he said, "Lola, you're embarrassing me. But, it's true. I do love this island—its history and all the animals that make it their home. It's unbelievable that something like this exists in the middle of our city. I've said it once and, I'll say it again: this should be a nature park. Frederic Law Olmsted's 1903 report agrees with me."

"Watch out, Harry's about to ride his favorite hobbyhorse," declared Lola, making everyone laugh.

Clearly, this island meant a lot to Harry. He'd guided them along paths that wound through dense undergrowth, beneath old trees, and across a rock-strewn dry channel to nearby Hard Tack Island.

At one point, Harry paused beneath an old oak tree, his face sad. "Fall, when the rains come, this is where I find the best mushrooms. I wonder if I'll get to pick them." That was the only time Harry mentioned the sacrifices he faced once he was in office.

As they followed him, Harry frequently paused to talk like a naturalist, pointing out fledging heron chicks flapping their wings on the edges of stick nests or gulping river carp dropped by their parents. According to Harry, nearly fifty species of birds lived here. Certainly, the surrounding water and plentiful black cottonwoods, white oaks, ash, and pacific madrone made for a sheltering habitat.

Now, with sundown taking hold, those birds added their chorus of cackles, clucks, whistles, churrs, and hoots to the cheer-up song of the plentiful robins. Sage was amazed such wildness existed within a mile of Mozart's Table and vowed to return.

Dusk settled around them and Harry rose from his log to toss more wood on the fire. Resuming his seat, he looked around and said, "If you don't mind, I'd like to tell you this island's history." At their murmured agreement he continued, "I'm sure the Multnomahs used this island before the white man came but that's history lost.

"Around 1846, a white man named Sherry Ross land-claimed the island and started a dairy farm on its 400 acres. His daughter was the first white child born in the Portland area. After some years, the island became a rowdy place where there was gambling, drinking, and you know what else. In the mid-1880s a bank clerk, named James Smith, was murdered in the island's saloon. Citizens' hue and cry over the murder shut down the saloon. Next, the police department claimed it. It would put its injured horses here to recover. That use ended when one of the horses missed life on the streets so much that it swam across the river and found its way back to the police stable.

"Since then, the island has been a recreation site. People boat here for picnics and to relish its fecund wildness. Like we've done today. My dream is to see this island and those three adjacent, become our city's crown jewel park. That's what Olmsted recommended."

The city's soon-to-be mayor took a deep breath, ran a hand through his unruly hair, and said, "I'm done lecturing. Though, I do thank you. You've been attentive as cats waiting to be tossed fish guts." He slapped his thighs, stood, and declared, "Let's get those sausages roasting."

Everyone laughed as the women rose to fetch plates, utensils, and bowls of food from wicker baskets while the men pulled out pocket knives to sharpen sausage sticks. An hour later bellies were full, the fire had died down, and the full moon was rising. They began packing up.

Sage walked through the underbrush to stand on the sandy beach. Across the water faint lights shone from house windows alongside the river and away up the hill. He wondered what the future held for this new western city.

"It's beautiful, isn't it?" Harry spoke at Sage's shoulder. "Portland is a jewel surrounded by incredible beauty in every direction. But for me, as Will Shakespeare wrote, 'What is the city but the people?' The people are what matter most to me—the people of my tribe with all their beauty and variety."

Sage turned to look at him. Harry's face was solemn as he continued, "I promise you that I will do my utmost to make this beautiful city a better place for every soul living here."

"I know you will, Harry. I have faith in you. We all do."

"I appreciate that support and what you all did for Lola and me. But, I must warn you. Don't hold illusions about what I'll be able to accomplish. I will argue mightily for what is good and right. But, in the end, most of my efforts will be futile. The Republican city council will certainly veto most of what I propose."

"That's a rather dim view of your future endeavors," Sage commented while wanting something optimistic to say. But, Harry was right. That was how change happened: small steps forward, then some steps back.

"My comfort lies in the long view, John. It's how I'll meet the disappointments ahead. You and your friends should do the same."

"The long view?" Sage parroted though he believed he knew what Harry meant.

"I'll use my office like a bully pulpit—the Teddy Roosevelt approach to making change. As mayor I'll state my progressive proposals loud and clear for all to hear. And, because we now have initiative and referendum, maybe some of those ideas will stick. Maybe the people will eventually vote my proposals into reality."

A quiet splash drew their attention to the flowing the black water. There moonlight glinted on a beaver's flat tail ripples as the animal swam upriver.

Harry turned back to Sage. "I'll take that beaver sighting as an omen. The Indians I've had the privilege to know believe the beaver to be a symbol of hard work, creativity, cooperation, and persistence. It means I must do my best to manifest all those qualities in the days ahead."

They were both silent until Harry cuffed Sage on the shoulder, saying, "We best head home. I'll go make sure the fire is doused. We wouldn't want to set the island afire as some have done."

Sage watched the city's next mayor disappear between the snowberry bushes' withering white blooms before his gaze turned to the humming city and he felt something akin to love. Not as passionate as Harry Lane's, but the emotion was there.

What would become of its beauty? In the future, would the people whose hands, hearts, and minds were now building the city, someday fall into a full-belly sleep beneath rain-tight roofs? Would the city's wealthy learn to loosen their grip on money and power? Would the city's people become a compassionate, caring tribe? Would the future yield even more Harry Lanes?

He pondered those unanswerable questions until Lucinda laid a hand on his arm and softly said, "Everyone is waiting."

The End

HISTORICAL NOTES

THERE ARE A FEW POINTS I need to make about the story before you start reading the factual information below. Some of the information will be familiar to those who have read other Sage Adair mysteries.

There is an excellent book to read if you'd like to know more about Dr. Harry Lane. Leon Speroff, M.D., has written a thoughtful and detailed biography of Lane in *Harry Lane, M.D.: Oregon's Progressive Physician & Politician*. Speroff does an equally admirable job of explaining the context and significance of the progressive era in Oregon and the U.S. to the country's evolution. Finally, I believe Speroff is the first historian to identify Lane's true and lasting historical significance.

Vincent St. John (who is called St. Alban in the Sage stories) has long been a hero of mine. *The Corpse on Boomerang Road: War on Labor 1899-1908*, by Mary Joy Martin, is a well-documented and credible history of St. John. It also recounts how corporate mine owners reacted to the miners' demand for better wages and safer conditions—including their efforts to jail and/or kill Vincent St. John.

The Oregon Historical Society research library and the City of Portland archives are wonderful sources of photographs and reference material contemporaneous to the time. As always, the folks staffing those two repositories are incredibly helpful and knowledgeable. For this book, I was also ably assisted by librarians at the University of Oregon.

Finally, for dramatic purposes, I altered the timing of certain events. The historical events described in the story happened during the time period, July 1904 to June 1905, with some alterations to fit the story line.

SETTINGS

Generally

1. Many of the settings described in the Sage stories come from photos taken in the early 1900s. That is true of the Fritz theater description which relies on photographs of its exterior and interior. Fire Chief Campbell declared Fritz's a fire trap and made many unsuccessful efforts to close it down. The City's power-wielding wealthy clique blocked his every effort.

2. Many buildings were becoming electrified in the early 1900s. The problem was that anyone with a generator could string electric wires so there were many different companies, often in the same area. That meant live wires were strung in buildings and across roofs, with no record of their location, who owned them, or where to shut them off. Because there were no regulations, Portland experienced a dramatic uptick in electrical-caused fires with growing numbers of fire fighters being injured and killed by the live wires. The Sage Adair mystery adventure, *Slow Burn*, uses this fact.

3. Telephone exchanges were also being created. Like the electric delivery companies, there were a number of different exchanges. Whether the resident had a telephone depended on whether an exchange had already strung wire in the area.

4. Prior to 1912, the year women finally won the right to vote in Oregon, women were involved in a myriad of progressive, public welfare efforts. One of their campaigns pushed the city council to adopt an ordinance prohibiting a physical connection between the inside of saloons and the whorehouses on the upper floors. It specifically outlawed interior stairways to those floors. As in the story, that intent was quickly circumvented by installation of outside stairways.

5. Another of the women's successful efforts was to shame building owners using an ordinance requiring that the owners' names appear on all buildings containing vice dens. That ordinance was

quickly repealed when the men's names on those buildings were often the husbands of the women who fought for the signage.

6. That Portland developed a large and healthy middle class is largely due to the effort of women and unions. Three prior Sage Adair mysteries *The Mangle*, *Bitter Cry*, and *Preservation*, focus on their achievements. What I find interesting is that Portland women achieved greater societal gains before they achieved suffrage, than they did after it was won.

7. The story's Chinese gambling den was inspired by a contemporaneous news article. In that article, the chief of police bemoaned the fact that raids on Chinese gambling dens were always unsuccessful because of all the hidden doors and secret passages.

8. Frederick Law Olmsted and his sons are national luminaries in the history of park development. Their landscape designs are too numerous to name, though most are familiar with the beautiful expanse of New York City's Central Park. Portland had few developed parks in 1900, only those now known as Washington Park, the Park Blocks, the Plaza blocks (across from city hall and the old courthouse), and Holladay park on the east side. It was John Charles Olmsted's December 1903 comprehensive park plan that gave rise to Portland's enviable park system of today.

9. Olmsted was brought to Portland at the urging of "nature lovers" that included Lester Leander Hawkins and Harry's friend, Dick Montague. Olmsted was hired to do two things: Consult on the landscaping for the Exposition and develop a plan for the city's future parks. In that city-wide plan Olmsted noted, "Another landscape feature of considerable importance to the city…is Ross Island and its adjoining island." To understand the importance of this Olmstead report, read the beautifully illustrated, *The Legacy of the Olmsted Brothers in Portland, Oregon*, by William J. Hawkins, III

10. Until researching for this book, I knew little of Ross Island's history or its natural environment. Harry Lane was a huge proponent of Olmstead's recommendation to make the island a city

park. That didn't happen. Instead, in 1928, the city sold it to a sand and gravel company that wrought much devastation.

11. Two important things have happened recently regarding Ross Island. The first is that it is on its way to becoming a publically-owned nature sanctuary. The second is that ecologists discovered that by filling in the channel between the Island and the nearby Hard Tack Island in 1926, the US Core of Engineers created the perfect stagnant environment for growing deadly algae. Consequently, plans are in the offing to reopen the closed channel between the two islands.

South Portland

12. Initially, the majority of the Jews settling in Portland, like the Meiers, the Franks, and a number of others, were very early immigrants from Southern Germany. They became highly successful and influential businessmen. Their wives were involved in many efforts to bring about a number of social improvements. In 1931, one of the Meiers, Julius, was elected Oregon governor.

13. A second influx of European refugees in the late 1800s, brought Jews coming from Eastern Europe, Italians from Southern Italy, and a sprinkling of Irish and Greek immigrants. The people of this second wave settled in South Portland, making it a vibrant, cooperative community. Polina Olsen has written at least three books about South Portland's history, with most of her information taken from firsthand accounts.

14. Vetter Fox, is a translation of 'Uncle Fuchs'. The character in the story is based on that significant figure in Portland history. He is significant because, beginning in the 1890s, he brought many Eastern European Jews to Portland. Some of those immigrants were members of his extended family, including those in the Director and Schnitzer families, members of whom went on to make important contributions to the city and state.

15. The character of Giuseppina Cereghino is based on a woman of that same name. She and her husband, Abramo, ran a

boarding house in South Portland. The historical society has a picture of their boarding house. They were an unusual couple in Portland because they came from two different areas of Italy. Because of widespread Sicilian poverty and starvation, most of the later Italian immigrants to Portland in that era were from Southern Italy. The *Italian Tribune* was widely read by these immigrants.

16. Unfortunately, the heart of the South Portland neighborhood was destroyed by developer interests in the 1960s. The city development commission promised that the new high rises and other buildings would include replacement, low-income housing for the displaced residents. That never happened. Instead, the area became a typical cluster of taxpayer subsidized high rent housing and office buildings.

North End

17. The description and numbers of brothels, gambling dens, and saloons were taken from reports of the day. Many saloons offered all three vices. People caught up in the pre-Lane raids were seldom sentenced to jail because the hidden owners of the establishments, "fixed" things.

18. When Harry Lane was running for mayor, over half of the city's budget came from vice licenses and fines. Those were considered the cost of doing vice business. That was a big issue in Lane's campaign and why he promised to tax the rich, instead of continuing what he considered to be the hidden taxes on those who could afford it least.

19. Many of the Sage Adair mysteries have scenes set in the vice-ridden North End, an area that is currently called "Old Town" or "Chinatown" or "Skid Road" or the "Pearl District." Despite prior research about the area, this book was the first time I learned about "shooting galleries." They were licensed by the city, but according to news reports, were operated in such a way that the shooters could never win. One proprietor was tried and found guilty of bilking a shooter out of $21. The saloon operator was

fined $19, but that money did not go to the victim. Instead, it was added to the city's coffers.

20. Most of the "better" brothels were located outside the North End. One of the most exclusive was on the street fronting the Park Blocks where the Sage Adair stories have Lucinda's top-of-the-line parlor house. Despite Portland's staid reputation of the time, there were at least 400 houses of ill repute. There were also many more men than women and very limited job opportunities for women. The jobs that existed were hard, extremely low-paying, and without a professional future—mainly household staff, laundry workers, and store clerks.

21. From its inception and, until the 1905 election, the City of Portland was largely controlled by the wealthy. They promoted taxes if it benefitted their real estate and other holdings. For example, streets were given. without cost, to the streetcar and train franchises in which many of the wealthy were shareholders. Everyone was taxed to build trestles over the city's many gullies so that the real estate developers could sell their land holdings on the far side of those gullies. Once the land was sold, the same developers fought and won against every effort to tax for the maintenance of the bridges or anything else for the common good. The Sage story, *Dry Rot*, details the consequences of this situation.

22. The rich men's opposition to tax increases kept the city police officers at starvation wages which meant two things: Low quality officers and intense susceptibility to bribery. This was a nation-wide problem.

23. The descriptions of how vice operated and the role of the special police were all taken from news and investigative reports of the time. Many brewery owners also owned saloons. As stated previously, over half of the city's budget came from fines and license fees levied on vice. Once again, that was because the wealthy opposed any tax increases. The net effect was that the lowest income people, those who frequented vice dens, were the ones supporting the city, rather than the wealthy citizens who benefited both from lower taxes and from their cut of the vice profits.

24. A group of young male professionals formed the Municipal Association. During the first 1900s decade they investigated and reported on vice. The information about the City Club saloon (called the Portland Club in the story), its profits, and its manager, Peter Grant, is taken from theirs and others' reports.

EVENTS

1905 Election

25. I had to fiddle with the election dates. Harry's political gatherings in meeting halls—of which there were more than sixteen—are accurately described as being overflowing. The huge rally in the armory also happened but not as early as in the story. Instead, that huge rally took place the night before the general election.

26. The 1905 election process differed from previous ones. It was the first time voters voted in a primary to select the candidates. Before that, the political parties made the selection at their respective conventions.

27. Until the 1905 election, the Republican machine controlled the outcome using voter fraud. Two shanghaiing crimps, known as Turco and Sullivan, always delivered the Republicans' fraudulent North End votes just as described. But, in 1905, the Democrats successfully engaged in the poll watching technique as described by Dick Montague in the story. Multnomah County Sheriff Word, an honorable man, assisted by having his officers arrest those who attempted voter fraud.

Lewis & Clark Exposition

28. For dramatic effect, the story has the Exposition opening about a month ahead of when it really opened. It did not open in May. Its opening day was June 1, 1905.

29. Photos appearing in books about the fair, as well as news articles, pamphlets, maps, and personal anecdotes in memoirs,

provided the story's descriptions of the Exposition's places and events. Books and other material held by the Oregon Historical Society Research Library describe the physical layout, buildings, and events that took place at the fair.

30. The Exposition was erected on 406 acres of land and water, situated at the base of the western ridge in Northwest Portland. The fair attracted over 1.6 million visitors during its four-month run, and featured exhibits from 21 countries. Portland grew from 161,000 to 270,000 residents between 1905 and 1910, a population growth that most attribute to the Exposition. Thus, the extravaganza fulfilled the city's money mens' dreams of attracting visitors to their establishments, legal and illegal, and buyers for their real estate. L&C expo board refused to give any of the $111,500 profits (3.8 million in current figures) to the city, despite the city's crumbling infrastructure.

31. As a fair promotional stunt, 18-year-old pilot Lincoln Beachey flew the City of Portland dirigible aircraft on a two-mile loop over downtown. He landed atop of the Chamber of Commerce building and also dropped fair advertisement leaflets on the *Oregonian, Evening Telegram,* and other buildings downtown.

32. While none of the newspapers at the time advertised the appearance of Little Egypt, at least two memoirs provide pictures of her at the fair while stating that she performed there. A number of belly dancers of that time adopted the name "Little Egypt." I couldn't discover which one appeared at Portland's exposition. The one in the story is modeled after the woman who is believed to have first used that name. She came from Chicago and had a very protective husband.

33. At a time when women's professional opportunities were extremely limited, the fair organizers chose a woman, Mrs. J.T. McCready, to manage the American Inn. The Sunday Oregonian called the Inn extraordinary, capable of housing 1,150 guests and having a dining room with seating for 1,000.

Carpenters at the Fair

34. In January 1904, Portland had 1800 union carpenters. When fair construction was just beginning in April 1903, the union carpenters working on the fairgrounds were paid less than the $3.50/day that was the standard, west coast rate. In response, they walked off the job, demanding the standard wage. Over two months later, they won that concession from the fair organizers.

35. In March 1905, Exposition carpenters struck again. This time the issue was that they were being forced to work nine-hour days whereas carpenters working elsewhere in the city only had to work an 8-hour day. Additionally, newcomer, nonunion workers were hired to work on the Exposition. The more highly-skilled union workers got blamed for the errors made by the nonunion workers. This problem was happening across all the trades working on the Exposition. So, a strike was called by all the trade unions. Fearing they'd miss the opening date, the organizers agreed to assign union workers and non-union workers onto different building projects and use an 8-hour day.

Tanner Creek Sewer Scandal

36. Again, for the sake of the story, I had to be flexible about the timing of the Tanner Creek sewer scandal. That scandal became public news in the late fall of 1904. I moved the event to March of 1905, to coincide with the 1905 election season, in part, because the Tanner Creek scandal was a huge election issue.

37. The story references dollar amounts in more than one place. It is important to know that $7000 in 1905 would have the purchasing power of $252,692 today. This means that the 1905 fraudulent profits from the Tanner Creek sewer corruption would have been enormous. Similarly, the story's claim that the Portland Club's vice activities created a $20,000 per month profit, was taken from a contemporaneous investigative report by the Municipal Association. In today's dollars, those illegal gains would total almost $800,000 a month.

38. The Tanner Creek Sewer scandal came to public notice because the wealthy homeowners served by the sewer were going to be billed for the work. When they learned of the re-done sewer's defects, they refused to pay, and hired an attorney. He fought for an independent inspection to justify their non-payment.

39. The material and construction inadequacies detailed in the story were taken directly from the newspaper and inspection reports. How the various city contract corruption schemes worked, was also taken from news reports of that time.

40. Mayor Williams tried to suppress the independent inspectors' report but it got leaked. He tried to counter the independents' report by hiring his own independent inspector. That was a mistake. His inspector not only verified the independents' report, but found even more problems. Despite this, Williams kept defending the city engineer.

41. "Riner" is the real name of the father and son contractors who perpetrated the sewer fraud. Riner's son and his employees were caught entering the sewer in the late night, planning to make corrections before the sewer objectors' independent inspectors conducted their survey. Of course, given its extensive defects, there is no way they could have remedied enough problems for the sewer to pass an independent inspection.

42. William Elliott was the name of the city engineer who enabled the Tanner Creek sewer corruption scheme. It seems irrefutable that Elliott was involved in the corruption. He was, in fact, indicted by the Multnomah County grand jury in January 1905, as were the Riners. During his trial, Riner's son testified that they had promised Elliott one-third of the final corruption "take."

43. It is hard not to conclude Williams was involved, along with Elliot, in the city contract construction corruption. When the mayor's own inspector verified the problems, Elliott resigned, only to have Williams immediately appoint him as the city's inspector on the Morrison St. bridge construction project. Moreover, William's Republican advisors were some of the city's

wealthiest men. Many of them were later found to have been involved in various nefarious schemes. Finally, Williams' wife was notorious for frequently exercising her excessive and very expensive tastes.

PEOPLE

Vincent St. John

44. Vincent St. John, called St. Alban in the story, was revered by working men and women for his intelligence, kindness, and dedication to the wellbeing of workers. The description of his appearance and character is taken from photographs and contemporaneous written descriptions of him.

45. St. John was one of the founders of the Industrial Workers of the World (IWW). It was created at a June 27, 1905, convention in Chicago. He subsequently led the IWW for six years.

46. St. John died at age 53. His death was largely caused by the lung damage he sustained while trying to save the Smuggler Mine miners trapped underground by the fire. They died because of a Boston corporation's cost-cutting measures. When it bought the operation, the company eliminated the door guard position that would have saved everyone's life by preventing the smoke from entering the mine. One of those St. John failed to save was his mentor and father figure.

47. Subsequent to the disaster, the union members increasingly demanded a return of previous safety measures. During one of these verbal exchanges the mine company's thug shot and killed a young, unarmed miner. A full out, unequal battle was barely avoided.

48. The attack against St. John occurred as described, except that it happened in Colorado. Most believed that the attack was ordered by the mine owners' association. St. John nearly died and when he recovered, he'd lost the use of his hand. That did not

stop his economic justice efforts nor did it make him more cautious about his safety.

49. Pinkerton agents hired by the Mine Operators' Association continuously followed St. John. He was also stalked by gunmen because of the bounty put on his head by the Association. St. John was arrested and charged with crimes he never committed and for which he was never convicted. St. John was also repeatedly, and falsely, labeled a "murderer" by the anti-labor press. A decade after the time of this story, St. John spent five years in Leavenworth prison because he voiced objections to the US entering WW1.

Charlie Siringo

50. Charles Siringo first appears in the Sage Adair mystery, *Dead Line.* He is modeled after a cowboy of the same name who worked many years for the country's pre-eminent detective agency. At one point Siringo was assigned to Central Oregon at the behest of Governor Chamberlain. The governor wanted firsthand information about the pending range war between the cattle men and sheep men. Siringo did not marry a woman named Xenobia or remain in Central Oregon raising goats.

51. Siringo wrote a book, called the *Cowboy Detective* in which he laid out the nefarious activities of the Pinkerton Detective agency. He later followed that book up with one entitled *Two Evil Isms: Pinkertonism and Anarchism.* His assertions in the story about the agency padding bills and churning up labor unrest to increase business are also found in two other books written by former management spies. I personally know of a Pinkerton agent who promoted strike line violence in the early 1970s.

52. The Tom Horn character in the story is based on a Pinkerton operative of that name. Siringo wrote about Tom Horn murdering on behalf of the big Wyoming ranchers. The agency paid Horn $600 per death provided the dead man was found with his head on a stone. It seemed fitting to use Horn's name because the Wyoming murder spree was not the only time he killed on

behalf of the agency. He boasted of having made seventeen kills. Horn was eventually hung in Caspar Wyoming after confessing to murdering a small rancher and a slew of others.

Charles Erskine Scott Wood (C.E.S. Wood)

53. Wood was a very prominent lawyer in Portland and accepted as one of their own by Portland's wealthy. He graduated from West Point, took part in the campaign against Chief Joseph and in other campaigns against Native Americans. Consequently, he became a friend of Chief Joseph, and once out of the army and practicing law, sent his twelve-year-old son to live with the Chief for the summer and continued to do so for a number of years. Wood forever regretted his participation in the wars against the Native Americans.

54. Wood often stated that he was an anarchist and follower of Prince Kropotkin. He counseled the I.W.W., defended anarchist Emma Goldman, Margaret Sanger, a proponent of birth control, and Dr. Marie Equi who demonstrated against US entry into WW1. He loved jokes and would send subscriptions of anarchist newspapers to conservatives he knew.

55. For a period of time, Wood shared a law practice with George Williams, before Williams became mayor.

Harry and Lola Lane

56. There is no historical evidence that anyone plotted to assassinate Harry Lane. Nor was Lola Lane ever kidnapped. Both incidents are fiction.

57. Harry Lane was born in Corvallis, Oregon on August 28, 1855. He grew up in Lane County which was named after his grandfather, the first territorial governor and senator of Oregon. Despite an impressive post graduate education in New York, San Francisco, and Europe, Lane chose to forego the privilege his achievements and family's historical status offered. Instead, he became a rabble-rouser and doctor to Portland's poor. He was, in fact, known as Portland's "Poor People's Doctor."

58. Lola Lane was born in Milwaukie Oregon in April, 1859. She was four years younger than Harry. Her stepfather operated a prominent navigation company's sawmill. When he died, the family returned to Portland, where she lived in a local boarding school. Upon graduation, she taught in Yakima and then for two years in Portland. She married Harry, a childhood friend, in 1882 when she was twenty-three. Lola was not an activist but did support the suffragette movement. The Lanes had three daughters, one of them adopted.

59. Harry's grandfather, Joseph Lane, led the US Army in battles against Native Americans in Southern Oregon and against Santa Anna during the Mexican war. His campaigns against the Native Americans were particularly brutal. Harry was appalled by much of his grandfather's legacy. So much so, that he chose to become an honorary grandson to a Salem newspaper publisher, Asahel Bush. The story behind this relationship is interesting. Bush was, at first, one of his grandfather's closest friends only to become his political enemy because of Joseph Lane's pro-slavery position during the civil war era.

60. Every indented speech by Harry in the story is a verbatim account of his words as taken from newspaper reports of the day. Harry won the mayoral general election by 1,217 votes, garnering 7,587 votes to Williams' 6,370 votes.

61. Lane was admirable in so many ways that it is impossible to list them all. His character was described as "witty, unafraid, and pugnacious." Having read some of his letters to his daughter, I would also add that he was wise, affectionate, and kind. This accords with Speroff's characterization of Harry as a "warm, tender, and caring husband and father." As a respected self-taught mycologist Harry discovered and classified a number of theretofore unknown mushroom varieties and wrote a number of published articles about mushrooms. He was the first president of the Mushroom Club of Oregon.

62. Harry led efforts to create the state's first TB hospital, pure food legislation, food health inspectors, school nurses, and many

other things that benefited the people of Portland and the State. He also led the city's efforts to send aid to San Franciscans following the devastating earthquake.

63. Harry was appointed director of Oregon's hospital for the insane but he only held the position for four years. He immediately attacked the rampant corruption he uncovered at the hospital. He lost the position because his anti-corruption actions earned him the strident and effective opposition of contractors, government administrators, and politicians. His well-known commitment to ending patronage, corruption and improving the lives of the asylum patients became an effective "selling" point in his mayoral campaign.

64. Harry and Lola were Unitarian in their religious beliefs, with the very influential Pastor Lamb, marrying them and remaining a close friend throughout their lives. Also a close friend was lawyer R.W. (Dick) Montague who was by Lane's side during the entire election campaign. He was a lawyer in Erskine Wood's law firm.

65. Harry was a fierce advocate on behalf of Native Americans. Harry spent his first ten years in Corvallis during which he spent much of his time with the local Indian tribe. In a 1914 interview, Lane said that his was an "utterly dreary" childhood except for the time spent with the Indians. He further said that he always wanted to be an Indian. I was unable to determine whether Harry spent time with the Kalapooya tribe of the Willamette Valley or with a tribe that had been forcibly moved from the Rogue River area as a consequence of his grandfather's bloody campaigns—the historical sources conflict on this point. My research on Indian values while writing *Unseen*, convinced me that Harry manifested many of their universally-held tribal values, especially that of elevating community well-being over one's self-interest.

66. Harry had tremendous respect for Native American cultures. He was one of a very few US senators who argued against the U.S. government's policies harmful to native peoples, he introduced countless pieces of legislation that would have improved

Indian lives had they not failed to pass. At a time when the policy was "Kill the Indian to Save the Man", he asserted the following on the floor of the US Senate:

> I think the whole scheme of our management of the affairs of the Indian is a mistake. It is wrong; it is expensive to the Government; it is fatal to the Indians. The poverty of the Indian population is through no fault of their own. The Native American people are prostrate while the white man is astride them and is at work taking everything they have. [The Sage Adair mystery, *Unseen,* highlights the situation Harry raises in this speech]

67. During his campaign for mayor, Harry never used personal attacks against his opponent, George Williams. Instead he focused on the bad acts of Williams' administration and its subservient ties with the city's wealthiest men.

68. Harry was the first mayor to value the inclusion of women in traditionally male roles. He appointed Dr. Esther Pohl Lovejoy as City Health Officer; Victoria Hampton as City Chemist, Sarah Evans as City Market Inspector, and Lola Baldwin as the nation's second policewoman.

69. Historians state that Harry had the most contentious relationship with his city council of any mayor in history. Of the 14 council members, 13 were wealthy Republicans and/or economic leaders. Over a hundred of Harry's vetoes were overturned by the council. Almost all of the council actions he vetoed were ones that furthered the interests of the wealthy and the large corporations.

70. Harry served two terms as mayor. His popular support with the public was high, and he easily won the U.S. senate seat after his last term as mayor even though he had lost the support of the official Democratic party. He lost that support because the people he appointed to office, and as advisors were chosen for their competency, not their political party. There were no scandals nor evidence of kickbacks or patronage during his terms as mayor.

71. One of Lane's first acts was to fire all of those in the North End's special police force, and all but one, of the city's vice detectives. Bribery was common among the police ranks because their salary was only $80 a month, even as extreme population growth and the influx of exposition-related workers and fairgoers increased their workload to unmanageable levels.

72. Harry's use of the "bully pulpit" worked. Leon Speroff found that, subsequent to Harry's term in office, the citizenry used the initiative process to vote in 25 versions of his thwarted ordinances and vetoes. They did so the month before Harry left the mayor's office to take up his position as Oregon's U.S. Senator.

73. There is some conflict between sources over where the Lanes lived in 1905. One source has the Lanes living at 28th and Holgate where a gas station currently stands. Speroff states the Lanes were living on eight acres at 8th and Holgate at the time of Harry's death. That location would have been directly across from Ross Island.

74. Harry died on May 23, 1917, while riding the train back to Oregon to defend his "no" vote on the U.S. joining WW1. He was one of six senators to oppose the entry. History has justified his vote. Lola Lane died in February, 1940, 23 years after Harry. She never remarried.

75. Harry and Lola are buried in the Lone Fir cemetery near an ancient redwood tree, right off the cemetery's main avenue. When looking for their graves it was discovered that Lola's was missing. Information provided to the graveyard keepers enabled them to find and uncover Lola's grave, next to Harry's, so that it can now be viewed.

76. As you can tell, I am a huge fan of Harry Lane. He deserves a City monument. Even by today's more enlightened standards, Harry took the right-side-of-history position on practically every issue. He always advocated for the "little guy." We need more Harry Lanes!

*Thank you for reading **Looters & Leeches***

*We invite you to share your thoughts and reactions with your library and on
Goodreads as well as on your favorite social media and retail platforms. Your comments help and encourage authors whose work you like and support.*

Request for Pre-Publication Notice

If you would like to receive notice of the publication dates of the next Sage Adair historical mystery novel, please contact Yamhill Press at

www.yamhillpress.com.

Other Mystery Novels in the
Sage Adair Historical Mystery Series
by S. L. Stoner

Timber Beasts

A secret operative in America's 1902 labor movement, leading a double life that balances precariously on the knife-edge of discovery, finds his mission entangled with the fate of a young man accused of murder.

Land Sharks

Two men have disappeared, sending Sage Adair on a desperate search that leads him into the Stygian blackness of Portland's underground to confront murderous shanghaiers, a lost friendship and his own dark fears.

Dry Rot

A losing labor strike, a dead construction boss, a union leader framed for murder, a rag-picker poet, and collapsing bridges, all compete for Sage Adair's attention as he slogs through the Pacific Northwest's rain and mud to find answers before someone else dies.

Black Drop

In this ripping yarn, President Theodore Roosevelt has left Washington D.C., embarking on his historic train trip through the American West. Little does he know that assassination awaits him in Portland, Oregon. The words of a dying prostitute warn Sage Adair and his allies that they will be blamed for Roosevelt's murder. Since life is never simple, Sage also learns of young boys who need rescuing from a fate worse than death. As the presidential train and the boys' doom rush ever closer, every crucial answer remains elusive. Who is enslaving the boys? Who plans to kill the president? Can either tragedy be stopped?

Dead Line

Sage Adair encounters murder and mayhem midst the sagebrush and pine trees of Central Oregon's high desert. This captivating land of big skies, golden light and deadly secrets is the home of hardy and hard people–some of whom intend to kill him.

The Mangle

During a blistering 1903 summer, Portland's steam laundry women are working ten hellish hours a day. Exhausted and ill, they demand a nine-hour workday. Sage Adair, and his mother, Mae, join their fight until women begin disappearing. Desperately searching for the missing women, Sage and Mae face grave danger midst suffragettes, prostitutes, social workers, white slavers, arsonists and heartless bosses. Inspired by actual historical events, this is the sixth book in the award-winning Sage Adair mystery series.

Slow Burn

Arson, murder, kidnapping and false accusations abound in this seventh book of the Sage Adair Series. What begins as a simple assignment—helping the city's firefighters unionize, catapults Sage onto firefighting's front lines and into solving the deeper mystery of who is burning down the city and why.

Bitter Cry

Night fog drives a young newsboy into a seedy saloon where his appearance catapults Sage Adair into a world of painful memories, child exploitation and frantic searches for missing loved ones. In the series' eighth mystery, Sage and his colorful allies find collaboration to be the path to survival.

Unseen

Sage Adair is working on mundane business accounts when an urgent message arrives. Within hours, he and his friends are struggling to comprehend the harsh reality of Indian reservation life. They journey into that strange and dire world to fight greed. Soon things turn ominous when an Indian Service inspector is murdered and time starts running out for a prominent tribal leader. As they and their tribal allies begin uncovering the reservation's secrets, a small boy disappears, taking the biggest secret with him. This ninth Sage Adair story inserts historical facts into a fast-paced adventure mystery unfolding within the deadly confines of an Indian boarding school and reservation.

Preservation

Once again, Sage is learning painful lessons. Like, what you eat might kill you. Diving deep into the heart of why, he finds angry doctors, endangered children, corruption, and murder. This time he and his trusted friends must join hands with the doctors, women, and farmers who are fighting the good fight. Because of their efforts, you can stand in the grocery aisle and read what is in the food you buy. This action-packed, historical mystery is crafted around the historical facts and the actions of yesteryear's real-life heroes and heroines. These are the progressives of the early 1900s who truly made America great.

NOTES